TERROR ON TUESDAY

Recent Titles by Ann Purser

MIXED DOUBLES
NEW EVERY MORNING
ORPHAN LAMB
PASTURES NEW
SPINSTER OF THIS PARISH
THY NEIGHBOUR'S WIFE

The Lois Meade Mysteries

MURDER ON MONDAY *

TERROR ON TUESDAY *

* *available from Severn House*

Terror on Tuesday

Ann Purser

This first world edition published in Great Britain 2003 by
SEVERN HOUSE PUBLISHERS LTD of
9–15 High Street, Sutton, Surrey SM1 1DF.
This first world edition published in the USA 2003 by
SEVERN HOUSE PUBLISHERS INC of
595 Madison Avenue, New York, N.Y. 10022.

British Library Cataloguing in Publication Data

Purser, Ann, 1933-
Terror on Tuesday
1. Cleaning personnel - England - Fiction
2. Country life - England - Fiction
3. Detective and mystery stories
I. Title
823.9'14 [F]

ISBN 0-7278-5956-0

Except where actual historical events and characters are being described for the storyline of this novel, all situations in this publication are fictitious and any resemblance to living persons is purely coincidental.

Typeset by Palimpsest Book Production Ltd.,
Polmont, Stirlingshire, Scotland.
Printed and bound in Great Britain by
MPG Books Ltd., Bodmin, Cornwall.

Grateful acknowledgement to Gilly and Jane, who know a thing or two about cleaning

One

'I used to carry a knife,' Lois said conversationally, 'when I was at school.' She had not bothered to lower her voice, and grinned at Derek's expression.

He looked at her across the pub table. Lois Meade, his wife of nearly seventeen years, still a smart girl and making heads turn, and still with the same challenge in her eye as when he'd first seen her serving in Woolworths. She'd just left school then, to the relief of her parents and teachers, and it had been instant lust on his part. He knew she'd had a fairly wild youth, but this latest revelation was new. They'd been talking about the lawlessness of today's kids, and about their own, who were safely at school, when Lois dropped her carefully calculated bombshell.

'No need to tell the whole pub,' he said calmly, rising bravely to the challenge.

'Yeah, well, things don't change all that much,' said Lois, downing the rest of her beer. She looked at her watch, and stood up. 'Time I went,' she said, and leaned across to kiss Derek firmly on the cheek. 'See you later, then.' She walked across the bar with her loping stride, and was gone.

'Ahem,' said a tall, soldierly man standing at the bar. 'I could not help overhearing Mrs Meade, and I must disagree. In my view,' he added, clearing his throat again, 'today's youngsters are totally out of control. Quite different from my day.'

Derek did not answer, but nodded and finished the ploughman's he had shared with Lois. He was rewiring the Waltonby pub, a long job, and she had joined him for his lunch break.

However, the barmaid, a confident, chatty nineteen-year-old, dark and quick, laughed. 'That was a long time ago,

Major,' she said. 'Things are bound to change. Now then, drink up and have another to give you strength.'

She straightened her short skirt, turned to refill his glass from the Teacher's optic, and winked at the delivery man who was dumping crates in the storeroom behind the bar. 'Hi, Darren!' she called. 'Time for a quick one?'

The bar was not full, being a weekday, but half a dozen or so people looked up and smiled. The unmistakable innuendo was to them an extra something to brighten the day. But the major, standing so straight, banged his hand down on the bar and said loudly, 'That's quite enough of that, young lady! This has always been a respectable pub, as our landlord should have told you.' He sniffed, turned around on his heel, and walked out, followed obediently by a small, brown terrier, one ear up and one down.

'What's eating him, Hazel?' said Derek, looking across at the barmaid. He'd seen the major in here most days since he'd started work on the rewiring, but had not taken much notice. One of those retired military blokes with not enough to do, he'd reckoned. Now he was curious; Lois had obviously roused him from his usual dignified silence. Derek waited for Hazel to finish dealing with the delivery, then asked her again, 'Funny kind of bloke, isn't he?' he said.

She laughed. 'Oh, he's all right. I expect I annoyed him, reminding him that he was old. Quite fancies himself, does the major! Likes to chat us girls up, in his slimy way. We go along with it, so long as he doesn't go too far. Geoff doesn't mind, do you?' she added, addressing the landlord, who had just come in with a plate of cod and chips.

The conversation became general, and Derek gathered that the major was called Todd-Nelson, lived alone in the village, came into the pub most days, and enjoyed the company of the young barmaids. He seldom talked to anyone else, and was very much a creature of habit.

Huh! thought Derek, not nasty habits, I hope. He didn't really approve of these young girls serving behind the bar, especially late at night when things could get rough. His own daughter, Josie, now fifteen, was already talking about the time when she'd be able to earn a bit of money serving drinks. 'Everybody does it,' she'd said. Like going clubbing, another of Josie's goals in life. He sighed, then put it out of his mind. Lois would handle it, when the time came. He was confident of that.

'Right, Geoff,' he said. 'Back to work.' He took his plate over to the bar, and Hazel smiled at him.

'Cheer up,' she said. 'It may never happen.'

Lois Meade sat in her small office, chewing the end of a pen and studying a list she had made on a piece of paper in front of her. The office had once been a doctor's surgery in a big, solid house, four-square brick, with a small garden fronting Long Farnden High Street. Lois had been the doctor's cleaner, and now here she was, moved from a council house in nearby Tresham, settled with her family, who had spread gratefully into the unaccustomed space. There was even a large garden at the back where Derek grew vegetables, and escaped from the usual turmoil of family life with three growing kids.

Josie, the fifteen-year-old, was first, then Douglas, nearly thirteen, and Jamie had been the last. Now eleven, he went with the others to school in the nearby town of Tresham. He sometimes called on his grandmother, who still lived on the estate and claimed she missed them all more than they missed her. 'Your Lois has got ideas above her station,' an elderly neighbour had said to Lois's mother, but she'd received a dusty answer, and Gran had encouraged Lois and Derek to make the move.

The telephone interrupted Lois's thoughts. 'Hello?' It was Derek, wondering if he should pick up anything on the way home. 'No, I don't want anything. Been to the village shop today. But listen, Derek, what time will you be home? I need some help, choosing a name.' She looked at the list in front of her. 'I don't like any of 'em at the moment. Perhaps you or the kids can think of something better.'

Derek had originally suggested Careful Cleaners for the business Lois was setting up, but she had shaken her head and said she could do better than that. Now she was having trouble. Farnden Cleaners? Superclean? Clean-up Squad? No . . . none of them was right.

'We'll do some brainstorming later, then,' she said.
'We'll do *what*?' said Derek.
'Never mind, see you,' she said, and put down the telephone.

Lois Meade had cleaned houses in Long Farnden for several years before coming to live in the village. It had been an odd story, sad in a lot of ways. The doctor's house, for instance, had come on the market because he and his wife had more or less run away from the great scandal. A woman had been murdered in the village, and he had been implicated. It had been enough of a stigma to put off purchasers, and the house was left vacant for months, the price sinking lower and lower, until Lois and Derek had looked at it, decided to ignore the bad luck name it had acquired, and bought it. Lois had liked the doctor, and felt no bad vibrations. On the contrary, as she went around the house she often thought of the good side of Dr Rix.

She had decided that on moving to Farnden she would no longer clean houses there, and had given in her notice all round. She knew only too well how enmeshed a cleaner can get in the private lives of her employers. It had helped, of course, when she'd been needed to assist the police with their enquiries . . .

But the children were still growing and ever more expensive in their demands, and she and Derek had pooled all their savings to raise a large mortgage. Lois decided to set up a business around the work she knew best, employing several girls to do cleaning on a proper, professional basis. She would fill in herself when the need arose, but in other villages, not her own. 'Cleaning people's houses,' she said in explanation to Derek, 'gives you a special place. They talk to you, you see things, private things, and it's best if they're not too close to home.' Derek knew exactly what she meant. After all, she'd had a lot to do with finding out who murdered that poor woman. She'd been evasive when he'd asked her to promise not to get involved with that kind of thing again, and he was glad to see her putting all her energy and enthusiasm into setting up the business.

The whole truth was a little different. Lois had secretly

enjoyed her foray into detecting, had got a taste for it. Things had got very tricky, even dangerous for her own family, which was why Derek wanted no more of it, but in the end there had been something satisfactory in it, like fitting in the last piece in a jigsaw puzzle. She had seen Constable Simpson out on his rounds several times, and he'd waved cheerily. And one day, when she came out of the village shop, Detective Inspector Cowgill was there in his car. He'd lowered the window and said, 'Morning, Lois. Glad to see you . . . don't want to lose touch . . .' And he'd smiled his chilly half-smile before driving off.

Lois got up and went into the big sitting room. They'd had to make do so far with their old furniture, but it looked cheap and small. As soon as she made some money from the business, that would be the first thing to do. If they were going to have a big house, they must try and live up to it.

Even as she thought this, Lois checked herself. This was exactly what she had said she wouldn't do. She knew what the villagers would say: 'That Lois Meade thinks just because they got the house cheap she can go up a few rungs on the social ladder . . . always did fancy herself, and she's only a cleaner . . .' Well, let them talk. Lois knew her own worth, was proud of her husband and his skills, and of her children. She had no wish to be bosom pals with those who considered themselves the village's elite. For one thing, she knew far too much about them. No, they'd soon see that the Meades were quite content to be who they were, and sod the rest!

Now she stood up, put down her pen, and left the room. In the kitchen, she opened the freezer and checked that there were enough beefburgers for the kids' tea, and prepared herself for the returning wolfhounds.

'Well now,' said Derek, pushing himself and his chair back from the kitchen table and patting his stomach. 'Now we've all got to think of a name for Mum's new business.'

A collective groan went round the table, and Josie said, 'I thought you were calling it Careful Cleaners? Dad's idea?'

Lois shook her head. 'Boring,' she said.

'Thanks very much,' said Derek huffily.

'I know,' said Jamie, always ready to help, 'what about Mum's Cleaners?'

'Don't be stupid,' said Douglas, shifting out of his chair.

'It's not bad,' Lois protested, seeing Jamie's face fall. 'I'll put it on the list.'

'And you can sit down, my lad,' added Derek to Douglas, 'until you've made at least one suggestion.'

Douglas sighed deeply, and Josie winked at him. 'I've got one,' she said. 'Why don't you call it Mop and Bucket?'

'That's good!' said Jamie, and Lois smiled.

'Yep,' she said, 'that goes on the list, too.'

'What about you, then, Lois,' said Derek. 'It's your business, after all.' Nothing, in his opinion, had come anywhere near Careful Cleaners. Told you everything you needed to know in two words.

'Dad's idea's on the right track,' said Douglas grudgingly. 'It's got alliteration, easy to remember . . .'

'Alliter what?' said Jamie.

'You'll get there,' said Douglas, and warmed to the subject. 'That's what you need, Mum. Something simple, catchy and easy to remember. After all, people're goin' to have to look you up in the phone book, an' that.'

Silence fell. Josie was fiddling with her hair, Jamie trying to kick Douglas under the table, and the rest thinking hard.

'I got it,' said Douglas triumphantly. 'New Brooms.'

'That's stupid,' said Jamie, getting his revenge.

But Lois and Derek beamed at Douglas. 'That's it, boy! Well done!'

'Well, I don't know what it means, even,' said Josie, 'let alone remember it.'

'"New brooms sweep clean",' explained Lois. 'It's an old saying. Everybody knows it.'

'I don't,' said Jamie.

'Nor do I,' said Josie.

'Oh well,' said Douglas, 'that proves it then, dunnit? Must be the right one.' And he stood up, made a great show of picking up his school bag full of homework, and stumped off to his room.

* * *

Later that night, warm and comfortable in bed, Lois and Derek were talking. 'Did you really carry a knife?' Derek said.

'O' course I did,' said Lois softly, tucking a friendly hand inside his pyjamas. 'Didn't you?'

Two

John Todd-Nelson, whose real name was Smith, stood in the back bedroom of his unremarkable house. Most of the houses in Waltonby were old, and built in rich, dark orange ironstone, and all were carefully maintained by their new-rich owners. Even old farmhouses that had seen nothing but muck and slurry for generations were now repainted and re-pointed, had restored features that added another few thousands to the price, and were occupied by young families who had arrived with the stated intention of 'joining in'. But Todd-Nelson's house, semi-detached, with pebble-dashed walls and peeling green paint, was not one of these. It was an anonymous house, giving no clues to the character of the owner, except perhaps hints of a private man, with little interest in what it looked like to other people.

Major Todd-Nelson, as he liked to be known, stretched, and flexed his biceps. A dozen John Todd-Nelsons flexed them with him in the reflections from mirrors lining the heavily curtained, spotlit room. What he saw pleased him still. Not bad for a man in his fifty-second year, he told himself, and began on the series of exercises he performed every morning of every day, all the year round.

Today, he spent an extra half hour in the exercise room, took special care with his shower, and brushed with disciplined vigour his thick, greying hair, only lightly touched with a warming tone, as it said on the packet. Taking an eyebrow pencil from a small box on his bathroom shelf, he carefully darkened his neat moustache.

Impeccably dressed now, his regimental tie (to which he had no right) perfectly tied, and his white shirt gleaming, he went downstairs to his meagre kitchen. He poured a small helping of cornflakes into a chipped white bowl, topped it up with milk from a bottle, and sat down with the *Sun* newspaper, turning first, of course, to page three.

Next door, in the other half of the pair of semis, the Reading family were at breakfast.

'I suppose sooner or later you'll get yourself a proper job, or at least think about going to college?' Hazel Reading's father was wasting his time. She was not listening – could not listen – because of the headphones clamped to her head. Richard Reading leaned across the breakfast table and snatched them away. 'Just listen to me!' he shouted, and his wife Bridie rushed out into the garden, shutting the door behind her.

Hazel was not impressed. 'What, Dad?' she said wearily. 'It's no good listening to you, because you always say the same old things. "Get a proper job" . . . "go to college" . . . I've heard it all before. And anyway,' she said, as she saw him open his mouth for another tirade, 'working at the pub is just temporary. All the girls do it . . . and it's a lot more fun than babysitting, *and* better paid!'

'All the girls?' her father yelled at her. 'Just you and who else?'

'And Prue,' said Hazel calmly. 'She's posh, so that should please you.'

Her father stood up, red in the face with anger. 'Prudence!' he snorted. 'That's a misnomer, for a start! God knows what her parents were thinking of, giving her a name like that! And I've no doubt you talked her into it!'

'She's very nice,' said Hazel, 'and learnin' fast. Still a bit wet behind the ears, but comin' along nicely.' And, turning her back on her father, she took the earphones and replaced them, turning up the volume in careless defiance.

Richard Reading opened the kitchen door so hard that it banged back on the worktop and the key fell with a clatter to the floor. He ignored it, and strode out into the garden, where his wife was nervously pulling up tiny weeds from an immaculate flower bed. Hazel, getting up from the table, picked up the key and replaced it, and then shut the door, quietly. She walked to the window and looked out at her parents. Her father's voice reached her, but she could not hear what he was saying, though from his expression she knew it was not pleasant. Her mother, still crouched over the flower bed, looked the picture of dejection.

'Bastard!' muttered Hazel, and left the room.

'Lois? It's Bridie . . . Bridie Reading . . .' Lois, knowing she was in for a longish call, sighed and drew up a chair. But she was wrong. This time, Bridie Reading just about managed to tell her what had happened, then burst into tears and put down the phone.

Lois had known her a long time. Bridie lived in Waltonby now, where Derek was rewiring the pub, only a few miles from Long Farnden. But Bridie, like Lois, had grown up and gone to school in Tresham, and they had been mates. Both had rebelled in perfectly predictable fashion – a little petty shoplifting, truancy, smoking and drinking under age – and Lois had always been the ringleader. Once married, both had settled down to a law-abiding life of housework, casual work to earn much-needed extra money when the kids came along, and – in Lois's case – loyalty to their husbands. Well, Bridie had been loyal too, so far, but Richard Reading was a very different kettle of fish from Derek Meade.

'Damn!' said Lois, her concentration gone. She had been in the middle of composing an advertisement for cleaners in the local paper: 'NEW BROOMS are looking for hard-working cleaners. No previous experience necessary, but applicant should be strong and willing.' But no, that hadn't sounded right. Willing for what? She had smiled, remembering some of her own experiences right here in this village, and had been just starting the ad again when the phone interrupted her.

Why didn't Bridie leave him? After all, Hazel was their only child, and practically independent now, living her own life, very confident for her age and quite able to maintain herself if necessary. Why did married people cling together when it was all such a disaster? Richard Reading was a particular disaster, cruel and violent, and had Bridie completely under his thumb. It hadn't been too bad when Hazel was little, and he was in control of both of them. But now his daughter had grown up with more spirit than her cowed mother. So far, it had enabled Hazel to stand up to him, and been the cause of violent rows, but Bridie was still a seemingly helpless victim. Lois considered what she could do – knew exactly what she would do in Bridie's place! – but decided that there was very little anyone could do unless Bridie made the first move. She resolved to call in there on her way into Tresham to see her mother, and then put it to the back of her mind.

'NEW BROOMS – a new cleaning service, requires hard-working cleaners. Must be strong and used to physical work.' No, that wasn't right, either. Sounded like an ad for a club bouncer. She looked at it, and erased the second sentence. Leave it at that, then? 'NEW BROOMS sweep clean! A new cleaning service, based in Long Farnden, requires hard-working cleaners. Apply box number . . .' That would do.

She pulled on her coat and went out to the garage. It was still a novelty to have a garage, though her battered old Vauxhall was too far gone to benefit. She got in and started the engine on the third attempt. As soon as I get the business going, she thought, I might get a van, white, clean and reliable, with 'NEW BROOMS sweep clean!' in gold letters on the side . . . She drove off in a happy dream.

The major was upstairs again, checking his laundry, which he took each week into Tresham. He could have bought a washing machine and done it himself, but he did not consider that man's work. Anyway, it was an excuse to go into town and have a drink in the Tresham Arms. He had one or two drinking acquaintances there, and he might see the new barmaid. She was young, very young, but a town girl with a nice line in chat, and plenty of curly red hair. She seemed to like him, too, always had a warmer smile of welcome for him, he was sure. And if not her, then it would be an old friend and useful contact, who was there most days. Yes, it was a pleasant hour, once a week, and did nobody any harm. He glanced out of the window, and saw an old Vauxhall draw into the curb outside. He drew back, still able to see who got out. He'd seen the young woman many times before, Bridie's friend from Long Farnden. She was dark and slim, and quick in her movements, well worth a second look. As he watched, she slammed the door, opened it and slammed it again, and then half-ran up the drive into the Readings' house next door. Thank God for that! He did not encourage visitors. He considered himself a perfectly sociable person in his contact with the outside world, but never invited a friend back. He had no real friends, he reflected, not *chums*, and considered himself better off without them.

No wonder Mrs Reading's friend had arrived! There'd been another of those shouting matches this morning. He could hear every word through the thin walls, and that silly woman had rushed out into the garden looking desperate, as usual. Ah well, that's what you get in marriages. Well out of it, he told himself, and took a last look in the mirror. Satisfied, he went downstairs, out of the front door, and locked it behind him.

'Bridie?' Lois tentatively stepped into the kitchen. She could hear sounds from the television, and walked through to the sitting room, where Bridie sat slumped in an armchair, her head fallen to one side, and her face pale. Lois walked over and touched her shoulder, noticing a bruise on her cheek. 'Bridie?' she said gently.

Her friend stirred and opened her eyes, then winced. 'Ouch!' she said, touching her cheek.

'Did he do that?' said Lois. Bridie nodded, and Lois said loudly, 'For God's sake, Bridie, you've got to bloody *do* something!' Lois was always hard on the kids for swearing, but, as Derek said, it was one law for them and another for her.

'You always say that,' said Bridie, pushing herself unsteadily out of the chair.

'And you never do anything,' said Lois. 'Here, sit down again. You're swaying in the breeze. I'll get you a cup of tea.'

She went back to the kitchen and put on the kettle. Then she collected up dirty plates and mugs and washed them quickly. She glanced at her watch. Her mother was expecting her for a snack at twelve thirty in Tresham, and she had to take her advertisement in to the newspaper office first. She made two cups of tea and took them through.

'You could get help, you know that,' she said, sitting down in front of Bridie. 'He's a violent pig, and always has been. What d'you think it's doing to Hazel? She's already old for her age, and looks as if she's seen it all at nineteen.'

'She has,' said Bridie flatly. 'But then, she copes. She's like him, you know. I don't worry too much about her. In fact . . .' She stopped, and her mouth quivered.

'What?' said Lois, frowning.

'In fact,' repeated Bridie, 'she doesn't need me, he don't need me, nobody needs me . . .' She paused, and then all in a rush, said, 'So the best possible thing would be for me to get out. Out of everything, I mean. Put an end to it.'

Lois stood up quickly. 'Oh, for heaven's sake!' she said. 'You don't mean it. An' what's happened to you, anyway? You were always up for anything . . . bunkin' off school, helping ourselves to this an' that . . . sorting out the randy sods! Come on, Bridie, don't let him win. He's got you so low you've given up . . .' Bridie began to cry. 'Well, if you won't take action, I will,' said Lois firmly.

'No! He'll take it out on me! It'll just make things worse, Lois, I promise you that.'

Bridie's eyes held real terror, and Lois said quickly, 'No, no, I don't mean to tackle him or anything like that. I just had this idea that might help. You know I'm starting the cleaning business – well, why don't you come and work for me? I know cleanin's not all that grand, but it'll get you out, and I'm paying proper wages.' She hadn't very high hopes of getting Bridie to agree, and so was surprised at her reaction.

'Yes! That's it!' she said. 'It'll be nuthin' to do with him, and I'll get to talk to other people, an' that.'

'Well then,' said Lois, thinking privately that it was not going to be as easy as that. First she had to get him to agree, or he'd give her hell even more than usual. Still, worth a try, and she knew Bridie was usually a fanatical housewife, with floors you could eat off. She stood up and said, 'I'll have to be off now, Bridie, but I'll get in touch. Just be thinking how to tell him.'

Bridie nodded. 'Lois . . .' She hesitated.

'What?' Lois was impatient now to be off.

'Sometimes,' continued Bridie, 'he's not bad at all . . . sometimes he's quite nice, really . . .'

'Oh God!' said Lois, and left.

Her car started first time for once, and she was on her way to Tresham at top speed, which in the Vauxhall was about forty-five miles an hour. As she drove into the suburbs of town, a plain, unobtrusive car passed her and a hand waved in salute. She saw through the window the familiar profile of Detective Inspector Hunter Cowgill.

Prudence Betts, Prue to her family and friends but still Prudence to her grandmother, stood behind the bar of the Waltonby pub and hoped that the major would not be coming in today. There was absolutely no reason for this, she told herself. He was the perfect gentleman, always polite and correct, and she had no cause to be anything other than pleased to see him. But he made her feel uneasy, with his constant stream of talk about old times that seemed to have nothing to do with the look in his eye. She'd not told Hazel about this irrational feeling, but wished she could be like her, taking the major in her stride, laughing at him behind his back and flirting with him in a mild kind of way as she served him with his Teacher's. Prue was happy enough with the young farmers, when they came in full of cheek and energy. She really liked them, and knew exactly how to handle them now.

Well, it was nearly two o'clock, and the major hadn't appeared. He was a strict timekeeper, and would certainly have been in by now. Prue relaxed. 'Nice day, Mr Meade,' she said, calling across the room to where Derek sat in the window, taking a break from his rewiring.

He nodded, his mouth full. He liked Prue Betts, and felt the customary disapproval at seeing such a young girl behind a pub bar. He knew, of course, that it was legal. Geoff would never allow an underage girl to serve. It was just that Prue looked so much younger – and was, a year or so – than Hazel. He'd done some work for her parents in the village school, where her father was headmaster. Prue was a precious only, and her father's pride and joy. Derek had heard she was waiting to go to university, filling in time and earning a few pounds, and he wondered what her parents thought. Maybe they reckoned it was safe enough, being in the same village. Anyway, you couldn't lock 'em up! He knew that well enough from his own Josie, unfortunately.

'Haven't seen the major today,' Derek said, making conversation.

Geoff Boggis answered him. 'Gone into Tresham,' he said. 'It's Tuesday, and on Tuesdays the major marches off to Tresham with his dirty laundry. Every Tuesday, without fail.'

'Walks all that way?' said Prue.

Derek and Geoff looked at each other. 'No, dear, that was a joke,' said Geoff. 'He took the bus as usual, 9.45 am outside the village hall, and back on the 3.15 pm, arriving at his front door at 3.25 pm precisely.' He drew himself to attention, clicked his heels and saluted.

Prue laughed this time. 'Why does he go on the bus?' she said. 'He's got a car. I've seen him cleaning it.'

'He says the parking's terrible in Tresham, which it is, and anyway, if we don't use the buses we'll lose them, he says. Makes it sound like a duty . . . take the bus, or straight to the guardhouse for twenty-four hours!' Geoff Boggis snapped to attention again, and Prue smiled.

She would have liked to ask some more questions about the major. Hazel had told her that he was an old lecher, and had several times asked her if she'd like to go and see his holiday snaps. She had been scornful, and Prue had felt a moment's pity for the major. Maybe just an old bloke who's lonely, she thought. No harm in him, most likely. Still, these days it wouldn't do, she knew that from her parents' frequent warnings.

'How's Dad and Mum?' said Derek. He'd liked both of them. Mr Betts was a bit stiff and starchy, but polite enough. Some people, when you worked in their houses, treated you like dirt, stepping over you like you were something the cat brought in. But Mr and Mrs Betts had been nice, talking to him about this and that. Regular cups of coffee had appeared, and when he'd finished the work, they made a point of saying how pleased they were with it, and how they'd certainly be in touch if they had any more electrical problems.

'They're fine,' said Prue. 'Dad's busy with meetings and such, and Mummy . . . Mum . . . is shopping for new clothes today. I expect she'll be back by the time I get home, full of it!' And full of questions for me, she added to herself. How did I get on? Who was in the pub? Who did I talk to? Was it all right, and did I manage the money, giving change and so on and so on. What they really wanted to know, of course, was did all the men gang up together and rape me on the billiard table after the pub closed? She sighed. Chance would be a fine thing. Her father had at first met her after work, especially if it was a late night shift. She had done her best to discourage him and he hadn't been there recently. She had a momentary vision of him taking on the young farmers single-handed, and laughed.

'You got a nice laugh,' said Derek in a fatherly voice. 'Mind you don't waste it.'

Now there's a nice man, thought Prue.

Three

The advertisement in the *Tresham Advertiser* brought in a big pile of replies, many more than Lois had anticipated. Some she knew at once she didn't want. Too many jobs already, or too reliant on others for looking after kids. Then she remembered how much she'd relied on her own mother. Well, now she didn't have to so much, what with school buses and after-school clubs. She looked again. Own car – that was something she had put in the advertisement, but even so some hopefuls had applied, saying they had bikes, or could get lifts. She shook her head. No, that ruled out quite a few.

'How many are you going to start with, gel?' said Derek. They were sitting at the big kitchen table with the applications spread out in front of them. One of them slipped off the edge and floated to the floor, and the cat, Melvyn, a stroppy ginger tom, pounced on it with muddy feet straight from the garden.

'Give it here!' said Lois sharply, and tugged at it. Melvyn hung on, and the letter tore in half.

'Better ditch that one,' said Derek. 'Must be a jinx on that woman.'

'Rubbish,' said Lois, and wrestled the other half away from the cat. She put the two halves together carefully and read aloud: '"Sheila Stratford, aged forty-five, married with grown-up kids, own car, reliable."'.

'Which is more than could be said for yours,' said Derek.

'"Hard-working and reliable, like my car . . .".' Lois laughed. 'I like that, shows a sense of humour and my God you need one sometimes. Sounds promising?'

'Where's she live?' said Derek.

'Um . . . oh, yep, that's good. She lives in Waltonby . . . I think it's the council houses on the Tresham road. You know, on the right hand side, just up from the pub. Definitely a possible.' Lois put the two halves on the pile of possibles, and picked up the next. 'Oh no,' she said. 'This one's sixty-eight and lives miles the other side of Tresham. Fallen on hard times, I shouldn't wonder, from the ladylike sound of her.'

'Prejudice,' said Derek. 'Give it here.' He read it quickly and smiled. 'Mrs Bigsby-Jones, I don't think you'll do,' he said, and put it with the rejects.

Finally, they had six possibles, including a twenty-eight-year-old man, who said he was useless at most things except housework, and he was excellent at that. Derek repeated his question. 'How many for a start?'

Lois shook her head. 'Don't really know,' she said. 'It'll depend on what they're like. I think the best thing is to hire say three or four of the really good ones, and then take on jobs accordingly. As we get known, I can always recruit more. There's word of mouth, too. If I can get recommendations, that'll be a good thing. They've got to be the right sort, not just good at cleaning. Got to know when to keep their mouths shut, an' that.' In her mind, Lois knew exactly what she was looking for, and that last quality was not entirely to do with the cleaning business. But Derek need not know that. She checked that the six all had telephone numbers, and went off to her office to make some appointments.

Derek tidied up the table and got ready to go out to work. He was proud of Lois, and determined to do what he could to help her set up this business, but he had a vaguely uneasy feeling that she was not telling him everything. Still, when had she ever?

'Cheerio!' he yelled, but there was no answer. Lois was already on the telephone to the first on the list: Sheila Stratford, of Waltonby.

As luck would have it, Mrs Stratford's husband answered the telephone and said that Sheila had gone away up north to her sister's. She'd be away for a couple of weeks, but was very keen to have a job with New Brooms, and would – if required – get in touch the minute she got back. Lois put down the phone, disappointed at this first frustration, but went on to the next one down on the list. This one was in her twenties, address in

Tresham, own car, one six-year-old and a next-door mother. She dialled the number and after a few seconds a light, flat voice answered. Yes, she was Joanne Murphy, and would be pleased to see Lois at any convenient time. She was doing a bit of bar work, but that was flexible. Lois arranged to see her the following morning at eleven o'clock, and put down the telephone feeling uneasy, but could not think why.

She had decided to interview the women in their own homes, then she could get a surreptitious look around, see how they lived. She knew only too well how easy it was to hoodwink employers. One story had stuck with her, about a woman who'd claimed all kinds of grand references and on the first day had pinched a valuable piece of silver and never turned up again.

She worked her way down the list, making appointments and checking details. 'We shall be working in villages around Tresham,' she said to each one. 'I don't intend covering Tresham at first, unless there are urgent jobs.' The kind of village client Lois had mind was the well-heeled worthy, well-known in the community and easily managed. Vicars, doctors, teachers, solicitors, accountants – they were the ones she had in mind. Not farmers . . . they were too tight-fisted, and anyway, seldom wanted cleaners. She'd heard one the other day declare loudly in the shop that he didn't need a char. He'd got a wife, hadn't he?

The sixth woman on the list was a talker. Lois could hardly get a word in, and mentally crossed her off the list. Then again, perhaps she'd better give her a chance. She arranged the appointment and went off to the kitchen to make herself a strong coffee. She felt tired and tense. When she heard the telephone ring, she went to answer it in a less than euphoric mood.

'Lois?'

'Yes . . . who's that?'

'Hunter Cowgill. You remember?'

'Of course I remember. What do you want?'

'Well . . . and how are you, too? Don't sound so suspicious, Lois. I said I'd keep in touch, and I just wondered how you were doing, now you're living in Farnden. How does the family like village life?'

'OK,' she said.

'So, how's the cleaning business going? New Brooms? A really good name, that. Have you got going yet?'

Lois remembered that there was not much that escaped Cowgill's eagle eye. 'No,' she said, 'but I've just fixed some interviews with possible women.'

She made an effort not to sound too hostile. In fact, it wasn't too much of an effort. In spite of all that Derek had said, she'd had a lurch of excitement at hearing Cowgill's voice. It wasn't that she fancied him . . . no, no . . . It was suddenly being part of that other world again, the shadowy, risky world of the dark side of the law. And having to think, to think hard about something else that wasn't family. A while ago, she'd volunteered to be a Special Constable, but was turned down: 'Get in touch with us later, dear, when your family has grown up a bit.' That had been the old bag at the police station. Well, Lois had early on in life found her own way of side-stepping the law. She was a respectable wife and mother now, but, as Derek said, her leopard spots were still there underneath. She certainly could listen to what Cowgill had to say now. No harm in that.

'Excellent,' he said. 'Well, I'd be most interested to hear when you start. Perhaps we could have a little chat? Just something I'm trying to set up . . .'

'Like what?' said Lois.

Hunter Cowgill was vague. 'Oh, you know, along community involvement lines . . . new thinking in police practice . . . all that . . .'

'What use would I be now?' Lois was curious. She hunched forward in her chair, holding the telephone closer to her ear.

'Much as you were before,' said Cowgill. 'Ear to the ground, that sort of thing.'

'Well,' said Lois, 'we'll be operating in the villages. But there's not too much in the way of weekly murders there, thank God.'

'There's always crime,' he replied, and sighed. 'Anyway, Lois,' he continued, in a brighter voice, 'it'd be good to see you again, so I'll give you another ring when you've got going, and we'll talk. Bye for now.'

Lois felt the usual pang of guilt. Her involvement had come so near to disaster last time, and she had then been tempted to promise Derek anything he asked. But now . . . well, it sounded more official. She would just think about it.

Four

When Lois had put Gary Needham on the list of six, Derek laughed in scorn. 'A bloke doin' housework!' he'd said incredulously. But Lois was intrigued. There could well be clients' places where it would be safer, or more tactful, or more useful, to have a man going in to strange premises. And anyway, the application had intrigued her. It was well-written, on good quality writing paper, and whoever he was had a nice line in self-mockery.

'I don't care what you say,' she answered Derek, 'and I know what you think. But I rcckon any man who's brave enough to opt for house-cleaning as a job – can you imagine his mates at the pub? – must be worth a look.'

'*If* he can spare the time from his knitting to go to the pub,' muttered Derek darkly.

Lois laughed. 'There you are then, you silly sod,' she said, 'that proves my point.' She passed by him on her way to get her coat, and he grabbed her.

'Now then, young woman,' he said, holding her against him, 'just because you're about to be a big tycoon, don't mean you can't take a bit of advice from your lord and master.'

She broke free good-humouredly. 'Must go,' she said. 'First stop, Joanne Murphy, then take Mum's shopping, and then Gary Needham. And no! Don't say a word.'

Derek shrugged his shoulders, picked up his jacket and followed her out to the garage, where he helped to start her car and waved her off down the road to Tresham. Why couldn't she be like other women, contented with house and kids and looking after him? But he knew that if she had not been exactly as she was, he would probably not have married her.

* * *

Lois drove into Tresham and it seemed as if the car turned automatically on to the short cut route to the Churchill Estate. She and Derek had started their married life here, and her mother still lived in one of the old people's bungalows. *Not* 'old people', Mum reminded Lois frequently, but widows and retired couples, who found each other's company more reassuring and familiar than trying to keep up with contemporary jargon and preoccupations.

She found Joanne Murphy in a semi-detached house still belonging to the council, with a garden reminiscent of the municipal tip, and a front door with so much paint chipped off that most of it was the original salmon pink undercoat. The door was ajar, and a whiff of stale air wafted out. Inside, on the door frame, Lois observed with a sinking heart a patch of deep grime where child-height hands had grabbed it when passing through.

'Hello?' Lois called in a loud voice to penetrate the sound of a television quiz game. 'HELLO!' This time she yelled as loud as she could and knocked so hard that her knuckles hurt.

'Who's that?' The woman's voice was followed up by her appearance at the door. She was wearing dirty jeans and a boy's T-shirt with a rude message stretched tight across her ample chest. 'Oh, 'ello,' she said, smiling crookedly. 'You Mrs Meade?'

Lois wondered whether it was worth even stepping inside, but she hadn't the confidence yet to end it there. The living room was untidy, dirty and sombre, chiefly owing to the windows not having been cleaned for months . . . or years . . . Lois's heart was now in her boots, and she sat gingerly on the edge of a rickety chair.

'Like a coffee?' said Joanne Murphy, quite relaxed and friendly.

Lois declined hastily. The television continued unabated, and no attempt was made to turn it off, or even lower the volume. Finally, after a few desultory questions about the woman's experience, the answers to which were before Lois's eyes, she stood up.

'Mrs Murphy,' she said firmly, 'there's no way I'd take you

on as a cleaner.' She turned slowly around in a circle. 'Just look at it . . .'

As Lois moved out of the room, Joanne Murphy got angrily to her feet, stubbing out her cigarette on a child's eggy plate left on the floor. 'What d'ya mean?' she said loudly. 'You got no right to come 'ere and bloody criticize! You can get out and stick your bloody job!' She pushed Lois towards the door.

This was a mistake. Up to now, Lois had kept professionally cool, but nobody pushed her around. Nobody. She whipped round and glared at the woman. 'If you dare touch me again,' she spat out, 'I'll have the law round here quicker than you can shove a fag into your foul mouth.'

The woman backed off, and Lois walked rapidly out to her car. Please God let it start, she prayed, her heart thumping with fury. It did, and she drove off without looking back. When her mother opened the door to her, she marched straight in, sat down in the clean, fragrant little sitting room, and sighed with relief.

An hour or so later, fortified by her mother's calm presence and strong coffee, she set off again for Gary Needham, two o'clock at number twenty-four, Tresham Park Road. She knew it was an attractive, expensive suburb, and had no idea what to expect. She told herself firmly that nothing could be worse than the unlovely home of Joanne Murphy, and turned into the pleasant tree-lined road with her spirits rising.

'What was he like, then, Mum?' said Josie.

The whole family sat around the big kitchen table that Derek had bought from a client on one of his jobs. It was Lois's favourite piece of furniture, the thing that had made her feel most at home in this big house, and she looked round at her kids and Derek with relief. It had been a very strange day, and she reminded herself that she had a lot to be thankful for. The young ones moaned every now and then at not having anything to do in a village, forced to get lifts and beg parents to take them where they wanted to go. But Lois had noticed a brightness in their eyes, clearer skins and less tension in all of them. It was the space, she'd decided, as well as the cleanest air for miles around.

'Room to breathe,' she'd said to Derek, as they watched the boys at football practice on the pitch behind the village hall.

Now they were all getting restive. 'Come on, gel!' said Derek, 'we want to know how you got on with the very charming Gary.'

Lois frowned at him. 'I'm warning you,' she said.

'Mum! What was he like?' said Jamie.

'Bloke doing housework?' said Douglas in his father's voice. 'Not my idea of a career . . . never heard of a careers session in school for boys wanting to take up housework!' He laughed a lot, and Jamie joined in loyally.

'Shut up, both of you,' said Josie, and finally it was quiet enough for Lois to speak.

'He was OK,' she said.

'Is that all? "OK"?' said Derek.

'Well, he was nice. I think he'll do.' Lois told herself not to be so mean. She knew they were all bursting for some juicy details, and there had certainly been some. Well, all in good time. 'Who wants more ice cream?' she said.

'Lois,' said Derek firmly, 'if you don't tell us exactly what happened, we shall tie you to your seat with the washing line and walk out!'

'Dad!' said Jamie, alarm widening his eyes.

'All right, all right,' said Lois, and put out a hand to pat her youngest on the top of his carrotty head.

She began at the beginning, when she had driven into Tresham Park Road and cruised slowly along looking for number twenty-four. It was a Tudor-style house, and two smart cars stood in the driveway. On each gatepost sat a bad-tempered stone lion, and the front door was an antiqued reproduction, with black iron studs and a ring handle. Lois had checked that she had the right number, and parked.

'I wondered what on earth I was doing,' she said to her attentive family.

'Or what that bloke was doing, more likely,' said Derek.

Lois nodded. She had had a strong feeling that it couldn't be right. Everything in her warned against going on with it. He was playing around, doing it for a lark, wouldn't last two weeks, would be rude to the clients, laugh at the other cleaners, and herself . . .

'Hello!' A bedroom window had opened, and a young man with an unfashionable mop of woolly hair leaned out. 'Mrs Meade? Come on in, I'll be down right away!'

He'd disappeared and the window shut. Seconds later the forbidding door opened, and Gary Needham, tall and thin, obviously nervous, had beckoned her in.

'Was the house bigger than ours?' said Josie, who had discovered that their own solid Victorian villa had given her quite a lift-up in the eyes of her Tresham friends.

'Not really,' said Lois, 'just different. Anyway, I didn't see much of it. We talked in the kitchen.'

'Blimey, that was a bad start,' said Derek. 'Shows what he thought of you.'

But it hadn't been like that, thought Lois. Gary had hopped from one bare foot to the other, asked her if she'd like a drink, apologized for the house being a tip, and allowed her to suggest they sat down in the kitchen, the only room that seemed to have a chair that was free from piles of books. Blimey, she'd said to herself, is there a tidy house in this town? She watched his face closely for signs of secrets and saw a twitching muscle in his cheek. Well, that could be nerves . . . only natural, under the circumstances?

'I must say straight away,' she'd begun, deciding firmly to take the initiative this time. 'I must say that if housework is the love of your life, then you haven't made much of a start.' She'd looked him straight in the eye, and he had grinned.

'Fair enough,' he'd said. 'Good point. But it's a lost cause in this house. Dad's a lecturer, and Mum works in the library, and then there's young Sam . . .'

'And you just recovering from a broken arm and a sprained ankle, and only getting your sight back after an operation?' Lois had stood up. 'And look at you!' she'd added. 'I couldn't send a scruffy-looking bloke in a dirty T-shirt and no socks into a client's house, not in a million years!' She had made swiftly for the front door, just in case. 'No,' she'd said, turning back to look at him. 'I'm wasting my time here, Gary. But best of luck with whatever it is you really want to do.'

'He didn't look much like a cleaner,' she said now, half to herself.

'Told you so!' said Derek triumphantly.

But Josie looked at her suspiciously. 'Why did you say he was OK, then?' she asked. 'Surely you didn't . . .'

'Well, yes, I did,' said Lois. 'There was something about him. He stood there looking hopeless, and then he said I could believe or not, but he *was* very good at housework. He'd had his own flat, and she could ask any of his friends, it had been like something out of a magazine.' Then he had said that what he *really* wanted to do was play his guitar in a rock band and be a big success. But so far this hadn't happened, and so he'd decided to try and make a living doing what he knew he was good at. *And*, he'd added, with a convincing emphasis she was to get to know very well, he could get his hair cut, put on a clean T-shirt and socks, and he could guarantee he'd be welcomed with open arms.

'Well,' said Derek, 'so you took him on?' Lois nodded. Derek was stunned, and shook his head in disbelief.

'What about the other woman?' said Josie quickly, seeing her parents were about to start an argument. Lois gave a pithy account of her interview with Joanne Murphy, and was surprised at the silence that followed. 'So?' she said, looking round the table.

'What was the difference, Mum?' said Douglas quietly. 'Two dirty houses, but one with a posh address? Two dirty cleaners, but one with a posh accent?'

Derek looked at him proudly, and opened his mouth to speak, but Josie got in first: 'The difference,' she said, lightly touching her mother's hand, 'is what Gran says. "Clean dirt" – that's the difference.'

'Got it in one,' said Lois, and stood up to clear the table.

Five

Joanne Murphy, now dressed in a low-necked, tightly-fitting top and brief miniskirt, jumped off the bus and patted her hair back into its shining blonde beehive. She had bought the wig in one of those dodgy joke shops in Adam and Eve Street, and was very fond of it. As she'd said to her neighbour, it covered a multitude! She walked with quick, small steps on very high heels, and in five minutes turned into the yard of Tresham's self-proclaimed oldest pub, the Tresham Arms. She left her jacket in the staff cloakroom, indulged in some sharp banter with the barman in the Lords and Ladies bar, and clacked along the stone hallway to the Coachman's, where, she was delighted to see, stood her old friend, Major Todd-Nelson.

'Good morning, my dear!' he said, with a fractional bowing of his head. Oh, how she loved to be treated with some respect for once.

Joanne adjusted her neckline, and put on her listening face. 'And how is Major this morning?' she said, pouring deftly, and out of sight, a glass of neat vodka which, had she been challenged, she would have said at once was water.

'Much better for seeing you,' he said gallantly. This was partly what he came for. His regular glass of Teacher's gave him a welcome lift, but an hour or so of sophisticated attention from this fine young woman would keep him going for several days. He admitted secretly to himself that there was something special about the innocent, fresh charms of young Prudence at the Waltonby pub, but this splendid woman in front of him, leaning on her arms on the bar and showing him a rounded plumpness that would haunt his dreams, was the real thing.

*   *   *

By evening, the major was back home, and Joanne Murphy was once more in thrall to the television, having forgotten all about her abortive attempt to become a cleaner.

In the Waltonby village schoolhouse, Prudence Betts's parents were having their customary conversation about Prue working at the pub in the evenings. Although the village had been proudly labelled one of the safest in the country, they felt uneasy until she was safely home in bed. And then there were the increasing number of occasions when she was very late – once it was one thirty in the morning – and when they complained, she always had a legitimate excuse ready. It was a special evening of Thai food, with mountains of washing-up; or shortages of staff; or extra training from Geoff Boggis. This last one raised their suspicions, and they asked one or two pertinent questions, but Prue had always been very good at giving away the least possible information with apparent total lack of guile.

'It's all good experience, Dad,' she'd said. 'You say you want us to see all sides of life. That's why you are teaching in the state system, you said, didn't you? Anyway, Auntie Betty keeps an eye on me.'

Her father sighed. You brought up your children to be articulate and questioning, and then it all bounced back at you, when you could have done with a bit of good old-fashioned respect and truthfulness to parents, and obedience and duty, and all of that.

'Very well, Prue,' he had said, 'but we expect you to behave in a responsible way, and to be honest and straightforward with us, as we try to be with you.'

Yuk! thought Prue, but smiled meekly and said, 'Don't forget, Dad, that Prue is an anagram of "pure".' This witticism reduced her mother to apprehensive alarm, and sure enough her father glared at her.

'That's enough, Prue,' he said. 'Just bear in mind what I have said.'

It was a busy evening, and both Prue and Hazel were needed behind the bar, to cope with the increased demands of a darts needle match between Long Farnden and Waltonby.

The pub was already filling up when Prue arrived, and Hazel waved cheerily, continuing her conversation with a couple of young farmers from the Long Farnden team. The two girls served beers and shorts non-stop for four hours, and then finally the victorious team made a noisy exit, followed by the more subdued Waltonby Arrows, who were boozily promising revenge.

'OK for you two girls to stay extra time to clear up?' said Geoff Boggis, winking at three of the older farmers, who had quickly enlightened the landlord on the time-honoured custom of drinking after hours in a small room at the back of the pub. They had a stack of doubtful videos with which they rounded off a jolly evening, and the girls were told to keep their eyes closed and mouths shut.

Halfway through the mound of stacking and drying, Hazel changed the subject of conversation from fanciable young farmers to her latest idea for annoying her father. 'You know that Lois Meade – wife of Derek, who comes in here – at Long Farnden? Her that's a friend of my mum?'

Prue nodded. She had chatted to Lois on the odd occasion in the pub, and had liked her. 'Didn't know she was your mum's friend, though,' she said.

'Went to school together,' said Hazel, and laughed. 'They claim they were trouble, but I reckon it weren't much more than shopliftin' a few sweets from Woolworths.'

'Anyway, what about Mrs Meade?' said Prue, trying not to yawn. She would not admit it to Hazel, but she was tired and thought longingly of her comfortable bed in the old schoolhouse.

'Starting a cleaning business, isn't she,' said Hazel. 'My mum's going to be one of the cleaners. Heard her telling Dad. He hit the roof, of course, but she means to do it. The thought that she might bring a bit of extra into the house smoothed him down.'

'And?' said Prue, thinking that all this was pretty boring.

'And I'm thinking of doin' it too. Dad'll be furious,' Hazel added happily. 'He wants me to go to college, or get a proper job. The usual thing. But I reckon it'd be really interesting, going to other people's houses and that. Mum's always made me clean up, so I know how. And I could fit in working here as well. What d'you reckon?'

This question was a formality, of course. Hazel did not rate Prue's advice on anything, and in any case had quite made up her mind. She had good reasons for wanting to stay around locally, not least because she was not at all sure what would happen to her mother if she left.

Prue said she couldn't think of anything worse than cleaning up other people's mess, and advised Hazel that she'd much better go to college and get some qualifications. She could hear her father's voice in her own, and was aware that Hazel was not even listening. 'Still,' she said, 'I expect you'll do what you want. You usually do. Anyway,' she added, 'I must go now. Mum and Dad'll be waiting on the doorstep. You coming?' Prue had assured her parents that Hazel would be walking with her all the way, which wasn't much comfort to them, but better than nothing.

'No, you go on,' said Hazel. 'I need to talk to Geoff about a rota and that, so's I can fit in a new job. See you,' she smiled. 'Mind how you go!'

There was no street lighting in the village of Waltonby, despite periodic forays into estimates and plans by the parish council. At intervals along the main street there were lights outside the front doors of the larger houses, and Prue had no fears about walking home alone. She was deep in thought about Hazel's cleaning ambitions, when a tall shape loomed out of the shadows on a dark stretch of road. She stopped dead in alarm, but then a familiar voice reassured her.

'Evening, Prue, my dear,' said the major. 'Isn't it rather late for a young girl to be out on her own?'

Six

Prue's mother had gone up to bed early, not because she was particularly tired, but because she was anxious to avoid the inevitable rising tension if Prue was late back from the pub. Mrs Betts agreed on every point with her husband, but considered that it was up to him to handle this aspect of Prue's growing into a young woman. She loved her daughter very much, and was intrigued to see how well she could handle her father. She supposed it was partly learned from herself. Right from the beginning, when he had been a promising fellow-student in teacher training college, she had known just how to get him in a good mood and keep him there. A mixture of flattery and acquiescence had been the recipe for success. Not forgetting, she reminded herself as she heard a car pulling up outside the schoolhouse, a powerful spicing of physical attraction.

Mr Betts also heard the car, and jumped up, pulling aside the curtains and staring out. He recognized the car. Two people were sitting there, and as he watched, the driver leaned across and appeared to kiss the person beside him. Mr Bett's pulse quickened, and when he saw the tall figure of the major get out of the car and walk round to let out the passenger, and the passenger was Prue, he boiled.

'What the hell do you think you are doing with my daughter!' Mr Betts' voice was harsh, and carried loudly up the garden path. Prue was walking towards him, and the major had started to get back in his car.

'Dad!' said Prue. 'For goodness sake! Go on back into the house and I'll explain.'

But Mr Betts was not going to let the major off so lightly. He pushed past Prue, stalked through the garden gate and wrenched open the car door. 'You'll be hearing from me!' he yelled. 'And you'd better have a pretty good explanation ready. Too late tonight,' he added, aware that several neighbouring curtains had been drawn back. 'First thing in the morning,' he added, and slammed the door shut again, provoking a dun-coloured terrier on the back seat into a frenzy of barking. The major stared at him without expression, then engaged gear and drove off.

Prue was waiting for him in the hall. 'Up to bed, young lady,' he said, 'I'll deal with you in the morning too. We don't want to wake your mother.'

'We'll deal with it now, if you don't mind,' said Prue, face set and hands trembling. She went into the sitting room, waited for her father to follow her, and then shut the door quietly. 'Now,' she said, 'you'd better calm down and listen, before you make even more of a fool of yourself.'

'Don't you speak to me like that!' her father blustered, but Prue motioned him into his chair and then sat down herself.

'Are you ready to listen?' she said politely. Her father said nothing, but covered his eyes with his hands. Prue sighed, and began to explain. It had been a shock when the major loomed out of the dark like that, and she had felt faint for a moment. He had apologized and persuaded her to go inside his house and sit down for a minute, until she regained her balance. 'He was extremely kind and gentlemanly,' she said. 'Made his dog shake hands with me and got me a glass of water. Talked to me until I felt better.'

'What conversation?' growled her father.

'He told me about his time in the army,' she answered.

'Huh!' Along with most of the village, Mr Betts had strong doubts about the major's army career.

'Yes, and he's been to lots of interesting places. He showed me photographs. Egypt, Africa, New Zealand . . .'

'Didn't know there was a war in New Zealand,' said her father, beginning to recover his wits.

'That was his holiday, Dad. Do try not to be so suspicious. The major is a nice man, and I've often had conversations with him in the pub. Hazel likes him, too, and her dad is just as horrible about him as you are.'

'Glad to hear Dick Reading has some sense,' said her father.

'Oh, it's useless!' said Prue. 'The man was kind, looked after me until I was OK, and then insisted on bringing me home.'

'And kissed you?' said her father, playing his trump card.

'That?' said Prue. 'That was just a peck on the cheek to cheer me up, because I knew I was in for a rocket from you!' She stood up. 'Well, now you know, and I suggest an apology to the major might be a good idea tomorrow. I'm off to bed now, and I just hope this stupid row has not woken up Mum.'

Mr Betts sat for a long time staring at the dying embers of the fire. Everything that Prue said sounded true, but he knew better than anyone what good liars children could be. Oh, damn it all. He'd have to tell her mother, of course, and maybe together they could find a sensible way of dealing with it. His own mother used to say that teachers made rotten parents, and he often had occasion to remember her words of wisdom. Yes, he'd tell Prue's mother in the morning, and she'd know what to do.

He remembered Prue's remark about Dick Reading. Much as he disliked the man, and despised him for undoubted violence towards his wife, he might go round and have a chat. See if he knew anything more about the major . . . Major! – a likely story!

Next morning, being Sunday, the village slept late. Mr Betts was, however, awake early, and tiptoed down to the kitchen to make tea. He walked back upstairs carrying a tray, and put it down heavily on the bedside table by his wife. He hoped this would wake her, and then he could tell her what had happened. She stirred, and he leaned over to kiss her awake. 'Morning, dear,' he said, just as he always did.

She opened her eyes and looked at the clock. 'But it's Sunday . . .' she said, protesting.

'Lovely morning,' he said, pouring out tea into two cups.

Mrs Betts' reaction to his account of last night's events was not quite what he had hoped for. In fact, she smiled. 'What a kind man,' she said gently, sipping her hot tea. 'Lots of things are said about him in the village, but I've always found him most polite and helpful.'

'He kissed Prue!' said her husband sharply.

'Yes, dear, but you said it was to cheer her up, knowing you'd be in a lather by the time she got in.'

'Not my exact words,' he answered crossly. 'The man should not touch young girls, even if there was no evil intent.'

'Evil intent!' said his wife. 'For goodness sake, don't exaggerate. You'll make things far worse than they are. If they are bad at all, which I doubt. Anyway, I think the best thing to do is nothing. Prue is quite safe, the major will probably know you've calmed down, and there'll be no harm done.'

Mr Betts thought it was not a good idea, under the circumstances, to tell his wife of his plan to see Dick Reading, but he had not given it up. Soon after breakfast – Prue still in bed and his wife reading the paper – he got his stick, put the lead on the dog, and set off, saying he was going to take advantage of the lovely morning. His luck was in, he thought, as he saw Reading in his front garden, tying back a rose that had come loose in the strong wind. High clouds scudded across a bright blue sky, and Mr Betts found it difficult not to feel cheerful. Perhaps he was making too much of a meal of it. Still, now he was here . . .

'Morning, Reading,' he said. 'Quite a breeze this morning!'

Dick Reading objected to being called 'Reading' by the village schoolmaster, but answered politely enough. 'Out for a walk?' he said, and walked to the gate, leaning on it to signal he was available for the exchange of a few words.

'How's Hazel?' Mr Betts did not quite know how to begin, but this was a start.

'Awkward as ever,' said Dick Reading. 'Don't know where she gets it from. I reckon they pick up all that cheek from the pub. Your girl works there too, doesn't she?'

Mr Betts could not believe his luck. 'Yes, indeed,' he said. 'They were both there last night, and Prue got brought back by the major, of all people. Don't know that I quite approve of . . .' His voice tailed away invitingly, and Dick Reading obligingly took up the subject.

'Wouldn't trust him an inch,' he said. 'Nor would you, if you knew what I know.'

Prue's father took a deep breath. 'Perhaps you wouldn't mind telling me?' he said tentatively. 'Could be important,' he added.

Dick Reading was only too happy. 'The man's a fraud,' he said. 'Friend of mine knew him, years ago, when he was plain John Smith. Never been near an army uniform, but at that time he was trying to get into the Territorials. Some whiff of scandal attached, my friend says, and he was chucked out. No, I wouldn't trust him as far as I could throw him.' He heard a voice calling from the house and turned round. 'Just coming,' he shouted, and turned back to Mr Betts. 'I've never said nothing about this,' he said, 'but I wouldn't hesitate to teach him a lesson if necessary. Just keep your eyes open, Betts, that's my advice.' He grinned as the schoolmaster stiffened, and then disappeared round the back of his house.

Mr Betts did not move. He glanced at the next-door house, but the major's curtains were all drawn closed. Should he go in, tackle him as he'd intended? No, he decided to let it be this once, but should there be anything, anything at all in the future, then he would act. He continued on his way, pulling the dog away from an interesting sniff, and did not notice the major's bedroom curtain twitch a fraction as he went.

Seven

Between Long Farnden and Waltonby, off the road and through parkland said to have been landscaped by Capability Brown, stood an Elizabethan mansion, once the home of an ancient family and now recently converted into a country house hotel. Dalling Hall was reputed by the locals to be haunted, and the new owners had taken up the story with enthusiasm. But for the sake of nervous souls they had removed sightings of the old lady in a long grey dress from the staircase of the hall to the tiny old church across the park, where the Dalling family had worshipped for generations.

Lois Meade had worked as a cleaner in the hall when it was in a transitional stage, still lived in by a single family. Those people had bought the estate from the Dallings, hoping to get grants to restore the crumbling mansion, but had failed, and sold it on to a hotel consortium with plenty of money to put it back to its former glory. Lois had left the job when the family moved out, but a couple of weeks ago had received a telephone call from the manager of the hotel, saying he'd heard about New Brooms, needed some extra cleaners, and was she up and running yet? She'd not wanted to turn him down, and so decided to say yes, do the job herself for a while, and see how things went.

This Tuesday morning, a Tuesday she was to remember, she parked well out of sight of the main building. All the other cars were BMWs, or Bentleys or Rollers. 'Don't worry,' she'd said to the manager, 'I won't lower the tone.' She went in through the staff entrance, and asked to see the other cleaners to establish a useful timetable. This done, she took her own things and climbed the stairs. She would start on the bedrooms – only three couples staying – and work her way downwards.

It was good to be cleaning again, she decided. It gave you time to think, and she had some thinking to do. So far, she had only two definites on her team. Bridie Reading had phoned with a new and positive voice, and said she'd be keen, if Lois thought she could do it. Gary Needham was the other definite. The more she thought about him, the more she hoped she'd done the right thing in hiring him. It was risky, but she could see there'd be clients where a man going in to clean would be useful. He had charm, too, and she had to admit that she had undoubtedly succumbed.

Then there was Sheila Stratford, back from her sister's, and ready for interview on Lois's way home from the hall. With any luck, she'd be OK, and then Lois could go on down the list. She could even start Sheila and Gary on at the surgery straight away, if all went well. A couple of weeks previously, the doctor had looked at Jamie's sprained ankle, and had chatted approvingly about New Brooms. He'd said immediately that he'd be her first customer, having just lost his regular woman.

Lois looked out of the window of the bridal suite and admired the view. You could be married at Dalling Hall, have your reception here, and honeymoon in this luxurious set of rooms, at a price. Gently rolling grassy slopes were dotted with sheep, and off to the right a wide lake, sparkling in the March sun, succoured at least forty wild duck, put there by the management and ready for execution by sporting guns in due course. Daffodils filled the garden, right up to the ditch that Lois had incredulously heard referred to by the previous owners as 'the ha-ha'. Not far away, the ancient church, set on a small mound with a doll-size moat around it, seemed to Lois to complete a carefully composed picture.

How many ladies of the Dalling family had stood here and looked across the park as she did now? Lois tried to imagine what it would be like, but failed. Her own life had been bounded by small spaces and small concerns, the minutiae of daily existence and struggle to survive. She knew perfectly well that compared with some, she and her family were lucky, especially since they had moved into Doctor Rix's old house. But hard work and frantic saving of every possible penny had enabled them to achieve this. The ladies of the Dalling dynasty must have taken it for granted, this huge house, the parkland and farmland that was theirs for as far as the eye could see, and beyond. Maids at their beck and call, and seamstresses putting in hours and hours of skilled work with flying fingers.

'Mrs Meade?' The sudden voice made Lois jump, and she turned round quickly.

'Goodness,' she said, 'I was miles away. Hello, Hazel, what are you doing here?'

Hazel Reading smiled. 'Looking for you, as it happens,' she said. 'Hope you don't mind, but the barman is a friend of mine, and he told me where to find you. I usually do a couple of hours in the bar here on the days they have weddings, so they know me.'

'Well, I have to get on,' said Lois, wondering what this was all about, and hoping it wasn't a message from Bridie that she dare not deliver herself and had sent her daughter instead. 'Is Mum all right?' she added. She supposed Hazel wouldn't be looking so cheerful if there was something wrong.

'Fine,' said Hazel. She pulled her short jersey down to cover a bare midriff. A handsome girl, thought Lois, but seems years older than her age. She had a dark, gypsy look about her, and reminded Lois strongly of the young Bridie.

'No, it was about your cleaning business, Mrs Meade,' continued Hazel. 'I know Mum's working for you, and I had this idea that you might give me a job too? I'm good at housework and that, and can work fast. You learn that in a pub, when everybody's shouting at you at once. It's good experience for all kinds of things. Even Prue Betts can do it now, and she was hopeless at first.'

'Prue Betts?' said Lois, remembering the name from one of Derek's jobs in Waltonby. 'Isn't her father the schoolmaster?'

Hazel nodded. 'He don't much like her working at the pub. Bit of a scene the other night, when that old Major Todd-Nelson took her home.'

Lois had heard of him, too. Bit of an old fraud, Derek had said. What was he doing with young girls like Prue? 'Was he a nuisance?' she said.

'No, Prue says there weren't nothing in it.' Hazel was

dismissive. 'He tried it on with me once or twice, but I soon put a stop to that. He's not a bad bloke. It's just one of the hazards of bein' behind the bar!'

'So what happened about Prue?' Lois was curious. It would not be so many years before Josie would be wanting to serve and flirt from behind the safety of a pub bar, and Lois wanted to be ready for her.

'Her dad bawled out the major, and Prue, but it didn't come to nothing more. My dad hates the major . . . says he should be told to leave the village and that. But he don't do no harm, I reckon. My dad always goes over the top . . . "Give the bugger a good thrashin" – you know the way he goes on.'

Lois did indeed know, and reflected that one of these days Richard Reading's good thrashings would bring him well-deserved retribution. 'Well, Hazel, I must get on.'

She picked up her tools, but Hazel stood blocking the doorway. 'What d'you think about the cleaning, then? Give me a try?'

Lois hesitated. Bridie had said nothing about this, and it occurred to Lois that she probably had not been told. Anyway, now was not the time or place, and she said as much to Hazel. 'I'll come round this evening, about seven. I need to see your mother, and we can talk about it then. Now,' she repeated firmly, 'I must get on, so I'll say cheerio.' She picked up her cleaning things, walked out past an irritated Hazel, and made for the bedroom at the end of the corridor, where two wedding guests had left it looking as though a hurricane had blown through. Her mind was still on Prue Betts, the major, and the thought that Hazel Reading seemed to know a great deal about many things. She might well be as good as she said, and just the sort of employee Lois was after. Especially bearing in mind the shadowy presence of Detective Inspector Hunter Cowgill, who had been so interested in Lois's plans.

Lois left the hall, and realized she was too early for her appointment with potential cleaner Sheila Stratford. She slowed down and looked across at the lake. She could park the car and go for a wander to look at the ducks. Or not, she thought, looking down at her thin shoes, which were fine for housework but useless for walking through wet grass and mud. There was the church. Maybe, if it was open, she could have a peek inside. She'd often wondered what it was like, so small and stuck in the middle of nowhere. There were services there on some Sundays; she'd seen that on notices pinned up in the hall reception. It'd probably be locked, but worth a look. She drove as far as she could get by car, then parked and walked up the last hundred yards of weedy path. A small bridge, only three or four metres long and bounded by iron railings, spanned the mock moat, and Lois came to the low, arched door, bleached by time and weather. She lifted a worn iron latch, and the door swung open heavily. A musty smell repelled her for a second or two, and then she walked forward, nearly falling headlong down a couple of steps that led down into the damp, dark interior.

Lois regained her balance, and waited until her eyes adjusted to the sombre light. It was very quiet. The first thing she noticed was the absence of chairs or pews in the main body of the church. Then, at the back, in what she supposed were the servants quarters, she saw three rows of age-blackened oak pews. So that's where the menials sat. In the centre of the church and all round its sides were Dalling family memorials, large, highly decorated and oddly forbidding. Some were in white or black marble, some painted in amazingly bright colours for their age. Some were plain stone, on which the lettering had almost disappeared, as the stone crumbled with age and damp.

'Sacred to the memory of Lady Eliza Dalling,' she read from a chalky white tablet on the wall. 'Died in infancy, aged two years, in the year of Our Lord, 1689.' Poor little soul. Then another, worse, named what must have been an entire clutch of children, all dying under twelve years old, and in the same year. Probably of some disease that would have been cured by antibiotics in a week, thought Lois, saddened at the list. Each had been a little child, lovingly welcomed into the Dalling family, laughing and running about the same rooms that Lois had just cleaned, skipping over the park through which she had driven. Then all died, little bodies lying still, with weeping parents kneeling in sorrow. Lois felt her eyes fill, and shook herself. For goodness sake, it was hundreds of years ago! But this was a place of death, and it had that terrible chill that had nothing to do with the absence of central heating.

It was also very quiet, but not a comfortable, peaceful quiet. It was as if the whole place was holding its breath.

Then she heard it. She whipped round, and there it was again. A faint sigh, a stirring of the air. Her immediate instinct was to run, but she checked it. She listened again. It seemed to come from the high, painted tomb at the other side of the church, where, in almost darkness, a recumbent stone figure lay waiting for the Day of Judgement. As she approached, she shivered at the thought of the old knight in his dull grey armour, and imagined his warrior face with drooping moustache. She was touched to see down at his feet the figure of a little terrier dog, head tucked between paws.

She looked around fearfully, but there were no more sighs, no scuttling mice or swooping bats. She peered again at the tomb. It must have been a nice little dog, keeping guard by his master for five centuries. Lois put out a hand to give it a friendly stroke, and recoiled. It was warm beneath her hand. 'Oh my God!' she screamed, her body rigid. And then, as she stared, rooted to the spot in terror, the little dog lifted its head and turned a bleary eye to look at her.

Eight

Derek had come home early after finishing a job with a couple of hours to spare. It wasn't worth starting something new, so he'd come back to Long Farnden and planned some time in the garden. He was just changing his shoes when the telephone rang, and he was surprised to hear Lois's voice. He didn't recognize it at first, she sounded so strange.

'What, duck? What did you say?' She was on her mobile, and the reception wasn't good. 'Come where? Oh, yes, oh, all right, then. Dalling Park. The church, you said? What on earth are you doing in the church? Lois? Lois?' But the line had gone dead, and he frowned, worried at the obvious panic in Lois's voice.

It didn't take him long to drive to Dalling, his foot down hard on the accelerator. Why hadn't she called his mobile, he wondered. Then he remembered he'd left it in the van when he got home. She'd probably tried it first, and when he hadn't answered got into a worse panic about whatever it was. He came to the grassy drive leading to the church and skidded on the turn, reducing his speed. He banged the car door shut and ran at the double to the church, flinging open the door and leaping down the steps into the silent interior. 'Lois! Lois! Where are you?'

He saw her then, sitting pale-faced in one of the black oak pews, staring at him, and mechanically stroking a dozy-looking, dun-coloured terrier curled up on her lap.

'Derek,' she said, 'what kept you?' She smiled uncertainly, and he breathed a sigh of relief. She got up from the pew, and walked towards him. 'Something very dodgy has been goin' on,' she said in a muffled voice, as he put his arms round her and the dog and held them tight.

'Hold on, gel,' he said. 'Give it a minute, then you can tell me.' If any bugger's done anything to my Lois, I'll kill 'em, he said angrily to himself.

'This dog,' she said, finally pushing back from him. 'I think it's been drugged. I found it over there, on the end of that tomb. It was just lying there, like a stone dog.' She stopped, took a deep breath, and continued, her voice more normal now. 'But there's more, Derek. Come over and see.' They walked over to the tomb, Lois still cradling the little dog, which seemed to have gone back to sleep. 'Look,' she said. 'Look inside the knight's helmet. It's . . . well, just have a look.'

Derek leaned over and peered at the head of the figure. 'Can't see much in this gloom,' he said.

'Look closer,' said Lois, 'look at his face.'

At that moment a shaft of sunlight shone through a diamond-paned window, high up in the side aisle of the church, a celestial spotlight, helpfully illuminating the knight's tomb.

'Face?' said Derek. And then: 'Christ Almighty! He's alive!'

'I don't think so,' said Lois quietly. 'But it *is* a real man.'

'Bloody hell . . . You're right,' choked Derek. 'And I know who it is.' He looked again, and then shook his head in disbelief.

'Who is it, then?' said Lois, though she was fairly sure she knew.

'It's the major,' said Derek. 'And you're right. He's dead as a doornail.'

'Better ring the police, then,' said Lois flatly. 'And while we're waiting, we can have a good look around. Here, dog,' she said, 'no good waiting for your master. We'd better put you in the van, though I expect the police will want to question you as an expert witness.' She gave Derek a wintry smile. 'Who would want to kill the major, Derek?' she said.

'Quite a few,' he said, 'from what I heard in the pub. Though none of it amounted to much, if you ask me. Still, better ring the cops, gel. Get on with it. Sooner the better.' And then he added, unable to keep a sour note from his voice, 'It'll probably be your pal Cowgill, the demon detective. No doubt you know the number.'

Lois ignored this, and looked at her watch. 'You'd better get back, Derek,' she said. 'The kids'll be home from school shortly, and one of us must be there. I'll wait . . .'

Derek frowned. Lois's face was still pale. 'Are you sure, me duck?' he said. 'I can just as well stay here for the cops, and you go on home, make yourself a cup of tea.'

Lois shook her head. 'No, I found him, so it'll be me they want to talk to. I'll be OK.' She took out her mobile, dialled a number and waited.

'Afternoon, Lois,' said Hunter Cowgill, stepping down into the chill.

After twenty minutes or so of being alone, Lois was relieved that the church was no longer empty, that somehow the presence of the law at the scene of the crime had warmed the place up. She knew some people believed the spirit hung around for a while before a dead person truly departed, and there was undoubtedly something still present in the silence of the church. After five minutes of absolutely nothing happening, Lois had started to hum a tune to keep the shadows from advancing. It was an old tune, one her grandmother used to sing around the house. Halfway through, she'd forgotten how it went, and stopped. Her shivers returned.

It had been perhaps half an hour before the panoply of the law moved in, and, last of all, now a welcome sight amongst all those strangers, Lois had seen Hunter Cowgill striding swiftly towards her, a half smile on his face. Well, it was all right for him: dead bodies were his stock in trade. But this was the first – no, second – that Lois had seen. And her dad didn't really count, because she had sat with him during those final hours, until he had slipped away in morphine-assisted sleep. There had been no sudden end, no point at which she could have said, now he's dead, my dad, gone. But coming across the major like this, in the middle of a day when she'd had an hour or so to spare and decided to satisfy idle curiosity, this took a bit of getting used to.

'I won't say I told you so,' said Cowgill, sitting down in the pew next to Lois.

'What?' she said sharply.

'On the phone, you said there was nothing for you to do, and I said there was always crime. And here it is, and you right in the middle of it.'

Lois stared at him. 'You don't think *I* did it?' she said, and was rapidly Lois Meade again. 'But then, of course I did,' she added, sitting up straighter. 'I knifed the old bugger, dressed him up in a suit of armour I happened to have handy in the kitchen cupboard, loaded him into the car boot, drove him here and hoisted him up on to that tomb thing . . . oh yes, and drugged this dog so he looked like stone.' She stared at Cowgill, and said angrily, 'Have I left anything out? Or will you arrest me now?'

'How do you know he was knifed?' said Cowgill. 'No, no, don't answer that,' he added hastily. 'Just tell me all about it, from the beginning. And don't look at me like that, Lois. I am making no assumptions at this stage.'

After that, he suggested she went outside and waited on the bench by the moat. 'Best leave the dog with the policewoman over there. You look frozen, and the sun's out now.' This was true, but he really wanted her out of the way when they got to work on removing the body of the major. It was not going to be easy, in that armour. And there were numerous tests to be done, photographs to be taken, notes to be made. 'I'll be with you in a couple of minutes,' he said, 'and when you've given me the bare bones of it' – Lois grimaced – 'you can go home, and I'll come and see you later.'

'What about the dog?' she said.

'We'll look after it,' Cowgill assured her, standing aside to let her out of the pew.

'But afterwards?' she persisted. 'What will happen to it?'

'Dog's home, something like that,' he said absently. The dog was not uppermost in his mind.

'Well, we'll have it, give it a home,' said Lois firmly, 'if nobody else will.'

'All in good time, Lois,' he said now. 'Other things to do first. Now off you go, there's a good girl, and I'll be with you shortly.' He should have known better.

'Sod that,' said Lois. 'I've got a family to see to. No difference between a bench outside and my own house, as far as I can see. I'll be there. Not that there's much to tell,' she added.

This was not entirely true. Before the police arrived, she had walked around the church, especially the tomb, noticing a number of things but touching nothing, of course. One thing was immediately obvious: there must have been more than one person. No one person, however strong, could have lifted the major in his full suit of armour up on to the high tomb. Two people, then? And when? Two men carrying a knight in battle rig was not a common sight in Dalling Park in broad daylight. There must have been a van, too. No, it would have been at night. That would have been easy enough, when the park was completely deserted. The key for the church? Kept by the verger, and easy enough to borrow and copy, if you had the means.

As she drove the car back to Long Farnden, Lois pondered on what she knew. It was pretty clear that it had been a well-planned job, needing time and manpower. But why such an elaborate plan? Anyone could have broken into the major's house in the middle of the night, killed him quietly, and got away before anyone noticed. Well, for a while, anyway. No, this was a nasty, bizarre murder, and the motive would no doubt turn out to be as twisted as the execution. Lois shivered again.

She parked the car in the garage and walked rapidly into the house, suddenly wanting normality, the kids and Derek. The school bus hadn't arrived yet, and Derek was alone. He stood at the cooker, Lois's apron tied round his waist, and a wonderful smell of frying greeted her. She looked at the table already laid for tea, and smiled. 'Thanks, Derek,' she said.

'No problem, me duck,' he said. 'And before I forget, one of your cleaning women rang – Sheila Stratford? – wondering where you were.'

'Oh God! I promised to call on her . . . went right out of my head. I'll ring her now.'

'Fine,' said Derek, and added coolly, 'and how was our old buddy, Sherlock Cowgill?'

Nine

Lois arranged to call on Sheila Stratford next morning, and then Hazel and Bridie Reading after that. 'Don't be too late,' Hazel had said cheerfully, 'I'm on duty at the pub at twelve. And hey, Lois, what about you and the major?'

As this was so soon after Lois had found the body, she wondered how Hazel knew about it so quickly. Then she remembered that the girl also worked in the bar at the hall, and word would have got back there from the church pretty quickly. 'The major is nothing to do with me,' she replied sharply, and added, 'and don't forget to tell your mother I'm coming.'

But first there was Sheila Stratford, who lived in Waltonby just down from the pub. Her references were good, one from the local vicar, and the other from her husband Sam's employer, a farmer in the village. Middle-aged, from a local family, with her own daughter and grandchildren living close by, Sheila Stratford sounded the kind of reliable, solid countrywoman that Lois had first envisaged for her team.

It is definitely the morning after for me, thought Lois, as she drove into Waltonby slowly, looking for the Stratfords' house. I could certainly do with a bit of sparkle from somewhere. Hunter Cowgill had called at the house after tea, and Derek had not been welcoming. In fact, he'd retreated to the garage, banging doors as he went.

'Take no notice, he'll come round,' Lois had said, making the inspector a cup of coffee. 'He still remembers Josie being in danger, an' that, and your lot doing their job.'

Cowgill had seemed sincere when he'd replied quietly, 'We all remember that, Lois.'

They'd talked about the major, and the circumstances of

Lois's discovery. Cowgill asked her how much she knew about him, and she'd told him all that Hazel Reading had said. When she had added that Derek had seen him several times in the pub, Cowgill said he'd need to talk to Derek, too, and was this a good time?

Derek had been reluctant, but had come back in and answered the inspector's questions. 'Didn't know the bloke at all,' he'd said. 'Just seen him at the bar, chatting up the barmaids. Best ask Geoff Boggis, the landlord.'

'We will,' Cowgill had nodded. 'But did you say he chatted up the barmaids? Bit old for that, wasn't he?'

Derek shook his head. 'Not in that way,' he'd replied. 'It was just a bit of fun . . . always the perfect gent, as far as I could see. You know the sort. Ex-army, or so he said.'

'Mmm,' said Cowgill. He had had a few more words with Lois, then looked at her exhausted face and wound it up. 'I'll be in touch,' he said at the door. 'And you know the form . . . anything more you come across, let me know through . . . no, on second thoughts, ring me direct on this number.' He scribbled on a piece of paper and gave it to her, and left quickly, nodding goodbye to Derek.

Lois put the paper into her apron pocket and began to wash up. As she took off the apron later, she felt the paper crackle. She pulled it out and read the number, and then something else: 'And don't forget Alibone Woods,' he'd written. Well, that was clear. She knew all about Alibone Woods.

Now she pulled up outside the Stratfords' house, the last in a row of six council houses, with a neat front garden and newly painted front door. Lois breathed deeply, relaxed, and prepared to be reassured. Sheila was very reassuring. She smiled, gave Lois a cup of hot coffee and a home-made biscuit, and answered her questions with just enough information and no gossip.

'Why do you want to work for me?' Lois said finally, sure that here was someone she could happily appoint her deputy when needed. 'I'm sure there's enough domestic work in Waltonby to keep you busy all week.'

Sheila nodded, and said simply, 'That's just it, Mrs Meade. I want to get out of the village. It's all too close, working for women who know each other. I don't like being the gossipmonger-in-chief, although I'd have every opportunity!'

Lois laughed. 'I know all about that! A degree in diplomacy – that's what you need,' she said.

And what else? Once again, Inspector Cowgill's words came back to her. She would have to glean information, she knew that. She would also have to use her cleaners, but not let them know about it. If they suspected, that would be much too dangerous. Well, it was probably not going to be easy, but first things first. She intended to recruit a good team to make a successful business, and Cowgill would have to come low on her present list of priorities.

Sheila Stratford beamed as Lois left. She'd got the job, and could start as soon as possible. Lois would give her a ring, intending to have a first meeting of all her cleaners, introduce them to each other, and give them prepared schedules. There was a spring in Lois's step that had not been there earlier, and she whistled as she got into her car and set off for the Readings'.

Her good mood was, for once, not shattered by Bridie Reading's greeting. Bridie looked cheerful and confident. 'Come on in,' she said. 'Hazel's here. Says you might want her on the team as well?'

'Mmm, well,' said Lois, 'we'll need to talk about that. And no thanks, Bridie, no coffee. Just had some, thanks. No, let's get on with it.'

She explained to Bridie about the intended meeting, and then turned to Hazel. 'You'd be a lot younger than the others,' she said, 'though Gary Needham is still in his twenties.'

'Gary Needham?' Hazel's expression was strange.

'D'you know him, then?' said Lois.

Hazel shrugged. 'Seen him around,' she said. Then she added with a odd smile, 'So there'll be a man on the team? Wow, Mrs M, that's cool! Could jolly things up a bit . . .'

Lois, seeing complications ahead, said, 'Now listen to me, Hazel, if I do employ you, you'll toe the line with the others. No special favours because me and your mum are friends. I shall expect respect, and the first signs of trouble you'll be out on your ear. You'll be working for all sorts of people, and you'll keep your clever comments to yourself. You will have to be punctual, polite and thorough in your work. I shall check on everybody at first, until I know how things are going.'

'So, is it on, then?' said Hazel, grinning broadly. 'Gimme a go?'

Lois sighed. Against my better judgement, she thought, but looked at Bridie's face, so bright and optimistic for once, and nodded agreement. 'A trial period,' she said. 'One month, and then we'll review it.'

'Does that go for the others, too?' said Hazel, bridling.

'I'm still thinking about it,' said Lois. 'But it's a definite for you, so take it or leave it.'

'I'll take it,' said Hazel, and to Lois's surprise she crossed the room and shook Lois by the hand.

'All right, then,' Lois said, 'and now on to the hot topic in Waltonby this morning.'

'The major?' said Bridie, settling herself comfortably. 'Well, ask Hazel. She knows all about him. Go on, love, tell Lois. She won't let it go no further.'

Much of what Hazel had to tell was barmaids' speculation. She and Prue had felt sorry for the major at first, and made a fuss of him. At least, Hazel had. Prue found it difficult, said Hazel, being brought up differently. In the end, both had had much the same experience. Leaving the pub late one Saturday night, Hazel had heard someone following her, and discovered the major a few paces behind. 'Just watching over you, my dear,' he'd said, and she'd not been alarmed. But then he'd come closer and taken her arm. 'When we got to his gate,' Hazel said to an attentive Lois, 'he sort of steered me towards his house. I tried to say I'd got to get home, and Dad would be furious if I was late, but he didn't take no notice. Said he'd got something to show me. In the end, I just pulled free and ran off.' She paused, and Lois waited. 'The worst of it,' Hazel continued, 'was him laughing. I could hear it all down the street. Gave me the shivers. I was more careful with him after that, though Prue did go in, *and* came out in one piece.'

'Doesn't he have any friends in the village?' said Lois, resisting the temptation to ask Hazel if she'd told her father.

Time for that later. She remembered Derek saying the major was always on his own in the pub, and never mixed with the others. She was curious to know where he came from, what he did for a living.

'Nope, no friends I've ever seen,' said Hazel. 'A loner, and no wonder. Though my dad says he knows for a fact he didn't have nothing to do with the army.' She and her mother exchanged looks. So Hazel had told her father, and there'd been repercussions.

'Didn't join in anything in the village?' said Lois.

Hazel shook her head. 'Went to Tresham every week, regular as clockwork. Oh, and I think Geoff Boggis said he used to do a bit of amateur dramatics. Some acting lot in Tresham, I think.'

Bridie, sitting quietly while her daughter was speaking, now chipped in, 'He'd be good at that . . . acting . . . Dick says he's been acting a part for years. He hates him, Lois. Or did . . .' Her voice tailed off as she remembered.

'Anyway,' said Hazel, 'why do want to know so much about him, Mrs M? You said yourself he was nothing to do with you.'

'I found him, didn't I?' said Lois.

Ten

The first meeting of New Brooms was a success. Lois had ushered her new employees into the big front room, and sunlight streaming in the window had warmed the atmosphere. Not that it was particularly cool. Bridie and Hazel had arrived first, and then Sheila Stratford, and, ten minutes later, Gary Needham. His unpunctual arrival had been the only blot on the proceedings. He'd apologized profusely, of course, and had a watertight excuse. Lois had not made much of it, apart from hoping this was not going to be a habit, and then got on with the business. It was only later that she remembered with some unease that all the women had smiled fondly on Gary and sympathized with his failure to get away from an urgent telephone call from his grandmother.

'Grandmother?' said Derek, as they sat over a sandwich lunch. 'That's an old one. Reckon you might have trouble with that one, Lois. Still, it's your business,' he added hastily. 'You'll know best.'

Lois laughed. 'Well done, Derek,' she said, and blew him a crumby kiss. ''Spect there'll be mistakes,' she added, 'and then you can say you told me so.'

She had explained how the cleaning business was to work, and Sheila Stratford had made some tentative but helpful suggestions. Lois had a list of clients, most of them the result of the advertisements for staff. There was clearly going to be no difficulty finding work for her team. She handed out the schedules, and Hazel was the first to speak.

'Oh, great, Mrs M! You've given me the vicar, old Rogers. He's not a bad old bloke. And everybody says he needs a good woman!'

'Yes, well,' said Lois, 'don't forget he's the Rev Rogers to you. And never mind about good women . . . you're there to clean his house, and that's all.'

'Blimey!' answered Hazel, with a grin at Gary. 'You don't think I'd—' She was cut short by a sharp kick on the ankle from her mother, and subsided obediently. Lois had also scheduled Hazel to work with her at the hall, where she could keep an eye on her.

'Everything all right for you, Sheila?' said Lois. She had allocated Sheila and Gary the doctor's surgery in Tresham, thinking the older woman would be a good influence. It was a partnership on the edge of town, and in a new, attractive building. 'Not too big,' she explained, and Gary said yes, he knew it well. His aunt was a patient there. Lois explained the need for absolute confidentiality: 'And that goes for you all,' she stressed. 'Whatever you see or hear, it is to go no further. The least bit of gossip'll mean the sack for New Brooms.'

She looked around. 'And Bridie? Everything OK for you?' She had given Bridie local jobs, sensing that her friend was not as confident as her extrovert daughter, and might like to be close to home. It had been encouraging, though, to see Bridie's happy face, and Lois had felt like touching wood. There was a lot riding on the success of New Brooms.

The rest of the week was spent shopping for cleaning equipment – a more expensive outlay than Lois had bargained for – and making sure that everyone knew what they were doing, and clients knew who to expect and when. Derek came and went, and kept out of Lois's way, except when he could see she was tired and needed propping up. The children were difficult. It had been bad enough having a mother who went out cleaning, but now she was running a business that was going to take up even more time; they felt left out and resentful. Josie was not so bad. She had admired Hazel Reading from afar on the school bus, and was pleased that she might see more of her now. But Douglas and Jamie were edgy and quarrelsome.

'They'll be all right, me duck,' Derek said periodically. 'Once you're up and runnin', it'll fall into place. Don't worry, leave 'em to me.' And he'd organized a trip to the Space Centre at Leicester for the weekend, hoping that would take their mind off their distracted mother.

The first Monday for New Brooms arrived with a gusting wind, drifting showers, and occasional bursts of encouraging sunshine. Lois had just waved Derek off to work, seen that all the kids had safely boarded the school bus, and was settling nervously in her office to await problem telephone calls, when a van drew up outside. It was a white van, with a large rose and the Interflora device clearly visible. A tap at the front door revealed a pleasant-faced woman bearing a large bouquet. 'Mrs Meade?' she said, and handed them over.

Lois took the flowers into the kitchen, thinking how lovely it was of Derek to think of such a thing. Then she opened the little gift card, and read the words: 'Congratulations and Good Luck to New Brooms. H.C.' Well, that wasn't too difficult. Hunter Cowgill. Lois breathed in the heady scent of lilies and roses, and wondered what to do. Since when did the cops send out bouquets, for God's sake? But then, Hunter Cowgill had demonstrated only too clearly that he was no ordinary cop. And how was she going to explain it to Derek? Sod it, she muttered, and began to unwrap the blooms. 'New Blooms!' she said suddenly, and began to laugh. There was no doubt a bunch of flowers cheered you up, whoever'd sent it. The telephone began to ring, and with a lighter heart Lois lifted it up, feeling ready for anything.

Eleven

The manager at Dalling Hall was incandescent. 'How did they do it?' he repeated, until Lois finally said, 'Look, I have no idea. I just found him. Yes, I know it's bad publicity, but you can be sure I shall not say anything. Mind you,' she could not resist adding, 'I don't see the press keeping quiet. Pretty juicy story, really. Dead body inside knight's armour in remote church. Upmarket hotel denies any knowledge, etc etc.'

She held the telephone away from her ear, until the shouting stopped. 'If I were you,' she said soothingly, 'I should think of a way of turning it into a good thing – you know, scene of the crime . . . come and play detective, that kind of thing?'

There was silence while he thought of that one. 'You know, Lois,' he said finally in his normal voice, 'you could be on to a good thing. Have to OK it with the police, of course, but it could be a big attraction. Well, I knew I'd think of something!' he added breezily, and rang off.

'Well, there's gratitude,' said Lois into the dead telephone.

She looked at her schedule for the team, and wondered how they were all getting on. Chiefly she wondered about Gary and Sheila. It was an unlikely combination, but could be good. Sheila would curb Gary's garrulous tendencies, very necessary when all the work had to be done before surgery opened. Neither of them had quibbled about starting really early in the morning. In fact, Sheila had welcomed it, saying her husband was always off to the farm at dawn; and even Gary had smiled and said how pleased his mum would be to see him out of bed before midday. Hazel had laughed at that, and Lois had made a mental note not to put those two together on any job. She lifted the telephone and dialled Sheila's number.

'How did it go, then? I'll just be checking for the first week with everyone. Hope you don't mind.' Lois wondered if she was being too tentative.

But this approach worked with Sheila Stratford, who replied in a warm voice that she was hoping Lois would ring, as she was really longing to tell her about their early morning in the surgery. 'First of all,' she said, 'I expect you'll be wanting to know if Gary was there on time! Well, yes, he was, waiting for me at the door!' They'd set to work straight away, and had found most of the consulting rooms tidy and little trouble to clean. But one, the old doctor's, was a real mess, things all over the place that should have been locked away. 'Gary said straight away he'd tackle it. Went at it like a dose of salts! He's a nice lad, Lois. I reckon you've got a good 'un there. No, there were no problems really . . . except . . .'

'Yes?' prompted Lois.

'It was just I had this funny feeling . . . silly really. Gary laughed at me, but he wasn't there when I heard it. Just a little noise now and then, like somebody having a rootle around.' Sheila paused, and Lois frowned.

'Could it have been one of the surgery staff, come in early?' she said. Blimey, Sheila was the last person she'd have suspected of nervous fancies! No, there was probably a simple explanation. 'Mice?' she suggested.

Sheila's good, wholesome laugh was reassuring. 'That's what Gary said,' she answered. 'But I've seen enough to know all the signs of mice – and rats, come to that! No, I expect it was birds in the roof, somethin' like that. Anyway, don't worry, Lois, we'll get it sorted. So, a good report, really, and both of us enjoyed it too.'

'Can't want for better than that, then,' said Lois, but put down the telephone feeling oddly uneasy.

Hazel and Bridie had both started in houses in Waltonby, though it had apparently been a struggle persuading Richard Reading that there was nothing to be ashamed of in having 'his women', as he called them, cleaning in their own village. 'Skivvying! Good God, what would my mother have said!' Quite a lot, Bridie had thought, remembering the old battleaxe who'd given her such a hard time before she died. Dick had inherited all her ire, and none of his father's gentle kindness, unfortunately. Bridie had not seen this before her marriage, but it had soon become apparent. Now, fortified by a new independence, and the full support of her daughter, she realized she could at least face up to his onslaughts without total collapse.

'Cheerio, then,' she'd said, as she set off for the big farmhouse in Waltonby's back road. Hazel had gone in the opposite direction, and had blown her mother a kiss as she turned the corner. Dick Reading had fumed on his own for a while, then slammed out of the house and set off for Dalling Hall, where he had a delivery to make.

Lois, still sitting by the telephone, reflected that perhaps she had had the worst of it. The others were off on exciting new projects, whilst she had little to do today except worry about them. She was glad she had decided to carry on with Hazel on Tuesdays at Dalling Hall. She was sure it was a good thing to keep her hands on the broom, in a manner of speaking.

Hazel Reading was in fine form, taking care to be brisk but thorough. The job was at a new stone house on the edge of Waltonby, one of a small estate built on a paddock that had once been grazed by sturdy ponies belonging to the village's carrier.

'Um, whatever you're having, Mrs Jordan,' Hazel said, halfway through her three hours and gasping for a drink. The central heating was overpowering, and the physical work of cleaning and polishing had warmed her up to a rosy glow.

'Do sit down for minute, then,' said Mrs Jordan, and put a cup of steaming coffee in front of Hazel. In minutes, it seemed, the woman had told her her life story, and Hazel had listened with interest. No information is wasted, she reckoned. You never knew when it might come in useful. She remembered Lois's strictures about gossip, and wondered if she dare answer any of the pointed questions fired at her. But the bar work in the pub stood her in good stead, and she managed to be polite and give very little information in return.

Upstairs again, and restored by the coffee, Hazel entered the main bedroom, and stepped back in alarm. On a tall chest in front of her was a grinning face, surmounted by a huge mop of chestnut curls. She must have gasped aloud, because Mrs Jordan came running up. She was laughing, and took Hazel by the arm. 'It's all right!' she said. 'Just a wig stand and my wig for the play! One of our cast painted the face on it for fun . . . so sorry it made you jump . . .' And then she was off on a long tale about the amateur dramatic company she belonged to in Tresham, and how she had a really big part in the latest production. 'Mind you,' she said, 'we've had a bit of shock. The man playing the lead part has . . . well, has dropped out . . .'

'Shame,' said Hazel, trying to get past the woman and into the bathroom, next on her list. Then something familiar chimed in her head. 'Amateur dramatics?' she said. 'You mean acting, an' that?' The woman nodded her head. 'And this bloke who's dropped out . . . you don't by any chance mean dropped off the perch?'

The woman frowned at this flippancy, but nodded. 'Yes,' she said.

'Ah,' said Hazel, starting on the hand basin with vigour, 'then I think I know who you mean. Was it Major Todd-Nelson? Because if it was, then you can take it from me he had it coming. Now, shall I give the windows a quick wipe?'

It was only on her way home, tired but still cheerful, that she realized what she'd said. Oh dear, Lois wouldn't like that. Still, with luck she wouldn't know.

In the Coachman's bar at the Tresham Arms, Joanne Murphy, who had so humiliatingly failed to join the team in New Brooms, leaned confidentially across the bar and whispered in the ear of the young man in front of her. Both of them looked unusually serious.

'But what are we going to do next?' said the young man. He was not the kind of customer the management encouraged, and the barman was keeping an eye on Joanne.

'Dunno,' she said. 'It's a bloody nuisance. Left us all in the shit, this has. Anyway, you'd better drink up and go. Old Ted along there don't like your sort in here. You'll get me into trouble, and I need this job, Gary. I'll get in touch as soon as I know somethin' definite.'

Twelve

Lois was glad to be out of the house and on her way to Dalling Hall. Yesterday had been a strain, but then the first day of any job is difficult. The difference is, she supposed, that before, she'd always been on her own, working for herself, confident that if a new cleaning job turned out badly, she could always leave. Now she was responsible for four other people, and if New Brooms succeeded, there would be more than four.

She glanced across at the huddled old church, with its surrounding moat and miniature drawbridge. It was a grey morning, and a hazy mist lingered over the fields. Lois shivered. When she hadn't been worrying about New Brooms, her mind had roamed around what she knew of the major's strange end. What had he done that was so terrible someone had to kill him? And the way he'd died . . . she'd heard no more from Hunter Cowgill about that. In fact, she'd heard nothing from him at all, and she'd quite expected him to be round again with more questions. Perhaps he was biding his time, filling in blanks from other sources. Maybe she'd get in touch, ask him about that poor little dog first, and then see what else came up. After all, she reasoned, if he wants my help again, there's got to be some exchange of information. On past experience, she knew that anything Cowgill deigned to tell her was usually negligible and stuff she knew anyway. Still, it was worth a try.

'Morning, Lois!' said the manager of Dalling Hall. His smile was restored, and Lois guessed he'd had a few bookings since they'd talked. Nothing like a juicy murder to bring out the ghouls. They'd probably arrange guided tours, thought Lois. 'This is where the major lay, and there's the broken effigy of the real knight, in the corner there. Such vandalism! And now come this way, please, where we have coffee laid on in the chancel and you can all purchase a specially written brochure on Dalling Hall and its historic church.'

'Is Hazel Reading here?' she asked, and was gratified to hear a voice behind her. 'Yep, I'm here, all ready to start. Mum sends her love. Can't say Dad feels the same, but who cares!'

'Yes, well, let's get started, Hazel,' said Lois, and led the way through winding corridors and into the Great Hall, with its limed oak doors at either end, huge portraits by the yard of English kings and queens, and the lovely beamed roof that not even the keenest interior decorator could spoil.

Apart from the occasional interruptions by scurrying staff using the hall as a short cut, Lois and Hazel were alone. Surreptitious glances told Lois that Hazel was unquestionably a good worker, and contrary to her expectations, silent. In the end, it was Lois who spoke. 'So you got on all right yesterday with Mrs Jordan?'

'Yep,' said Hazel. 'She was OK. Bit daft, an' that, but OK.'

'How d'you mean – daft?' said Lois.

'Oh, you know, couldn't stop talking the minute I arrived. Followed me about. Asked questions all the time. Oh yes, an' this'll make you laugh! She had this weird head with loads of hair in her bedroom . . . talk about severed head! 'Course, turned out it was a wig on a wig stand, wasn't it. Give me quite a turn for a minute.'

Lois, who had talked initially to Mrs Jordan about the job, looked surprised. 'A wig? She didn't look like the sort.'

'No, she don't wear it around. She's in this drama group in Tresham, an' it's for a play she's in. Well, I suppose it's all right for those that like it. My life's dramatic enough, without playin' at it.'

'You mean your dad,' said Lois quietly. Hazel's face was turned away from her, as she polished an old side table with loving care. There had been a break in her voice. Hazel Reading's tough, uncaring front that she presented to the world was hard won. Lois wondered why the girl didn't leave home, go off like others and make her own life.

'Yeah, Dad,' replied Hazel. 'Still, our daily dramas won't turn into tragedies, not while I'm there.' And so Lois had her answer.

'That Gary,' said Hazel, changing the subject, 'how did he get on with Sheila Stratford? Funny bloke, but not bad, I reckon. I can just see him getting up speed with the Hoover!'

One of Lois's first rules for New Brooms had been an absolute ban on discussing one cleaner with another, so she just laughed and said time would tell. She guessed the doctors would soon complain if they weren't satisfied.

'And that goes for us here, too,' said Hazel with a flourish. 'Done my side, so shall I come over and give you a hand?'

Cheeky devil, thought Lois, but she smiled, and the rest of the morning they worked together equably enough.

It was while they were having a coffee break that Hazel remarked casually that Prue Betts had stopped working as a barmaid. 'She's not going to college yet, so it's a bit of a mystery. The lads in the pub say she told them her dad came on a bit strong about the major, and the dangers of alcohol and stuff, and soon after that Prue left. Shame, really. I liked her, and I reckon she enjoyed it. Grew up quite a bit, did Prue! Haven't seen her lately, so I expect he's told her I'm a bad influence.'

'Is he like that, then, her dad?' said Lois lightly.

'Not nearly as bad as mine,' said Hazel with a grimace. 'But he is a teacher, and you know what teachers are. Thinks his family should set an example in the village, an' all that rubbish. But he's very fond of Prue, and they don't have many rows . . . Anyway, Mrs M, it's time we got goin' again. Can I do the bridal suite? It'd be nice to think I might need it one day.'

It had been easier at the hall with the two of them. Somehow Hazel's chirpy enthusiasm made much lighter work of it. Feeling pleased with the day, Lois returned to her sunny office and checked the answerphone. Nothing alarming, thank goodness, but the last message made her smile. Must be telepathic, she thought. 'Hunter Cowgill here,' the deep voice said. 'Could you give me a ring, Lois? Oh, and I hope New Brooms are sweeping clean.'

She dialled the number he'd given her and when he answered, said, 'I was going to ring you anyway. What's happened about the major's dog? I said I'd take it, and Derek's agreed . . . reluctantly, but he said we could have it.'

'It's being well looked after,' Cowgill replied. 'An old lady heard about him and was very keen. He's quite a nice old chap. The sergeant got quite fond of him.'

'And the major?' said Lois. 'Don't think he was a nice old chap, not from what I've heard.'

'Ah, yes,' said Cowgill. 'Well, that's why I rang. Can you manage a meeting? A few points have come up, and one or two questions you might help with. And,' he added hastily, remembering Lois's previous insistence on two-way exchange, 'I can give you a few pointers, if you're still interested.'

'Oh, I'm interested all right,' said Lois. 'Any bloke who invites young girls into his house late at night is of great interest to me, even if he is dead. Could be part of something bigger, and my Josie is, well, you know . . .'

'No need to remind me, Lois,' said Cowgill. 'Right, then. Ten o'clock tomorrow morning in Alibone Woods. And park your car where I showed you, out of sight.'

Lois sighed. Trudging through muddy woodland paths was not much in her line, but she could see Cowgill's point. No one was going to talk to Lois Meade if they thought she was in league with the cops. 'Ten o'clock,' she said. 'I'll be there.'

'You know that girl, used to be on the school bus? Her dad's a teacher at Waltonby school?' Josie had spoken with her mouth full, head down, polishing up tomato sauce from her pizza plate.

'Did you say Waltonby?' said Lois.

'He's head teacher,' said Douglas. 'My friend went to school there, and he liked him.'

'What about the girl, Prue Betts?' said Lois, frowning Douglas into resentful silence.

'Yeah, that's her,' said Josie. 'Well, she's in hospital. Her friend said, on the bus today. She didn't know what was wrong with her. Apparently her mum's upset, but not saying anything. What d'you reckon's happened, Mum?'

Lois looked hard at her daughter, and thought she looked shifty. Knows more than she's telling, Lois considered. She knew better than to grill her, but just said that whatever it was she hoped Prue would soon be recovered and back at home.

Then when Derek came in, he was full of it. 'Seems the parents aren't sayin' anything, and have told Prue's friends to keep their mouths shut, so it's not appendicitis, is it? Somethin' they don't want talked about. Doug in the pub says they'd had a row, Prue and her dad. Stopped her working in the pub. But he was sure old Betts would never knock her about, nothin' like that. That Dick Reading, yes, all the blokes in the pub know about him. But Prue's dad's one of them non-violence, preachy sort.'

Josie and Douglas exchanged glances. 'Them quiet ones are always the worst,' said Douglas, with comic maturity.

Josie hooted. 'O 'course, you'd know all about it, wouldn't ya.'

Douglas reached over the table, took a half-eaten orange from Josie's plate and ran off upstairs, followed by loud strictures from his parents and admiring laughter from Jamie.

When things had quietened down, Lois turned to Derek and said quietly, 'I don't like it, Derek, there's something funny goin' on.'

'Well, no doubt you and your huntin' chum will find out what it is,' said Derek lightly.

Thirteen

Alibone Woods were full of the sounds of invisible creatures. Birds and rabbits rustled in the undergrowth, and a black crow clattered away over the trees in alarm at Lois's footsteps. At this time of day there were no walkers, and the bluebells that in Spring attracted hundreds of visitors had died away, leaving slippery mats of rotting leaves that caught Lois unawares. As she picked her way along the twisting path, wishing she'd remembered to put wellies in her car, she saw Cowgill's tall shape leaning against a tree in the clearing where they had arranged to meet.

As he heard her approach, he turned to greet her. 'Morning,' he said. 'Thanks for coming.'

His face was the usual impassive policeman's mask, but Lois thought he had a particularly sombre look about him this morning. 'What's up?' she said, getting down to business.

He raised his eyebrows. 'Well, for a start,' he said, 'an elderly man has been found dead on a tomb in Dalling church . . .'

'All right, all right,' said Lois, 'but what's new? Must be something for me to be standing in the middle of a muddy wood with—'

'And I appreciate your coming,' Cowgill interrupted, 'especially when your New Brooms is just getting off the ground. How's it going, by the way?'

'Fine,' answered Lois. 'But what did you want? I've got to go over and introduce Gary Needham into a new job later, so I can't stay long.'

'Ah yes,' said Cowgill. 'Tell me about young Gary. Satisfactory, is he?'

'I don't know yet,' said Lois, shrugging. 'So far he seems fine.'

'And the others?' said Cowgill.

Lois frowned. She didn't want to talk about her team to Cowgill. Lines had to be drawn. She shrugged. 'Well, there's Bridie and Hazel, and I've got a woman from Waltonby signed up, too: Sheila Stratford – very nice woman.'

'Yes, we've already talked to her,' said Cowgill. 'Her husband works on the hall farm, and she sometimes does flowers in the church.'

'So what else, then?' she said, hoping to get him on to something new. But he came back to Gary Needham.

'Young Gary,' he said. 'Anything you can tell me? First impressions, family background, that sort of thing? I know you well enough to know you'd have made enquiries.'

Lois sighed. Cowgill never gave up, she knew only too well, so she told him how she'd first thought Gary a complete waste of time, just what she did *not* want. Then she described her change of mind, and how at the first meeting of all of them together, Gary had seemed to fit in well. He had a knack of being able to handle the others' doubts about him. And, more importantly, he'd proved his claim to be an excellent cleaner. She did not tell him about the noises Sheila heard at the surgery on the first morning. This had nothing to do with Gary, surely.

'So have you got something on him?' she said.

Cowgill shook his head. 'Not really,' he said. 'He's been seen with some unlikely characters in Tresham . . . clubbing, all of that . . . but no, nothing necessarily wrong.'

'Clubbing!' said Lois. 'Don't talk to me about that! Our Josie only mentions it six times a day and pesters the life out of us to let her go with some older kids.'

'Don't let her,' said Cowgill flatly. 'If you can stop her, that is,' he added.

'Oh yes, we can stop her,' said Lois. 'Now we're in Long Farnden, she can't just flounce out and disappear. Needs us for transport, fortunately. What else did you want to know?' She had told him nothing much, really.

'Anything odd come your way, in the cleaning jobs?' said

Cowgill. 'Overheard anything in the hall, or reports from the cleaners? You know anything you say is in strict confidence, anyway.'

Lois told him about the major's acting activities, and about Hazel's encounter with Mrs Jordan and her wig. She asked him if he knew about the drama group? He did, of course, but was interested in Hazel Reading.

'Quite a bright spark, that one,' he said. 'Knows the scene pretty well.'

'What scene?' said Lois. She remembered now how she had always found his enigmatic remarks extremely irritating.

'Oh, you know,' he replied, 'latest crazes, pubs, staying afloat. Her mum's a friend of yours, isn't she, Lois? And her dad? What do you know about him?'

'Too much,' said Lois. 'He's a sod, as I expect you know. Still, Hazel's got him sussed out, and Bridie seems a lot happier now she's working for Brooms. Nothing bad enough for you to step in there,' she added quickly.

She was waiting for him to ask what she knew about Prue Betts, and sure enough, just when they'd started to walk back to the cars, he said casually, 'Don't suppose you know the Betts's at Waltonby? Prue Betts, worked in the pub with Hazel? Father's the school headmaster?'

Lois stood still. 'No, I've only seen her in the pub. But now she's in hospital, the family have clammed up, and my Josie knows something. If she tells me, I'll let you know. Sounds a bit dodgy. Is there a connection, then, with the major?'

Cowgill shook his head. 'Too early to tell,' he said unhelpfully.

'What d'you want me to do, then?' said Lois. 'Apart from grassing on everybody I know.'

'No need to be like that,' said Cowgill. 'But I'd like to know more about these amateur theatricals without them knowing I'm interested at the moment. See what you can glean. Oh, and by the way, you haven't asked me how the major got into that suit of armour, or how we got him out. Not like you, Lois, to miss the obvious!'

'I've had a lot on my mind, in case you'd forgotten,' said Lois sharply. 'But tell me, anyway. I had wondered. Thought maybe somebody had half-inched a suit of armour from the hall, though I can't say I've ever noticed one.'

'Imitation,' said Inspector Cowgill.

'Come again?' said Lois.

'Polywhatever sort of stuff . . . the suit was made of it. Very well made, painted up to look just like the real thing. Just like you'd have on stage, in a play. We cut him out with very little trouble. Well, here we are,' he added, his voice now quite cheerful, and before she could reply, he'd thanked her again, said he looked forward to hearing from her, and disappeared at speed in his car.

'Fancy a night out at the theatre?' said Lois to Derek.

He stared at her. 'You gone crazy?' he said. He could just about be persuaded to go to the cinema, if the film was about football, but theatre was a foreign land to Derek, and he did not intend to venture abroad.

'There's this amateur lot in Tresham,' said Lois. 'Seems they've got a good comedy on, so the girls were telling me. Medieval stuff, damsels in distress, knights on white chargers, all that kind of thing.'

'Oh my God!' said Derek. 'Are you serious? Ah,' he added, 'wait a minute. Did you say "knights"?' Lois nodded. No flies on Derek. 'So,' he continued, 'there's an ulterior motive for this outing? Something come up to do with the major, now no longer a member of that poncey lot? Last seen givin' a very convincing performance as a dead knight in armour in Dalling Church? Come on, Lois. I'm wasn't born yesterday. If you want to go sleuthing in Tresham, take one of your pals. Bridie Reading'd like a night out for once. Take her.'

Lois shrugged. 'OK,' she said. 'Thought you might like to come along and give me a bit of a hand. Two pairs of eyes are better than one.' Derek did not reply, burying himself behind the sports page of the evening paper. 'Fine, thanks a lot,' said Lois. 'I'll ask Bridie, then. And next time you want me to drive you and your pissed pals back from a match, think again!'

She dialled the Readings' number, and Richard Reading answered the telephone. 'Oh, it's you,' he said grumpily. Like all bullies, he was temporarily deflated now his victim had turned on him. But he was biding his time, he told himself. Keeping a low profile. He had plans, he'd told his reflection in the shaving mirror that morning, and not unconnected with Lois Meade. 'I'll get her,' he said, and deliberately left Lois hanging on for several minutes before fetching Bridie in from the garden.

'Hello? Oh, hello, Lois. Did you want to know . . . ? Oh, nothing to do with New Brooms. A play, did you say? Well, I don't know . . . it doesn't sound much in my line. Oh, hang on, here's Hazel just come in. Wants a word with you.' Lois heard Bridie telling Hazel about the play, and wondered what it was Hazel wanted.

'Mrs M? I was going to ring you. That Mrs Jordan . . . you know, the one with wig! Well, she's asked for more hours next week. Seems they've got extra performances of this play. Very popular, she says. Will that be OK?'

Lois confirmed this, and then, on the spur of the moment, asked Hazel if she'd like to see the play. 'You'd know what Mrs Jordan was talking about then,' she said. To her surprise, Hazel seemed keen.

'What about Mum, though?' she said. Lois could hear Bridie being far from keen in the background, and then Hazel said, 'Right then, Mrs M, what time and where?'

They made the necessary arrangements, and Lois put down the telephone. She looked at Derek, slumped in the armchair, snoring gently. Of course he wouldn't want to go to a play. What was she thinking of? Poor bugger wouldn't want to go off to Tresham after a hard day's work.

She walked over to him, and leaned over, kissing the top of his head. 'I love you, Derek Meade,' she said. 'I love you just as you are, football, pissed pals and all.' He did not stir, but when she'd gone out of the room, he opened one eye and smiled.

Fourteen

Hazel Reading sat in Tresham Hospital at the bedside of a very pale, hollow-eyed Prudence Betts. The nurse had been reluctant to admit her into the private room where Prue lay sleeping. Hazel had had to force a small tear, and stress what close friends they were, before she was told, 'Five minutes only. And if she doesn't wake, then out you go.'

Hazel's watch showed she'd been there three minutes. Two minutes to go, but maybe they'd give her a bit longer. This was very important, and she needed to talk to Prue urgently. She looked around, making sure nobody was watching, and gave Prue's white hand a gentle pat. No reaction. She tried again, and this time Prue stirred. Her eyelids flickered, and then she was looking at Hazel, though her eyes were clouded, unfocussed.

'Prue?' whispered Hazel. 'How're you feeling? No, don't try to speak. Just listen. They're going to chuck me out in a minute, so try an' take this in.' She paused, looking anxiously at the still figure. To her relief, Prue nodded. It was a very slight nod, but there, without doubt. 'Right. Now then, it's goin' to be all right. You're not to worry at all. All over now. Get better quickly, ducky, and don't worry. See you soon.'

The nurse came into the room, looking at the watch pinned to her uniform. 'Time's up,' she whispered. Hazel stood up, and blew a kiss towards Prue, who had closed her eyes again. The nurse waited, holding the door open until Hazel had left without speaking. As she hurried down the long corridors and out of the hospital, she felt tears springing out and down her hot cheeks, and this time they were unforced.

*   *   *

'This should be a bit of fun, Mrs M!' said Hazel, her natural chirpiness restored.

They parked in the multi-storey in Tresham, and walked down the main street. All the shops were closed, of course, but quite a few people were still about. They passed a group of kids standing in the wide doorway of the library. 'Hi, Hazel!' shouted one of the girls, and the others turned round and stared.

'Friends?' said Lois. There was a lot she didn't know about Hazel Reading, and she was curious.

'Just a girl I used to go to school with,' said Hazel lightly. 'Now, don't we go down here?' They turned off down a dark passage that led into a back street of terraced, red-brick houses. Some were neat and newly-painted, and others had dirty curtains permanently drawn. Lois shuddered to think what went on behind those.

'It's down here somewhere,' she said. 'A converted shoe factory, they said.'

From the scruffy, narrow street, they entered a new world. A rich benefactor had bequeathed a large sum of money to the Tresham Dramatic Society's theatre for restoration, and as Lois led the way inside, it was as if they were entering a warm, red velvet-lined box. The theatre had a capacity of around two hundred, had raked seating, and a colourful safety curtain, hand-painted with the comic and tragic masks of drama. There was the promise of a richly rewarding evening, and Lois and Hazel sank into crimson plush seats with rising excitement.

About ten minutes into the play, Lois felt Hazel stir in her seat and lean forward, as if to get a better look. Then she heard a sharp intake of breath, and Hazel turned towards her, mouthing something silently. Lois couldn't get it. Hazel repeated it into her ear in a very soft whisper, but not soft enough for the man in the row behind them. He shushed at Hazel, making much more of a racket than she had with her whisper, but she subsided in her chair.

Lois stared hard at each of the three cast members on stage. Two men and a woman, all heavily made up, bewigged and dressed in elaborate costumes. The audience had warmed up, and the antics of one of the men, tall and thin, with an accentuated gangling gait, brought roars of laughter. Lois looked more closely at his face under an untidy wig. There was something about it . . . Then he turned and looked full-face at the audience, grinning at their reaction. Gary Needham. Gary was the gawky young fool, and playing the part very well indeed.

At the interval, Lois and Hazel struggled out of the auditorium with the chattering crowd, and made their way to the bar. 'What would you like?' Lois wondered if she'd remembered to put enough money in her purse for the gin and tonic she was sure Hazel would request.

'An orange juice, thanks,' said Hazel, 'but this is my turn. You paid for the tickets. So what'll it be?'

Lois said she'd have a glass of white wine, if Hazel could ever make it to the crowded bar. Finally they had their drinks and were settled at a small table in the corner.

'How about our Gary, then?' said Hazel. Her expression was serious, and Lois wondered why she did not find the spectacle of Gary making a fool of himself as funny as she did.

'He's good,' said Lois. 'Wonder why he didn't tell us he was in it? Still, why should he, really . . . He's got trouble enough with Brooms, him being the only man in a woman's world, an' all that. I know what Derek will say when I tell him!'

'Load o' bloody fairies! That's what my dad would say,' said Hazel, still unsmiling.

'Oh, come on, Hazel,' said Lois. 'It's not as bad as that! Give the lad a chance. You have to admit he's doing very well on stage, anyway.'

'And what else,' muttered Hazel to herself, and got up from the table, saying she had to go to the toilet. Lois sipped her drink, looking round at the crowd. It was like a private club, she thought. They all seemed to know each other, and over in the corner she caught sight of Mr and Mrs Betts, the schoolmaster from Waltonby and his wife. They were in earnest conversation with another couple, and she thought she recognized the tall, straight back of the man. Then he turned, and she saw that it was Detective Inspector Hunter Cowgill, and he was coming towards her.

'Evening, Mrs Meade,' he said, as if they were casual acquaintances meeting socially. 'Very good performance, don't you think? My wife and I are thoroughly enjoying it. Especially young Gary,' he said. 'I expect you'll be going round backstage to congratulate him after the show,' he added, and it sounded like an order.

Sod that, thought Lois, and said nothing. Cowgill turned to go, and Lois looked around for Hazel. A shrill bell rang, signalling the end of the interval, and Lois made her way back to her seat. Where had the girl got to? Just as the curtain rose, a commotion at the end of the row proved to be Hazel making her way across feet, handbags and rolled-up coats, until she reached her seat.

'Sorry,' she whispered. 'Long queue for the Ladies.'

'Shush!' hissed the man behind them, and the theatre became silent, waiting for the opening of Act Two. The audience, now thoroughly warmed up by laughter and interval drinks, responded vigorously to the continuing high jinks on stage, and Gary's character drew more laughs than any other.

As the play ended, Lois was slow to get to her feet. 'Come on, Mrs M!' said Hazel. 'Let's beat it. Follow me . . .'

But Lois frowned. 'No, just a minute, Hazel,' she said. 'Maybe we should go round backstage and have a quick word with Gary? Tell him how much we enjoyed it? That's what people do, don't they?'

Hazel stared at her. 'Some do,' she said. 'D'you really want to? I mean, we could tell him tomorrow, or whenever?'

Lois shook her head. 'No, I think we'll go now. It'd be nice for him. Come on,' she said, decisively now, and led the way. They found the stage door in a dark, narrow passage at the side of the theatre, and knocked.

'Yes?' said a woman's peremptory voice. No light fell on her face as she stood leaning against the door frame.

'Can we speak to Gary Needham for a minute, please,' said Lois.

'Well,' said the voice, 'look who's here . . . Gary!' she yelled. 'Your adoring public is at the door!'

'Come on, Mrs M,' said Hazel, tugging at her sleeve. 'Let's get out of here.'

But Lois was annoyed. She was being patronized, and did not like it. 'You can cut that,' she said sharply to the woman, whose voice sounded oddly familiar. Maybe because she'd just seen her on stage. 'Just get Gary Needham,' she added, 'and be quick about it.'

Then Gary's figure appeared in silhouette against the light from inside. Lois found herself pushed to one side by Hazel. 'It's me, Gary, and Mrs M is here with me, wanting to congratulate you on your performance,' she said quickly.

'Oh, right,' said Gary uncertainly. 'Hang on a minute. Too crowded in here.' He fumbled round the door frame, found a switch, and suddenly a light shone from above the door, illuminating Lois and Hazel. Gary stepped out into the passage. He had gathered his wits now, and said how very nice of Mrs M to come round. He was so sorry he couldn't invite them in, but there wasn't room to swing a cat, let alone a glass of champagne! 'Like the show, then, Hazel?' he said, finally looking in her direction.

'Yep,' she said. 'You were good. Very lively. Must be exciting when it goes well. Get a high from it, do you, Gary?' she added.

Lois wondered at Hazel's dry, clipped tone, and broke in quickly. 'We had a great evening. Never knew we had such talent in New Brooms!' she said, and then, puzzled by the failure of what should have been a jolly five minutes celebrating Gary's triumph, returned with Hazel to the car.

They drove for five minutes or so in silence. Then Lois said gently, 'What's up, Hazel?'

'Nothing.'

'Right,' said Lois, 'if you don't want to talk about it. But don't forget I've known you since you were a screaming brat. If you're quiet, it means something's up.'

The silence persisted for another five minutes. Then Hazel sighed. 'Trouble is, Mrs M,' she said, 'you don't know enough, and I know too much.'

In the darkness inside the car, Lois did not turn her head. Good thing I'm driving, she thought, and don't have to look at her. She might find it easier. 'About what, in particular?' said Lois.

'Oh, you know, everything,' said Hazel wearily. 'Stuff I hear in the pub, around the place. You and Mum think you had a wild youth, but you don't know nuthin'. Anyway,' she added, 'it's nothing to do with me, nor you, and we're best out of it.' She seemed about to say more, but hesitated.

'You might as well tell me,' said Lois. 'There's nobody else. Your mum's not up to listening, is she? And I can't see your dad being much of a help.'

'*I* don't need any help, Mrs M,' said Hazel emphatically. 'And I'll just say this. Gary Needham's fine as a cleaner. Can't be faulted, according to Sheila Stratford. But keep an eye on him, Mrs M. I been askin' around people who know him, and he's one to watch.'

Lois drew up outside the Reading house, and saw the front door open. Richard Reading's belligerent figure emerged. 'Hazel?' he yelled. 'About time too!'

Hazel turned to Lois. 'I won't ask you in,' she said with a grin, 'and thanks for the evening out. It was great.' Then she was out of the car, pushing past her father and gone from Lois's sight.

'Night, Dick!' Lois called. No sense in antagonizing him more than necessary. She didn't know about Gary yet, but she did know that Dick Reading was one to watch.

She turned the car round and headed off towards Long Farnden, thinking about Gary and his subdued reaction to seeing them. And that woman who'd opened the door . . . definitely familiar, and not from the stage. She'd spoken to her before, she was certain. Then it came to her, and the revelation was a shock. She had last heard that voice in a grubby, untidy room on the Churchill Estate in Tresham. It was Joanne Murphy, and Lois could not think of a more unlikely place to meet her again.

Fifteen

'First thing tomorrow,' Lois said, her back against the old Rayburn, drinking cocoa and warming up, 'I shall ring Gary and ask him to come over and see me.' The radiating heat relaxed her as she told Derek about the evening's surprise appearance of Gary Needham. She left out her brief conversation with Hunter Cowgill, but included the unpleasant exchange with Joanne Murphy.

'What the hell was *she* doin' there?' said Derek. 'The way you told it, she was a lazy slag who spent most of her time watching telly and smoking.'

'Yeah,' said Lois thoughtfully, 'but there's more, apparently.'

'Something you're not telling me, Lois,' said Derek. She shook her head, and he took her empty mug and rinsed it under the tap. 'Well,' he continued, 'just remember what I said. Don't you get involved in that major business. Could be a lot more there than meets the eye.'

'That's the trouble,' said Lois, 'nothing meets the eye. So far, nothing at all. Haven't heard a *really* bad thing said of Major Todd-Nelson. Except from Dick Reading, of course, and you can't count what he says about anything. The major was a lonely man with a weakness for young women – an' I mean women, not girls – and a member of an amateur dramatic society. Maybe not a very nice man, but there's plenty of those. But there's something, Derek, ferretin' away under the surface. Like one of them nasty insects that burrow under the skin.'

'So long as it's not under our skin, I'd advise you to leave it alone,' said Derek. 'And now to bed, sweet maid,' he added with rare dramatic inspiration, making Lois laugh.

They went up the wide stairs arm in arm, and just before

they settled for sleep, Derek said seriously, 'That old bloke probably *was* up to something rotten,' he said. 'I've heard some muttering in the Waltonby pub since he was done in. It'll all come out in good time, ducky, so don't you get mixed up in it. Let that Cowgill bloke sort it out on his own. That's what he's paid for.' He turned over, and Lois yawned.

'Mmm,' she said, 'Night, Derek. Sleep tight.'

Next morning Lois rang Gary early. 'When you've finished at the surgery,' she said, 'can you drop in here on your way to the pub?' She had assigned this job to Gary, and so far he was more than satisfactory.

The landlord, Geoff Boggis, had told Derek that he'd no fault to find at all. 'Fast and efficient, you can tell your Lois,' he'd said. 'And he doesn't gossip. You hear all kinds of things in pubs, but Gary doesn't want to know. Does his work, has a coffee and a quick chat about nothing in particular, and then goes. That's how I like 'em.'

'Sure, Mrs M, I'll drop in,' said Gary. He had adopted Hazel's name for her, and somehow it seemed right. Just that touch of respect she hoped to have from younger members of the team. Derek had laughed when she told him that. 'You'll be goin' on a management course next,' he'd said, and although he was joking, Lois had subsequently given it some thought. Still, they were doing fine so far. The surgery was a daily customer, likewise the pub and the hall, and the rest of the week had filled up nicely. Next step would be more cleaners, but at the moment Lois had decided to establish a solid base before expanding.

Gary arrived punctually, and Lois took him into her office. 'Not much time, Gary,' she said, 'so I'll come to the point.'

He looked puzzled. 'Something wrong?' he said.

'Far from it,' she said. 'Very good reports about your work. I thought I'd tell you that. And I just wanted to ask you something about a woman I saw when we came round backstage last night.'

Gary's expression changed. 'Oh yes,' he said, 'it was really nice to see you and Hazel. Never dreamt you'd show up! I was a bit embarrassed, I don't mind saying—'

Lois interrupted him. 'No need,' she said. 'But about this

woman. I could swear it was one who applied when we were starting New Brooms.' She thought of telling him how she'd turned down Joanne Murphy, and how disgusted she'd been at the whole set-up, not least the woman's reaction to being rejected. But she thought better of that. No, first wait and see if he knew her. 'She sounded just like Joanne Murphy,' she said, and waited.

Gary's expression did not change. He shook his head slowly. 'Can't remember that name,' he said. 'It's a big cast, mind,' he added, 'and some of 'em I only know by their Christian names. Let me think . . .' Lois watched him closely. He looked unruffled and not very interested. Then he brightened. 'There is one of the walk-on characters called Jo,' he said. 'Could that be her?' He picked up a rubber band from her desk and began twisting it in his fingers.

'Maybe,' said Lois. 'Anyway, she was the one that called you out to see us.'

'Yep, that was her,' he said, and looked at his watch. 'Shall have to be getting going,' he said, 'if Brooms wants to keep its reputation for punctuality.' He smiled at her, apparently relaxed and friendly. As she went to the door with him, he turned back and said casually, 'Oh, and by the way, why did you want to know about Jo?'

'Just curiosity,' Lois said. 'I hate not being able to recognize people. You know how it is . . . can't get it out of your head. So thanks for calling in. I did want to tell you how pleased everyone is with your work, anyway. See you next week.'

After he had gone, Lois sat for a while in her office, thinking. So it *was* Joanne Murphy, and Gary seemed to have no particular connection with her. But in that case, she said to herself, getting up ready to set off for the hall, why had he twisted that rubber band until it finally snapped?

In the schoolhouse in Waltonby, Mrs Betts prepared a lunch tray to take upstairs to Prue. She had returned home from hospital and gone straight upstairs to her room. The doctor had advised taking it easy for a few days, and suggested that a holiday away from Waltonby would be a good idea. When she had said Prue had cousins in the Lake District, he had been enthusiastic and waffled on about daffodils 'Beside the lake, beneath the trees', and the beauties of Lake Windermere. Prue had not seemed at all keen, but Mrs Betts intended to work on her. Worried and anxious as she had been, there had also been anger and a feeling of being betrayed. Hadn't they given her every advantage? Prue's father, she knew, had wanted a boy – still did – but had decided very soon that Prue would do equally well, and with any luck she would fulfil his decided views about equality of the sexes.

Mrs Betts had told nobody her own view, which was that Prue was a dear little girl and should play with dolls, prefer frilly dresses, and in due course become, perhaps, an infant teacher, which would prepare her very well for looking after her own family in the future. But it was best not to argue. She backed up her husband in his plan for Prue's education, and in her own quiet way made sure that the more frivolous side of a girl's growing-up was taken care of. The result, she had thought, was a daughter with pleasing looks and nature, a good brain, as her husband put it, and a healthy interest in the opposite sex.

A small voice answered Mrs Betts's knock on the bedroom door. She went in, and found Prue sitting up in bed, staring out of the window at the children in the playground.

'They're very lucky, those kids,' Prue said.

Her mother put the tray on the bedside table and sat on the end of the bed. 'How do you mean, darling?' she said quietly.

'Well, look at them. All in their lovely red and grey school uniform, dashing about without a care in the world. Except that one,' she added, 'over there in the corner.' Mrs Betts looked. A small girl sat on her haunches against the school fence, huddled up, the picture of misery. 'That was me,' said Prue. 'The outsider, the teacher's daughter. Nobody wanted me in their gang, nobody told me secrets. They thought I'd run off to Dad, and they'd be in trouble.'

Mrs Betts frowned. 'Are you serious, Prue?' she said. 'You never said anything at the time, and I'm sure your father would have noticed if there was anything wrong with you.'

'I was good at hiding it,' Prue said. 'It wouldn't have been any good telling Dad. He had a job to do, and that came first. As it should.' She turned towards her mother. 'You could have sent me to another school, though,' she said. 'If you'd thought. It was fine once I went on to Tresham. Only the school bus to contend with then.'

'It is easy to find excuses, Prue,' her mother said in a firmer voice. 'Easy to put the blame on to others . . . especially your parents . . . when things go wrong. Anyway,' she added, standing up, 'try and eat some lunch, and then you can come down and have tea with us later on. It's not good to sit up here on your own and brood.' She settled the tray on Prue's lap, and turned to go.

'Mum?' said Prue. Mrs Betts stood still, waiting.

'I'm sorry,' Prue said.

Detective Inspector Cowgill sat in his car outside the schoolhouse reading from a file of papers. After ten minutes or so he dialled a number on his mobile phone. 'Lois?' he said. 'We need to talk. Developments,' he said cryptically. 'Three o'clock suit you? No? All right, then, four o'clock. What about the kids home from school? Ah, good old Derek. Usual place, then. Bye.'

He opened the car door, shut it noiselessly, and walked slowly towards the school.

'Why do people always call just when we're sitting down to a meal?' said Mr Betts. 'No, I'll go,' he said to his wife, who had half-risen from her seat. He walked into the hallway, and she heard him say in an irritated voice, 'Yes? What do you want?' There was another voice then, quieter, and after that her husband's tone changed. 'Oh, I see,' he said, 'you'd better come in then. I'll get the wife. Prue's in bed upstairs, and still far from recovered.'

Mrs Betts sighed. It was a good thing they were having salad. She covered the plates and went into the sitting room to find her husband talking quietly to a tall, serious-faced man in a dark suit.

'This is Inspector Cowgill,' Mr Betts said, and the man shook her firmly by the hand.

'I shan't keep you long,' he said. 'And I do apologize for

coming at lunchtime. I thought it would be least disruptive for the school.' He took the chair indicated by Mr Betts, and said, 'Better get straight down to it. We know what happened to Prue, and are very sympathetic with you both. Very worrying time, of course, and this is not entirely connected with it. I realize that. But if you could just give me some idea of what kind of girl she is, how she spends her free time, who her friends are, that kind of thing, it would be a great help with our present investigations. Then perhaps I could have a quick word with her. I promise not to upset her, or stay too long.'

His quiet air of authority did the trick, as usual, and Mr Betts opened up at once, describing the good academic results of his daughter's schoolwork, her future place at university, his hopes for a brilliant career.

Mrs Betts said nothing, until Cowgill addressed her directly. 'And do you have anything to add?' he said kindly.

Mrs Betts thought of her conversation in the bedroom with Prue, and hesitated. She glanced nervously across at her husband, and then said quickly, 'She was unhappy at the village school. Found it difficult, with her father being headmaster. We didn't know. She only just told me.' And then, to her extreme chagrin and her husband's amazement, she burst into tears and hurried from the room.

'It's the stress,' said Cowgill reassuringly. 'My fault. It's probably too soon. Don't worry, Mr Betts. We'll leave the talk with Prue for a bit. Maybe tomorrow. And thank you for being so helpful. Give my apologies to your wife for upsetting her. Now, you go and help her, and I'll see my way out.'

Mr Betts, used to being the one in control, stood by the kitchen door uncertainly. 'Are you all right, love? he said to his wife, who sat at the table with her head in her hands. 'Anything I can get you? Anything I can do?' He moved round to where she sat and put his hands on her shoulders.

She shook her head. 'Unless you can put back the clock,' she said, 'there's not much we can do.'

Sixteen

'Isn't there somewhere else we could have these meetings?' said Lois, picking her way delicately through marshy ground in the woods.

'Can you think of anywhere?' said Hunter Cowgill equably. 'Just seems the most likely place I know, but I'm open to suggestions.' He could see Lois was in an irritable mood. He knew her well enough now to know that this usually meant she had something to tell him, and had not quite made up her mind whether to do so.

'I'll think about it,' she said, as they came to the clearing. She perched on the edge of the tree stump while he paced to and fro in front of her, saying nothing.

After a minute or so, Lois said, 'Well? You said there'd been developments. What are they?' Let him begin the exchange. She had not quite decided whether to tell him all she had discovered at the theatre, or just an edited version. She was very anxious not to draw his attention to Gary, who was proving a very useful member of her team. Loyalty was vital, she had stressed to the others, and this went for herself as well. New Brooms was in its infancy, but already she felt a kind of protective fondness for Hazel, Sheila and Bridie . . . *and* Gary. And anyway, there was absolutely nothing against him, she told herself firmly.

'You've probably heard something,' he said. 'In fact, I'm hoping you'll know more than we do. There's just a possibility it could have something to do with the major.'

'Very clear,' said Lois. 'You'll have to do better than that.'

He grinned. 'Patience, Lois,' he said. 'I'm getting round to it. Plodding cops are not renowned for their quicksilver minds. No,' he added quickly, realizing he had given her the perfect opening, 'it is the business of Prudence Betts. You remember we spoke about it?'

'Yes,' said Lois. 'The kids were full of it, but they didn't know why. Naturally, it was all round the school bus. The favourite seemed to be a suicide attempt, and then a poor second was accidental death from overdosing. So, which was it? Or was there a third?'

Cowgill looked straight at her, with no trace of a smile. 'It was serious, Lois,' he said. 'Prue nearly died, and it was only her father's prompt action that saved her. I can't tell you exactly what happened at the moment for obvious reasons. Her parents are distraught, and desperate to keep the whole thing to themselves. We are involved, and are treating it as urgent. That's why I wanted your help.'

'Well, if you can't tell me more than that, I don't see how I *can* help,' said Lois. Cowgill's gentle reprimand had brought her back with a jolt to the seriousness of what she had willingly got herself involved in. If Prue had nearly died, then she instantly put herself in the Betts's shoes.

'Oh yes, I think you can help,' said Cowgill, and he had that look on his face that warned Lois he was up to something. She had learned early in their acquaintance that he was a true policeman, not above a little manipulation of people who were useful to him. 'Prue is very friendly with Hazel Reading, isn't she? And Hazel seems to confide in you quite a bit. Perhaps you two could get together, see if anything comes up. Girls hang around together these days, tell each other things that never reach their parents.'

'Nothin' new in that,' said Lois. 'My mum and dad were the last people I'd have told. No, you're right, Hazel probably does know a whole lot more about it. I'll do my best, if only for them poor Betts's sakes.' She stood up, thinking that this Prue thing had probably made him forget about the theatre. She was wrong, of course. Hunter Cowgill was practised at getting around to things in his own way.

'Right, thanks,' he said. 'And now it's your turn.'

'My turn?' said Lois. 'I've told you all I know about Prue at the moment. And you still haven't told me what it might have to do with the major . . .'

'Ah, yes, well, we do know that he used to talk to her in the Waltonby pub . . . seemed to be particularly fond of her . . . and once, when she'd been working late, took her back to his house.'

'And showed her his etchings when they got there,' said Lois innocently. One of the things she liked about Hunter Cowgill was that he was – in spite of being a plod – pretty quick on the uptake.

With no change of expression, he said, 'Tell me more about that.'

She told him what she knew from Hazel, and realized the seriousness of the implications. Not that the major could have harmed Prue so recently that she'd ended up in hospital . . . he was too dead for that. But she could see the oddness of the situation.

'Now,' said Cowgill, 'about the theatre set-up. Anything untoward spotted there? You and Hazel seemed to be enjoying young Gary's performance. Mind you, my wife said it was the funniest thing she'd seen for years. Quite a gift, that lad.'

'Yep,' said Lois breezily. 'He's good at cleaning, too. Had really good reports from clients, so far. I like him, and he gets on well with the others.'

'And when you went backstage?' said Cowgill.

How did he know? Lois bridled at the thought of being spied on, and said, 'Blimey, you got eyes in the back of your head?' Then she remembered he had suggested it.

'Natural enough to want to congratulate Gary,' he said. 'We were going to do the same, but my wife didn't want to wait. So I left it to you. Was he pleased?'

Lois hesitated. It would probably be best to tell him about Joanne Murphy, and take the heat out of his curiosity about Gary. And anyway, she was not averse to the idea of the police taking an interest in Joanne Murphy. She was the tricky one, without a doubt, the one who niggled away at Lois when she thought about the major and his peculiar end. So far, there was no connection that she could see, except that Derek had said he'd seen the major in the Tresham Arms once or twice, chatting up a barmaid who, though considerably tarted up, seemed to answer Lois's description of the cleaner she did not hire. Yes, perhaps she'd let Cowgill do some sniffing around that scruffy cow and see what came up.

'Well,' she began, 'there was this woman who opened the stage door. I'd seen her before . . .'

Bridie Reading was enjoying herself. Lois had said that she could take over the vicarage from Hazel, who was, Lois thought, better suited to a farmhouse stuck right out in the middle of fields which, though isolated, had the appeal of three young sons working a big acreage of land. She wanted Bridie not too far from home, in case anything should go wrong in the family. She couldn't say exactly what might go wrong, but she had never trusted Dick Reading and saw no reason to do so now. You never knew which way a bloke like him would jump. There was another reason. Bridie was an ingenuous soul, who blurted out whatever was on her mind at the time, and since Lois looked on Dick as one of the possible suspects – hotheaded, bigoted, and with a known record of campaigning against the major – she hoped for more information on that front. Working at the vicarage would not be more than routine, and so Bridie's conversations with Lois were more likely to centre on her own home.

'Morning, Vicar,' Bridie said, as the elderly cleric opened the door to her.

The Reverend Christopher Rogers had been the vicar of Waltonby for twenty-eight years, and was nearing retirement. He was neither loved nor disliked. He had carried out his duties with willing thoroughness, and had a reputation for 'doing a good funeral'. But apart from that, he often thought he could be invisible. A small congregation, elderly like himself, turned up to go through the familiar prayers and hymns, and he never sprang any surprises on them. *Hymns Ancient and Modern* held sway, and he had no time – nor did his congregation – for the happy-clappy style of the vicar in the next parish. Indeed, several who attended Christopher Rogers's church were escapees from badly-strummed guitars and hymns with alien tunes. It had been an Easter hymn sung to the tune of 'What shall we do with the drunken sailor?' that had sent the latest couple, a retired bank manager and his wife, to sit contentedly in the back pew of Waltonby church. The Reverend Christopher Rogers had greeted them kindly, and tried to forget their accounts of his neighbour's packed and noisy church every Sunday. He had long ago ceased to go about evangelizing in his own parish, and a growing feeling of guilt was propelling him inexorably towards retirement.

'Come in, my dear,' he said.

He was relieved that this nice woman had taken the place of her rather stroppy young daughter. Hazel had done the work well, he had to admit. But her young, positive presence in the quiet vicarage was disturbing in its vitality, in the way she strode about from room to room, humming loudly and regaling him with items of local news she obviously thought would interest him. He could not accuse her of gossip. There was never anything personal in her conversation, but relayed with relish were such things as updates on the proposed new community hall; or the cat that got stuck up a tree and had to be rescued by the fire brigade.

'What a waste of their time, Vicar!' she'd carolled. The most recent was an unlikely story of a donkey that had escaped from old Mrs Brown's paddock on Good Friday, and turned up at the church door, braying to be admitted. 'Thought you'd be interested, Vicar, it being Easter an' that,' she'd said with a perfectly straight face.

Now Bridie set about her work quietly. She didn't say a word unless addressed, and at precisely eleven o'clock sat down at the kitchen table to drink her coffee as quickly as possible. This suited the vicar admirably, and he made a note to telephone Mrs Meade to say how happy he was with the new arrangement.

'What are you doing home?' said Dick Reading to his daughter, who sat reading a magazine and drying her hair at the same time. 'Not out skivvying like your mother?'

'I've finished,' Hazel said flatly, not taking her eyes off the magazine. ''Til this afternoon.'

'You can get me some lunch, then,' her father said, washing his oily hands at the kitchen sink. 'That bloody car isn't right yet.'

'Why don't you get a new one, then? That old thing has had it. Nobody I know has a car that old.'

'Money doesn't grow on trees, young lady! Even now your mother's earnin' a mammoth wage from her millionaire pal, it don't mean we can splash it about. And anyway, it's a good car. Once I've got it sorted, it'll do us.'

Hazel took no notice of him, and continued reading. Furious at being ignored, he cast about for something to annoy her into a reaction.

'As for you not knowin' people with old cars, what about that bloke that's cleanin' for Lois? That's the worst old crate I've ever seen. You're not tellin' me it's passed an MOT lately. Very suspect, that one. And I don't mean the car,' he added.

This had the effect he'd hoped for. Hazel switched off the drier and looked up at him. 'You know nuthin' about Gary Needham,' she said sharply. 'And I'll thank you to mind your own business. My job, my friends and my time are my own affair. You get on with your life, and I'll get on with mine. And get your own lunch,' she added, stalking out and slamming the door behind her.

'Bloody kids,' muttered Dick Reading. 'Give them everything you've got, and they turn against you just the same. Needs a good hiding, that one, and goin' the right way to get it.'

By the time Bridie arrived home after her morning at the vicarage, Dick had worked himself up into an evil mood. The minute she walked into the kitchen, she knew things were bad. He was sitting at the kitchen table, a mug of coffee in front of him, reading – or pretending to read – the paper. 'Did you find the cheese sandwich I left for you?' she began tentatively. No answer. 'It was in the fridge . . . oh, I see, you haven't had it yet. Were you waiting for me?' she asked nervously. Still no answer. She took the sandwich out and put it on a plate, which she set down on the table. 'There,' she said, 'you eat that and I'll cut another one for me.'

He looked up at her now, and very deliberately stood up. He walked over to the bin, and slowly tipped the cheese sandwich and plate into it.

'Dick! Don't throw the plate away!' Bridie said.' I'll eat

the sandwich. That's waste, that is!' He advanced towards her and she retreated, holding up her hands. 'For goodness sake, Dick,' she pleaded. 'What's wrong? That cheese was really fresh . . .'

He had her by the arms now, his strong fingers digging into her flesh. He finally spoke. 'I don't care how bloody fresh it was,' he said, his voice horribly quiet. 'I have been working on our bloody car all bloody morning, and find when I come in for a decent lunch that all my bloody wife has managed to produce is a bloody freezing cold cheese bloody sandwich!' His voice had risen to a crescendo, and Bridie began to whimper.

'Shut up!' Dick yelled. 'You and your precious daughter ought to be chained up! Out all day skivvying in people's houses, and no time to get your own husband a square meal. It's got to stop!' he added, and when Bridie silently shook her head, he flung her away from him so hard that she caught her foot on a chair and went sprawling against the door.

'Get up!' Dick advanced towards her, fists clenched. She got up on to her hands and knees and crawled away from him, sobbing bitterly and trembling violently. He started towards her, his foot raised for a vicious kick, and suddenly the door flew open.

'Get out!' It was Hazel, her face dead white and her eyes burning. She held her mobile phone in one hand, and as he turned towards her, she began to dial. 'I'm getting the police,' she said. 'And if you come anywhere near me or Mum, ever again, you'll never see either of us again. We've had enough. Now get out!' She finished dialling and held her phone to her ear.

Dick Reading stood still. Uncertain now what to do, he fell back on an emotional appeal. 'Sorry, gel,' he said. 'No, don't do that – don't ring the police. I never touched your mother – did I, Bridie?' He appealed to his wife, now sitting head in hands at the table. She silently shook her head. 'Come on, now, Hazel,' he said. 'Everybody loses their temper once in a while . . .'

Hazel stared at him. He could hear the tinny sound of the telephone ringing at the emergency number. 'Hazel!' he repeated. 'Please, love, for God's sake, I'm your father!' Now he could hear the voice asking for details.

Hazel stared at him, then at her mother, and slowly disconnected the call. She sighed deeply, and went over to put her hands on her mother's shoulders. 'Go away, Dad,' she said. 'Just go away and don't come near us until teatime. Mum and me have got to talk.'

Desperately relieved, Dick Reading backed out of the kitchen, and they heard him start the car and drive off.

'What are we goin' to do, Hazel?' said her mother. 'He'll never be any different . . . perhaps if I give up working for Lois . . . ?'

'No!' said Hazel firmly. 'What we're going to do right now is have a cup of strong coffee and somethin' to eat. Then we'll talk. You put the kettle on, and I'll make us some egg and bacon. Unless you want a bloody freezing bloody cheese bloody sandwich?'

When she saw a faint smile appear on her mother's face, she wanted to cry.

Seventeen

Gary Needham's old car was parked in a gateway entrance to a field outside Waltonby. He appeared to be asleep in the sun streaming through the car windows, raising the temperature to a soporific degree. His expression was serene, and when Joanne Murphy tapped on the window, first softly and then in sharp irritation, he did not move.

'Oh, Christ,' she said. 'Not again.'

She walked round to the passenger side, and opened the door. Seating herself next to Gary, she opened her capacious bag and pulled out a small bottle of water. Without hesitating, she unscrewed the top and tipped the entire contents over his supine head. With a protesting splutter, he woke up, rubbed his eyes and seemed to have difficulty focussing.

'No need for that,' he said thickly. 'Just having a snooze. Have to get up early to go to the surgery with Sheila, you know . . .'

'Of course I know, you fool,' Joanne said. 'And for God's sake get yourself together. We have some serious talking to do.' Gary sighed. Joanne's idea of serious talking was not his, and he edged as far away from her as possible. Her cheap scent was making him feel sick.

'Need some air,' he said, and opened his door.

She leaned over him, causing him to retch, and slammed the door shut. 'You stay right here,' she said. 'We have to get a few things straight. So far, you've been pretty hopeless. That job at the surgery should have been a doddle, but so far you've turned up bugger all. And that mess-up with Prue whatever her name is. I'm warning you, Gary,' she continued. 'If you don't start coming up with the info, there'll be trouble.'

'Trouble from who?'

'Trouble from me,' snapped Joanne.

'You and who else?' said Gary, smiling in spite of himself at this relic of the playground.

To his surprise, Joanne Murphy subsided like a flat tyre. 'Oh come on, Gary,' she said. 'You know as well as I do who else. We're stuck with this now, and it has to work, else we're all in the shit. You've bin around a long time, for God's sake.' She sighed. 'I wish I'd never seen that major bloke. But it's too late now, so let's try a bit harder, huh?'

The implied threat in her voice jarred on Gary's jangled nerves. 'Don't try that,' he said. 'There's nothing on me, and you know it. If anybody's in the shit, it's you. So just watch it, *Mrs* Murphy, and I'm warning you, if you tell any lies about me, you'll regret it.'

Joanne got out of the car in a flurry, and then leaned back in. 'Better move on,' she said. 'You got some dustin' and polishin' to do this afternoon, no doubt. Get yer pinny on, pathetic little twit!' And then she was gone, stalking off down the road to where a car with darkened windows awaited her.

Derek, driving home from a swift half at the Waltonby pub, passed Joanne Murphy walking down the road, then noticed a familiar-looking old car parked in a field gateway. By the time he reached home, he had remembered whose it was. And when he told Lois, adding that he thought the tarty barmaid from the Tresham Arms had been talking to Gary, she was much more interested than he had expected. 'Bit of a romance, gel?' he suggested. 'No need to go over the top. You can't get involved in your team's private lives. Fatal. Everybody knows that.'

There is only one thing to do, Lois told herself. Confront him with it. But how can I, when, as Derek says, what he does with his spare time is entirely his affair? But he lied to me, that's certain, and that's a different thing altogether.

The weekend passed with the usual family activities, disagreements and reconciliations. The boys went off with Derek on Saturday afternoon, and Josie spent hours trying out new make-up in front of her bedroom mirror. She was off to a party in the evening, being collected by an older sister of a friend from Tresham. Around seven o'clock, when the boys and Derek were back and tea was finished, Josie came down the wide staircase into the hall.

Lois was passing through, and looked up. 'My goodness!' she said. 'You look nice, Josie, really nice. That new stuff makes you look years older, girl. Just you be careful at this party . . .'

'Oh Mum, don't nag!' Josie said. 'It's just kids from school . . . in my class . . .' She hoped her face did not reveal the lie. In fact, she had given in to persuasion to join a group of older girls who were going to the Cinderella Club in Tresham. 'Just for an hour or two,' they'd said. 'Nobody'd know you weren't same age as us. It'll give you a taste of it! One of us'll run you home.'

Josie lurked about in the hall until the doorbell sounded, then quickly greeted the girl, yelled 'Cheerio' to her family, and was gone before either Lois or Derek could come out of the kitchen.

'Well,' said Lois suspiciously, 'she got out quick!'

The club was heaving. Josie stuck close to the other girls, but as one after another they peeled away to talk to others, she found herself standing alone in a corner, too nervous to join in. I'm the Cinderella all right, she thought. She felt conspicuous and vulnerable. Best thing would be to go to the loo and return when her friends came back. The women's toilet was empty, and she leaned against the wall, fighting against tears. Then the door swung open and a woman came in.

'Hi,' she said, and disappeared into a cubicle. When she came out again, she glanced curiously at Josie. 'You all right, sweetie?' she said.

Josie nodded. 'Just the noise,' she said. 'I'm like that.'

The woman nodded. 'Yeah,' she said, 'gives you a headache sometimes.' She fished in her handbag, and pulled out something small and white. 'Here,' she said. 'This'll help. I'll be around if you need anything.'

She disappeared quickly, and Josie looked down at the little white tablet in her hand. Blimey, that was quick. A sudden urge to get out and be home again overtook her, and as she heard voices approaching, she did what she always did when stuff was offered. It was easy enough to pretend and then get rid of it. She went quickly into a cubicle, flushed the pill away, and emerged with her head down. She didn't know the laughing group of girls who came in, and none of them noticed her.

'Where're you going, Josie?' It was one of her friends, seeing her on her way out. 'Come and join us!' The girl's pleasant, laughing face reassured Josie for a moment. Perhaps she should go back in. After all, nothing bad could happen to her now, now she knew the score.

It was midnight when Josie came creeping back into the house.

'In here!' said Derek peremptorily, taking her by the arm and pushing her into the kitchen. 'Shut the door, Lois,' he added, taking no notice of Josie's protestations that she was tired and wanted to go to bed.

'Right,' said Derek. 'Now let's have the truth.' His voice was harsh, and Josie cringed.

'Dad—' she began, but her mother interrupted.

'Just a minute, Derek,' she said. 'Let's have her side of the story first. Give the girl a chance.'

'Chance!' said Derek. 'She's lied to us, come back here with God knows who, and looks like somethin' the cat brought in! She'll be lucky to get the chance of a bed to sleep in!'

Lois gently pushed Josie into a chair, and sat down with her, taking her hand. 'Now then, love,' she said. 'Where've you been? Dad phoned that friend, and they said there was no party. You'd better tell us straight . . . it's easiest in the long run.'

The last two hours had been hell for Lois. She couldn't forget Josie's disastrous entanglement with Melvyn Hallhouse, a lad who'd been much too old for her and turned out badly. She thought she'd forgotten that particular nightmare, but it had re-emerged in full force as she watched the clock and heard Derek's shocked voice telling her there was no party. They had given themselves until midnight before they phoned around other friends, and then Josie had come in, like Cinderella, on the last stroke of the clock.

Josie had reckoned that contrition and tears would be her

best defence, and so sobbed out the whole story, including the woman with the tablet. This was not a great surprise to Lois. Her kids were part of the drug generation, though not, she was reasonably sure, an active part.

'What did she look like?' said Lois urgently, and Josie's description was clear enough. Then, sniffing back her tears, she repeated a desperate apology for lying, for causing them so much worry . . . again.

'I hate bein' fifteen!' she blurted out finally. 'Why is everything so bloody horrible? I just wish I was dead!'

'Like that girl in the paper?' said Derek, pushing across the picture of a lovely girl who had been found dead by her friends after an evening clubbing. 'Is that what you want?'

Lois shook her head at him and took the paper away. 'No, Derek,' she said. 'She doesn't mean it. Best thing now is to go to bed and get some sleep. We can talk some more in the morning – after all, it's Sunday, the day of rest.'

Rest! That was a laugh. She knew she wouldn't sleep, and tomorrow would be a dismal day, with Derek stamping round in a temper, Josie refusing to get up, and the boys retreating to the sanctuary of their rooms.

She followed Josie upstairs and peered into the total darkness of her daughter's bedroom. 'Night, love,' she said.

A small voice answered her, and then added, 'Oh, and Mum, you might like to know that bloke was in the club, that Gary who works for you. Right little raver, he is.' Lois did not reply, but shut the door quietly and went along to her own bedroom.

'Gary Needham was there,' she said to Derek, who was undressing slowly.

'Wonderful,' said Derek. 'That's all you wanted to know, isn't it, me duck. I dunno, Lois,' he said, 'we seem to be gettin' into another bloody mess. You'd better get us out of it quick, else I shall do it for you.' He climbed into bed, turned his back on her and put out the light. It was some time before Lois could get Josie's description of Joanne Murphy out of her head.

Eighteen

A couple of weeks went by, and the Josie drama faded. Derek had threatened her with fire and brimstone if she lied to them again, and family life returned to normal. New Brooms settled into its routine, and Lois began to enjoy the feeling of being in control. There was no shortage of work, and she knew that once their reputation was established she would have to think about further recruiting. But for the moment she made sure each job was done satisfactorily, and that the team was happy with the way things were going.

On another front, she had failed to ask Gary Needham once again about Joanne Murphy. He must have been talking to her that day when Derek had passed by, and she felt increasingly uneasy about him. He, on the other hand, had continued to be charming, helpful and seemed to be loving the job. She knew she should tell Cowgill what she suspected, but did she want to put him on Gary's tail? Give it a bit longer, and there might be something more definite to tell.

Monday morning, and Lois was up early. She had just put on the kettle for Derek's early cup of tea when the telephone rang. Blimey, who was that at this hour?

'Lois? This is Sheila.' Her voice was thick and indistinct.

Lois knew at once what she was going to say. 'You sound terrible,' she said.

'A cowd, thad's all,' croaked Sheila, 'bud I don't think I cad go to work today.'

'No, no,' said Lois, thinking rapidly that she'd have to do the surgery herself, 'get on back to bed, and I'll ring you tonight. Don't worry, Sheila, we'll manage. Take care, bye.'

'Bound to happen sooner or later,' said Derek. 'Can't you get Hazel to turn out? She ain't got kids to see to.' But Lois said no, she'd rather do it herself. 'Oh well, then,' said Derek, 'it's a bit o'luck I can stay at home until they're gone to school. Better get goin', Lois.'

Gary was there before her, sitting in his car reading a paper. When he saw her approach, she thought a shadow of alarm crossed his face, but then he was out of the car, smiling and saying, 'Is this a spot check, Mrs M?' She told him about Sheila, and said they'd better get on, since they now had a late start.

Gary was helpful, as she'd expected, telling her their routine, and making sure she knew exactly what they had to do. 'Most of the rooms are tidy, and lots of the cupboards are locked, of course,' he said. 'There's just the old doctor's room that's a shambles. Anyway, I do the doctors' rooms, and Sheila does the rest. Are you OK with that?'

Lois nodded, and began work. She found herself keeping an ear tuned to where Gary was cleaning. It wasn't easy, with the linear layout of the surgery. A long corridor bisected that section of the building, with doctors' rooms on either side.

'Mrs Meade, room number two, please,' said a voice. She whipped round, her heart thumping, and then realized it was Gary, fooling about up the corridor.

'Just get on with it,' she said crossly, and he disappeared.

Half an hour or so later, Lois had made a decision. This was a perfect opportunity to have a word with Gary. No need to give it unnecessary weight by asking him to see her at home. Just a casual word, she decided. She walked on soft-soled shoes up the carpeted corridor to find him. He was in room number three, with the door half open, and she could see that he was reading a document he must have picked up from the doctor's desk. She stopped dead, uncertain what to do. He went on reading for a few seconds, then sensed her presence.

'Mrs M!' he said, putting the piece of paper down hastily on the desk. 'I didn't hear you coming.'

'Obviously,' said Lois sharply. 'What were you doing reading that letter?'

'It's not a letter,' said Gary, swallowing hard. 'Well, just a handout from a drug company. Doctors get them all the time. It caught my eye, that's all. Look, you can see for yourself.' He picked up the paper again and held it out to her.

She shook her head. 'Bloody hell, Gary!' she said. 'You know we don't touch private papers! Put it back where you found it. I've a good mind to give you your cards right now, you stupid idiot! Now just get out . . . right out, and go home. I'll let you know what I decide.'

Gary shrugged. 'Not a criminal offence,' he muttered.

She ignored him, and left the room, but when he'd gone, she went back to room number three and looked into the doctor's in tray. It was the same piece of paper, she was sure, and read it without picking it up. In no uncertain terms, the drug company set out the side effects and dangers of over-prescribing a new painkiller, known to be used illegally by kids in the States. The letter stated baldly that hundreds of young people had died from misusing this drug, and warned doctors to be particularly vigilant.

By the time Lois reached home, her instant rage at catching out Gary had subsided. After all, it wasn't as if he'd had his fingers in the till. She told Derek at lunchtime, and his reaction was what she expected. 'Get rid of him, gel,' he said at once. 'I told you he'd be no good, and he isn't.'

'But he's very good at his work,' Lois protested.

Derek exploded. 'What's the matter with you, Lois? The nasty little sod is obviously up to something, probably ferretin' about for the latest on drugs, and you witter on about being good at cleaning! For God's sake, woman, think about it! For all we know, it might have bin him dishin' out God knows what at the club Josie went to . . . and you said that woman she saw could have been the slut you turned down . . .'

'It was,' said Lois quietly. When Derek lost his temper with her, she always listened. 'At least, I'm pretty sure it was, from Josie's description.' She felt sick, remembering how Joanne Murphy had threatened to get back at Lois for rejecting her. Not through Josie, surely? Nobody could be that evil! Oh yes, they could, Lois told herself.

'Well, for Christ's sake, Lois, get rid of him. And then let's stay out of this whole business. Josie's got her head screwed on, more or less, and we can keep an eye on her.

You can easily find another cleaner, and then leave all that other stuff alone.'

Lois was quiet for a minute or so, and then put out her hand to take Derek's. 'You're most likely right,' she said. 'But I took him on and it'll have to be me that fires him. If I do. My decision, really, and it'll have to be quick. He'll be waiting.'

'Let him wait!' said Derek. He sighed. Lois was right. It was her business, and he'd not take kindly to her telling him how to rewire a pub. But she was still his wife! 'Just get your priorities right, Lois,' he said. 'Our kids come first. And if there's any sniff of danger to them, I hope you'll know what's the right thing to do.'

After he'd gone back to work, Lois sat motionless for an hour, staring out of the window and getting her thoughts in order. Finally she made her way through to her office and lifted the telephone. 'Inspector Cowgill?' she said. 'Can we meet?'

Nineteen

The storm began when Lois was halfway to Alibone Woods. Her ancient windscreen wipers were not really up to the job, and she could barely see the road ahead. As she turned off into the track where she concealed her car, she splashed into deep puddles and muddy potholes. I hope to God I can get out of here again, she thought. Well, I can't blame Cowgill today. He'd taken her request very seriously, and suggested the next day, when she had planned to go into Tresham to see her mother, and would be passing by the woods anyway. 'You sound worried,' he'd said. 'Can it keep 'til tomorrow?' She had assured him it wasn't that urgent, though after she'd put down the phone, she had realized she had no idea of how urgent it was. Like Derek, she began to feel caught up in something too close to home. She tried not to think of the children out there . . . on the school bus, in the playground, on their way home through the village. She fought back mental pictures of Josie being dragged screaming into a car with darkened windows, of Douglas reeling home covered in bruises and cuts, and Jamie yelling for his mum as he was dumped unceremoniously into the boot of the same car.

Lois was early, and there was no sign as yet of Cowgill. She found an old umbrella under the back seat, and got out into the rain. It was much lighter now, and she trod – in wellies this time – along the familiar track to the clearing meeting place. As it came in sight, she saw something that caused her to stop dead in her tracks. Someone was there already. Leaning against a tree? Watching out for her? It was a man, she could see that, but his attitude was odd. He was standing up, certainly, but he seemed to be looking down at the ground, and not moving. A shower of raindrops fell from the tree above her, and she dodged to one side, shaking the water from her head. She looked again. Still no movement. He must have heard her, so what on earth . . . ?

Walking forward slowly, Lois glanced behind. Surely Cowgill would be here in a minute. She could hardly go running back now. Her wellies would slow her up, and this man, whoever he was, could easily catch her. If he wanted to, that is. He had certainly shown no interest in her so far.

As she got closer, she saw why. The woods spun around her, and she grabbed at a low branch for support. Slowly, slowly she crept forward, hand to her mouth. Now she could see that the man was tied to a tree, right next to the broad stump where she perched for her meetings with Cowgill. The rope went round and round, anchoring him in an upright position. Only his head was free, and lolled hopelessly down.

Lois took a deep breath and marched forward, dizziness gone. She came up to the bound figure and peered at his face. He was dead. There was no doubt about this. He was the second dead man she had seen in the last month, and as she heard the crackle of twigs under Cowgill's approaching feet, she knew that this second death, and who it was, and where it was, was no coincidence.

Lois had assumed there would be immediate telephone calls, summoning police doctor, ambulance, and all the paraphernalia she had witnessed at the major's spectacular demise. But Cowgill just stood and looked. Then he put his hand on her shoulder and said quietly, 'You all right, Lois?' She nodded, and then he said, 'Right. Nothing we can do for him now, so let's have that talk. Can you manage that?'

Again she nodded. 'Can we go over there?' she said.

'He can't hear us,' said Cowgill, and Lois looked at him bleakly.

'I know,' she said. 'But he never liked me, and I'd rather not have to look at him.'

She was calm, and had rehearsed what she wanted to say. It was brief, well-organized, and put Gary Needham in a very bad light indeed. As a consequence, she was surprised at Cowgill's reaction.

'No,' he said, 'don't sack him. If you can cope, keep him on. We're getting well on into this, and Gary Needham can lead us even further.' He paused.

'Your turn,' said Lois flatly. 'What's it all about? That Joanne Murphy'll probably have another go at my kids. And how can I send Gary to jobs when I don't trust him?' She turned involuntarily to look at the motionless figure. 'And what about *him*? What did he do to deserve that?'

Cowgill shook his head. 'Can't tell you more than you know, except that Joanne and Gary are bit players in this particular theatrical production. Let's say the play can't go on without them, but we're after the producer.'

The image did not impress Lois, who lost her temper. 'It's not a bloody game!' she shouted at Cowgill. 'Derek is furious with me, and my kids are in danger. The cops are supposed to protect us, aren't they? And you're a bloody cop, aren't you?'

Cowgill held up his hand in self-defence. 'Lois, calm down,' he said. 'If I thought your kids were in serious danger, I'd do something. But take it from me, that approach in the club was probably routine. Joanne Murphy may not even have known Josie was your daughter. No, it'll be much more dangerous if we don't get to the heart of all this, and you can help. You *have* helped already.' He became brisk. 'Now, get on out of here. I'll give you five minutes to get away, then I'll summon the troops. And don't forget, I'm always accessible, night or day.'

With one last look at the sagging corpse, Lois stumbled her way back to the car, and drove carefully out of the woods and on to the road. But instead of continuing to see her mother, she turned back towards Long Farnden. She needed to be by her telephone, ready to take the inevitable call. She didn't know whether it would be Bridie or Hazel, but they would be needing her, nothing surer than that. After all, however much you hate your father – or husband – it'll be a great shock to hear he has been found dead, tied to a tree, with a knife stuck into his heart.

Twenty

Hazel and Bridie Reading sat in Lois's kitchen, mugs of tea in front of them, and the talking had finally stopped. Yesterday had been a nightmare for them, and for Lois, too. But now the police had gone for the moment, and the two Readings had come over to Long Farnden to be with the person they trusted most.

Lois had felt this keenly, since she was not able to be straight with them. She could not tell them she had been in the woods, or that she had found Dick's body. She had to keep secret that she knew the inspector in charge, and that she was more than interested in that other death. As she sat quietly at the table, waiting until they wanted to talk some more, she reflected that both victims had been men variously disliked. The major had had no real friends in Waltonby, and she knew that both Hazel and Gary were contemptuous whenever his name was mentioned. She knew that Dick Reading was tolerated at work only because he was very good at it. He had no friends there, and none in the village. News of unhappy marriages is soon common knowledge, and the whole of Waltonby knew of Bridie Reading's tribulations. Not that anybody but Lois had tried to help. Still, Lois was the first to admit that Bridie was her own worst enemy. She would do nothing about Dick's violence, refused to talk about it to anyone but Lois, and repeatedly made her promise not to pass it on, saying she would be the one to suffer.

Lois's thoughts wandered on. Dick Reading had often cursed the major, threatening all kinds of retribution if any kind of approach should be made to his own daughter. Had some unknown person revenged the major? She shook her head, and Hazel looked at her curiously. 'It's really nice of you to ask us over,' she said. 'But I expect you'll be wanting to get on. It's just that . . .' She dried up, all her customary bravado gone.

Bridie helped her out. 'We just needed to tell you, Lois, that if we're not wanted to help the police, we'd like to carry on working.'

'Oh, Bridie, I don't expect that!' said Lois at once. 'For goodness sake, there'll be loads of things to do, and you'll both still be in shock. No, no . . . we'll manage somehow.'

'You can't,' said Hazel baldly. 'Not at this early stage in New Brooms. Not enough staff, and you can't get replacements in time. No, Mrs M, we'll keep going, if you don't mind. It'll be a help. Me and Mum have decided, if it's OK with you.'

Lois looked at their pale faces and wondered what else she could do. She had lost count of the number of times she'd wished Dick Reading was out of the way for good, times when Bridie's face had been purple with bruises, and Hazel a frightened little girl hiding in her room. But not dead. She'd never wished him dead, though she knew she could not mourn for him. Somebody had made sure he was dead, though, and Lois knew that whatever Derek said, she had to do all she could to help clear up the mess. Whoever had murdered Dick Reading had done his wife and daughter no favours.

In a grubby bedroom on the Churchill Estate in Tresham, Joanne Murphy lay stretched out on her bed, blowing smoke rings up to the ceiling. Her eyes were half-closed and a jangle of angry music came from a radio beside her. She did not hear the footsteps coming along the landing, and sat up with a start as the bedroom door opened.

'Tony?' A burly man stood smiling at her. 'Fancy a Chinese?' he said. 'Sort of celebration, you could say?

'Later, maybe,' said Joanne, stubbing out her cigarette. 'Now come 'ere, you great idiot, and let's 'ave a celebration right away.'

It was some time later that Joanne and Tony perfunctorily tidied the bedroom, checked that the kid was at her grandmother's as usual, and took the big black car with darkened windows into town. 'First stop the theatre?' said Tony.

Joanne looked at him. An unlikely member of a theatre audience, she thought. Huge shoulders, no neck and a shiny shaved head sitting squatly on his body. Pea-sized brain, she thought to herself. But this didn't matter. She had enough brains, and he was the brawn. She giggled, thinking how satisfactorily brawny he was, and how safe she felt with him around.

They pulled up outside the little theatre, and Joanne got out. 'You wait here,' she said, 'shan't be long.' They were parked on yellow lines, but this did not bother Tony. He had mates who could fix most things, including traffic wardens. It was early evening, and the street was beginning to come alive. It had been respectable once, full of workers from the shoe factories, families who had moved from slums into neat terraces of houses that seemed to them like palaces. Then it had gone through a phase of dereliction and abandonment, and now once more there was new paint, fresh curtains and pots of flowers. Ethnic minorities had taken over, and were proud of it. But here and there were the remnants of the bad old days. Peeling paint, filthy windows, and doors that were never opened more than a few inches. Tony's mates lived in these houses, a network of low life that came and went in the shadows, dealing and dodging and betraying one another without compunction.

Twenty minutes went by, and Tony began to get restive. Where the hell was she? She'd told him to stay put, but he was bored. How had he got into this . . . taking orders from a bloody woman? Still, that was how it went. She took her orders from somewhere, he had no idea where, and he passed on whatever was necessary, making a profit like they all did. And she was a good lay, no doubt about that!

Joanne emerged from the alleyway at the side of the theatre and got in the car. 'He's not there,' she said. 'Stupid little runt! Anyway, I've left word with the so-called stage manager, and he'll pass it on. Come on, Tony, let's get out of here and get some food. I'm starving after all that exercise, you evil brute!' She leaned across and kissed him full on the mouth while he flailed around, taken by surprise.

'Christ, Joanne,' he said, 'how about getting a takeaway and goin' back to my place?'

'Suits me,' she said, and leaning back in her seat, she licked her lips like a snake in the sun.

Gary Needham was in a panic. He knew he should have been at the theatre to meet Joanne, but he'd finished work late. For the first time, his client housewife had claimed he'd not finished the job properly and threatened to ring Lois Meade. And now he *had* to see Hazel Reading. The network had faithfully reported Dick's death, and Gary was scared. He needed to talk to Hazel urgently, find out what she knew – what anyone knew. Although he'd tried her home number dozens of times and not found her, he was reluctant to try her mobile. She could be anywhere, and, what is more important, with anyone. No, he would have to go over to Waltonby and try to track her down. It was more important than risking the wrath of that disgusting Joanne Murphy.

His old car chugged along like a reluctant carthorse, and by the time he reached Waltonby his panic had subsided. Nevertheless, he was extremely relieved to see lights at Hazel's windows. Chances were that she was in, keeping her mother company. Gary knew all about Bridie and Dick, and about Hazel, too. He'd quite fancied her once, and still respected her. When she'd just arrived in the first class at school, he was about to leave. But the word had quickly got around that one of the new girls was very promising. By the time Hazel was thirteen, she had a string of spotty admirers, all of whom got the bum's rush. This mass rejection naturally stimulated burgeoning male instincts for conquest, and for the rest of her school career Hazel had an enviable time. When Gary came back from his various attempts at stardom, he saw her again, flashing around Tresham on her bike, and wondered if he should have a go. But she wouldn't have looked at him twice, he was sure. Their paths had crossed steadily since then, both of them involved with Tresham undesirables. Then, when he met her at New Brooms, he learned more about her domestic situation and pitied her. He ran up the path to ring the doorbell, hoping against hope that she would answer the door.

'Gary? What do you want?' Hazel stood in the doorway, and he was shocked at her pale, drawn face.

He gathered his wits, and asked if there was somewhere they could talk. 'Oh, and I'm really sorry about your dad,' he said quickly. 'Must've been a terrible shock.'

Hazel nodded and seem to be considering whether or not to let him in. 'Mum's here,' she said. 'But we could go upstairs to my room. She's asleep at the moment. Doctor gave her some pills. I don't want her worried, so it'll have to be quick.'

He followed her in and up the stairs on tiptoe. With the bedroom door shut, he turned to face her. 'What's going on?' he said. 'Have you got any idea?' Hazel looked at him, and then sat down suddenly, her shoulders drooping. He saw that she was crying, and put his arm around her.

She scrubbed at her eyes with a screwed-up tissue. 'You don't think I did it?' she said in a muffled voice.

Gary said nothing. He had no idea how much he could trust Hazel. 'Yeah, or me,' he said, with a poor attempt at an ironic laugh. 'What d'you think?'

Hazel shook her head. 'I dunno. Don't suppose you'd have the bottle. No, Dad was up to something. He was always bloody well up to *something* . . .'

Gary sighed. He walked across to the window. 'Look at it,' he said. 'Just look at your idyllic village. Twilight in the Garden of Eden, most people would think. And it's as rotten underneath as anywhere else. Anyway,' he added, 'I'll go now . . . if anything comes up . . . can you let me know?'

She stared at him, frowning. 'It's a bloody mess, Gary,' she said, and as he brushed past her on the way out, she realized he was shaking violently.

Twenty-One

It was two in the morning on the luminous bedside clock when Lois suddenly sat bolt upright, her eyes wide open and staring at nothing.

'Lois?' muttered Derek, turning in his sleep. 'Whazza-matter?'

'Nothing,' she said quickly, 'just a bad dream. Go back to sleep.'

It was true: she had had a dream, but one that was so ridiculous that she knew even while she was dreaming that it was rubbish. But then it had changed, and what came next was so frightening and plausible that it woke her up with a start. She had seen quite clearly the meeting place in the woods, and Dick's body tied to a tree, but as she watched from some invisible hiding place, she saw Bridie and Hazel. They were adjusting the ropes, and then stood back to admire their handiwork. They were laughing, and even as she woke up Lois had felt the terrible nausea of shock.

She slid quietly out of bed and crept downstairs to the kitchen, being very careful not wake the kids. She had to think, and once the day started there was so little time for careful thinking. Pouring a glass of orange juice, she sat down at the table. Melvyn the cat, curled up in the old armchair beside the Rayburn, opened one eye and looked at her, then went back to sleep. The shelf clock measured out the time with its uneven tick. It was very peaceful, and Lois relaxed. The second part of her dream had been just as much rubbish as the first, she told herself. First of all, Hazel and Gary had appeared in police uniforms and arrested a protesting Derek in front of all the kids. And then she had seen Bridie and Hazel at their murderous task. But Bridie was her oldest friend, and she knew that however bad it had been, she would never have committed a violent act. But Hazel? She had a fierce hatred of her father. Lois had seen plenty of evidence of that over the years. There was no doubt that her will was strong enough, but neither of them were physically up to manhandling a live or dead Dick Reading into the woods. He was a big bloke. An accomplice? No, this was getting ridiculous. She would just go back to bed, forget the dreams and concentrate on whatever facts came her way.

She heard a sound, a footfall on the stairs, and then the kitchen door opened. It was Josie, peering into the kitchen with a worried frown. 'Mum? Are you all right?'

'Fine,' said Lois, smiling reassurance. 'Just couldn't sleep. Sometimes it helps to come down and sit for a bit.'

'I couldn't sleep either,' said Josie, slumping into a chair opposite Lois.

'Something worrying you?' said Lois, feeling her heatbeat quicken. These days, anxiety for the kids was always lurking in the background. She did not share Cowgill's casual certainty that Joanne Murphy had not known who Josie was, and now she looked closely at her. In her cotton nightdress, and with her dark hair loose around her shoulders, she appeared younger than usual. *Even* younger than usual, Lois thought. Fifteen years old was still childhood.

'I keep thinking about Hazel's dad,' Josie said. 'I didn't like him, but he was her dad. Why would anyone want to kill him, Mum?' She was near to tears, and Lois stretched her hand out across the table.

'We don't know yet, love,' she said. 'But they'll find the killer. Nothing surer . . . very few get away with it.'

'They haven't got the bloke who killed that major over at Waltonby, have they,' said Josie flatly. 'Was he something to do with Hazel's dad?' she added, sniffing loudly.

Lois shook her head. If only she knew! Then she could tell Cowgill, and the whole bloody mess would be cleared up. They sat quietly, holding hands across the table, for a few minutes, and then Josie spoke again. 'Mum,' she said, and hesitated.

'Yep, what?' said Lois.

'They were talking on the bus today,' Josie continued.

‘O ’course everybody knew about it. One of the boys said his mum knew the major. At some drama thing in Tresham. Said he reckoned he was gay and that’s why he got killed. Jealousy, an’ that.’

‘But . . .’ said Lois, wondering what to say to this, ‘but what about him fancying young girls? I thought that was the gossip about the major?’ So this was what they talked about on the school bus. Well, they’d done the same in her day, swapping scurrilous stories and one-upping each other, getting wilder all the time.

‘Oh, you mean Prue Betts,’ said Josie knowledgeably. ‘Yeah, well, she was asking for it. Not as goody-goody as you think, Mum. She was one of the gang.’

‘What gang?’ said Lois sharply.

‘Oh, you know, clubbin’ and dabblin’ in this an’ that. They think they’re so clever that nobody knows. But it’s all over the school. We all know who they are, and where they get it from. You can smell it sometimes. Soon as we get off the bus one of the boys lights up.’

Lois knew better than to ask which boy. ‘What d’you mean, you know where they get it from?’ she said, very wide awake now.

‘Oh, Mum,’ said Josie wearily, ‘it’s not that difficult. All the gang put money in, and one of the boys buys the stuff. Then they share it out.’

‘But do the teachers know?’ said Lois, trying to keep the alarm out of her voice. She knew Josie would clam up at the slightest hint that her mother might take some action.

Josie shrugged her shoulders. ‘Dunno,’ she said. ‘If they do know, they don’t do nuthin’.’

Silence descended again. Then Lois made up her mind. ‘Josie,’ she said. ‘I know you’ve got more sense than to join any bloody gang, so I’m going to tell you something that you probably know already. There’s no future in drugs. Don’t believe anybody who tells you otherwise.’

‘Dad uses drugs,’ said Josie stubbornly.

‘What?’ snapped Lois.

‘He drinks, don’t he? And he used to smoke. I’ve seen him pretty drunk once or twice, so what’s the difference?’ Josie looked at her mother's face, and relented. 'Anyway, Mum, you can save your breath. Me and the others don't touch the stuff. Don't need it, thank God, though it's been offered plenty enough times. You can stop worrying about that. And what I just said about Dad . . . I know you think there's a difference. I'm not sure, but I'll take your word for it for now.' She stood up, came round to Lois and gave her a hug. 'Night, Mum,' she said. 'See you in the morning.'

Lois nodded, and walked over to the armchair. 'Move over, Melvyn,' she said, and sat down beside him, wiping away sudden tears. After a while, she dozed off, and that was where Derek found her when he came down in the morning.

As she drove through the park to Dalling Hall, Lois caught sight of the church, solid and safe-looking in the distance. She remembered reading in history lessons that at one time you could get sanctuary in a church. Once inside with the door shut, nobody could touch you. But that wasn't why they put the major in the church, that was for sure. He was there so he couldn't touch anybody outside. He was dead for that reason, probably.

She stopped the car at the end of the footpath to the church, and got out. She was early anyway, and a few minutes wouldn't make any difference. Hazel would carry on without her. It occurred to Lois that Hazel might not turn up after all, but she would discover that soon enough.

The narrow oak door was ajar, and Lois hesitated. It was early in the day, surely, for the church to be open? She pushed the door and looked in. At first she couldn't see much in the gloom. She walked down the steps and stood still until her eyes adjusted. Then she saw she was not alone. The shadowy shape of a man came into focus, in the far corner, where one of the less elaborate of the tombs of the Dallings seemed to have its lid standing on end, propped up. The man was as motionless as she was.

'Who's that?' Lois said, her voice strong and impatient. She'd had enough of shadows and mystery. There was no answer, but the shape moved, and as he came into the light from one of the high-up windows, Lois could see he was big and bulky. The light caught the top of his shaved head, and his expression was not friendly.

'Get out!' he said. 'If yer know what's good for yer, get out!' he repeated.

'Sod you!' said Lois. 'I've got as much right as you . . .' She just had time to see him taking off his jacket before he was on to her, and she could neither see nor breathe.

Twenty-Two

'Well, well,' said Joanne Murphy, teetering on high heels and arms akimbo, 'so who have we here? I'll be buggered if it's not Mrs Mop herself!'

Lois spluttered, getting her breath. She could still taste the sourness of the man's jacket. He'd put it over her head and squeezed, and then unaccountably let go suddenly, pushing her back so that she landed on a pew, gasping and rubbing her eyes. Of course, now she saw why she had been released. Joanne Murphy had arrived in the nick of time. An unlikely rescuer, but Lois thanked God she'd appeared. Her head felt muzzy, but it occurred to her straight away that Murphy must have some authority over the gorilla who was now sidling back towards the open tomb.

'Get that sorted, Tony,' Joanne said sharply, and then turned back to Lois, who was trying to stand up. No bloody Joanne Murphy was going to talk to her like that. But she was pushed back roughly into the pew. 'Just a minute, I've got something to say to you before you go anywhere.' The brassy blonde wig shone in the light coming from the upper window, and Lois noticed heavy make-up, transforming the sluttish woman she remembered from their first encounter. Perhaps she should pretend dizziness, let her speak and see what came out.

'God knows what you're doin' here,' said Joanne.

Big Tony in the corner sniggered. 'That's good, Jo,' he said, 'yer know, this bein' a church an' that . . .'

She ignored him, and continued to stare at Lois. 'You're in the way, Mrs Mop,' she said. 'We can't 'ave you bustin' in 'ere, interruptin' a bit o' business between me and Tony.'

Lois shook her head, as if to clear it, and said nothing. This was like something out of a bad movie. She hoped it would have a happy ending.

'Now this is what you're gonna do,' continued Joanne. 'We'll let you go, and you'll forget you ever saw us. Forget *everything* you saw,' she added, glancing back at the tomb. '*And*,' she said with great emphasis, 'if you *don't* forget, I shall know about it, and you'll be sorry. Not just sorry, but bloody finished. I know how I'd feel if one o' my kids went missin' . . . you know, how they do, endin' up in fish ponds an' that.'

Still Lois said nothing, but if Joanne Murphy had bothered to notice Lois's change of expression, her cockiness might have been somewhat dented. But she noticed no change, because she was high on triumph and revenge.

'So clear off,' she said, 'and don't you bloody well forget what I said. Go on, bugger off!'

Lois stood up. She finally had words for Joanne Murphy and her henchman: 'Touch my kids,' she said, and her voice was cold and clear, 'and you're dead.' And then she walked swiftly out of the church.

'You all right, Mrs M?' Hazel was waiting for her at the hall, and frowned at Lois's pale face.

'I'm OK,' said Lois. 'How about you? And how's your mum?' She had expected a call from the Readings, changing their minds about working on. But here was Hazel, neat and attractive, cleaning equipment in hand.

'Mum's fine,' she said. 'Well, you know, not fine, but coping. She's gone to the vicarage, so she'll be all right. He's a nice old bloke, that vicar, and it's quiet and peaceful there.'

Lois nodded. 'Let's get on then,' she said. 'Sorry I'm late – got held up.' Well, that was true. She was still very angry, and noticed Hazel looking at her hands, which shook as she plugged in the cleaner. She was angry mostly with herself, for putting herself at the mercy of that ratbag. And that oaf, scrabbling away in the corner by the tomb – what the hell was he doing?

'Don't you think so, Mrs M?'

'Sorry?' said Lois. 'What did you say?'

'Are you *sure* you're all right?' Hazel looked at her curiously.

Lois nodded and managed a smile. 'Yep,' she said, 'now let's get cleaning.' After a while, her swirling thoughts settled down to one question. How often was that church used? She walked down the long corridor to find Hazel, and asked if she knew. 'Is the Waltonby vicar in charge of Dalling church as well?' Lois had judged her young cleaner accurately. When Hazel had first worked for the vicar, she had bombarded him with friendly questions, just to put him at his ease, she said. And so she knew precisely that he was indeed in charge, and took a service once a month at six o'clock in the evening for the few people scattered around in park houses and any odd guest from the hall.

'He told me he sometimes forgot, it not being very often, and then sometimes the man who was supposed to open up, he forgot his key. So it was all a bit unreliable. Anyway,' she added, 'why d'you want to know about Reverend Rogers?' Hazel spoke casually, but Lois was acting strangely this morning, and Hazel was worried.

'Just wondered,' said Lois. 'You know how if something bothers you, you have to find out. My mind wandering, that's all.'

With promises from Hazel that she would let Lois know immediately if Bridie needed help, they parted after work and went their ways. Lois drove slowly past the church, looking to see if the big black car was still there. But of course it was not. They would have scarpered long since. She toyed with the idea of going back to look at that tomb in the corner, but decided against it. Everything would be back in place. No, she would go on home, get lunch for Derek, and consider what to do next. One thing was definite: the kids were going nowhere on their own from now on. They'd have to find some way of doing it without alarming them, but Lois did not trust Joanne Murphy one inch. She took her threat very seriously, and knew that as soon as possible she would have to alert Hunter Cowgill. A telephone call straight away was the best idea. She pulled over into a lay-by, and dialled his number.

* * *

Cowgill sounded concerned, and assured Lois that everything necessary would be done to protect the kids. She worried about this, knowing that they could not be shadowed every hour of the day. Cowgill listened closely to what she had to tell him about the church, and agreed that a talk with the vicar would be a good idea. 'Why don't *you* talk to him, then?' said Lois, already backtracking on her idea.

'I'd rather lie low on that one,' he said unhelpfully.

'Huh!' said Lois. 'Anyway, chances are he's pretty ga-ga. That's how Hazel sees him, anyway.'

'That one probably thinks anybody over forty is ga-ga,' said Cowgill, with amusement in his voice. 'Just call in on some pretext – checking on Bridie's work? – and have a chat.' Lois wondered at his apparent familiarity with Hazel, but then remembered that of course he'd had hours of conversation with her and Bridie about Dick's death.

Early in the afternoon, Lois dialled the Waltonby vicarage number. 'Christopher Rogers here,' said a gentle voice. Lois reminded him who she was, and said that she was interested in Dalling church. She wondered if he had any records, history, legends, anything like that. 'Why, yes,' he said. 'All churches have interesting records. Anything particular you were looking for?'

Lois cast about for something convincing. 'Just the family, really,' she said. 'I'm working at the hall and got interested. You know, how they lived and children dying young, an' all that.'

'Why don't you call in some time?' he said, just as Lois had hoped. 'I could look out some papers.'

'Tomorrow?' said Lois swiftly. 'About two o'clock?'

'Well . . . er . . . yes, that would be all right,' said Christopher Rogers.

'Thanks,' said Lois, and rang off.

Twenty-Three

The vicarage at Waltonby was an impressive old house, all pinnacles and turrets, with a large garden and glebe meadow where a neighbour kept two engaging donkeys. The stonework of the house had mellowed pleasantly, and when the sun shone, it glowed as if blessed. For the Reverend Christopher Rogers, living in this idyll was not always so pleasant. Built for a cleric with private means and a staff of four or five to run the establishment, it had sadly deteriorated in a more atheistic age. Now he lived mostly in his kitchen and study, opening up the large, chilly drawing room only for Parochial Church Council Meetings and the occasional visit of the bishop. He was, fortunately, a keen gardener, and the approach along a short driveway welcomed visitors with flowers and shrubs. His vegetable garden provided him with a vital supplement to his regular diet of sausages and fish fingers.

His ordered routine had been temporarily disturbed by Hazel Reading, who had breezed through the house once a week, opening windows, rearranging papers, tidying books into the wrong places in bookshelves, and generally causing him to dread Fridays. But now her mother, Bridie, had taken over, and she was so quiet and considerate, always asking before attempting any reorganization, and Christopher Rogers was contented once more.

This morning, Bridie had made him his cup of milky instant coffee and brought it to him in the study. 'I've put a couple of biscuits out for you,' she said, setting down the small tray on to his desk. 'Anything else you need?'

What a pleasant woman, he thought, and how brave of her to turn up under the dreadful circumstances. 'Thank you, my dear,' he said. 'And I'm to see your boss this afternoon – quite a busy day for me!'

This was news to Bridie. Hazel had said something about Lois asking questions about the vicar, but she had thought nothing of it. She knew her work was satisfactory, because Father Rogers had said so, several times. He had been careful to stress that Hazel had been wonderful, too, but perhaps not quite right for an old codger like himself! Bridie could have told him it had been a big surprise to her that Hazel had wanted to work for New Brooms in the first place, let alone discover that the girl seemed to be enjoying it. She was, though, well aware that Hazel had stayed in Waltonby, doing a local job, primarily to defend her mother against a violent husband. Now that Dick was gone, in such unbelievable circumstances – she swallowed hard – she supposed Hazel would soon be off to pastures new.

'Well, I'm sure Lois won't bother you,' she said now, smiling at Father Rogers. 'She's an old mate of mine, and one of the best.'

By the time Lois lifted the heavy iron knocker on the vicarage door, Father Rogers had gathered together a few books and papers relating to Dalling Hall and its ancient church. He'd met Lois before, of course, when she came to arrange the cleaning service, and he would not have judged her a natural student of local history. A good-looking woman, brisk, efficient, obviously a good wife and mother, yes, all those things; but not . . . ah, well, you could never tell.

'Come in, come in,' he said, and Lois stepped into the tiled, dark hallway. It was cold, but Lois was glad to note that a fresh smell of polish and soap had taken over from the musty atmosphere that greeted her on her first visit.

'Everything all right with Bridie?' she asked, and smiled at the vicar's enthusiasm. 'Yes, well, I didn't expect either Hazel or Bridie to work for a while, but they wanted to keep busy,' she added in answer to his solicitous enquiries.

He offered tea, but Lois shook her head. Vicarage tea was pretty pallid stuff in her experience, and anyway, she'd only just had a snatched sandwich at home. 'Perhaps later, then,'

Father Rogers said. 'Bridie left us a tray all ready, and I'd hate to disappoint her.'

What a thoughtful man, thought Lois, and wished that all her clients were so easy. Just before she'd come out, the pub had rung to say Gary had left a hot tap running in the ladies' cloakroom, and this was the second time it had happened. What was she going to do about it? They couldn't afford to waste hot water, and might have to think about making other arrangements. She'd promised it wouldn't happen again, and regretted once again that she'd allowed Cowgill to persuade her to reinstate Gary Needham. His mind was not on the job, that was clear, and she hated to think where else it might be.

She forced her thoughts back to Father Rogers, who was spreading out books and papers on his desk. 'You might like to browse through these,' he invited. 'It could be said that the history of the Dalling family is the history of England in a microcosm,' he added, and Lois nodded politely, not having the faintest idea what he was talking about. But she tried hard to follow, and found herself becoming interested.

Through wars, early deaths, whole families of children lost in infancy, political liaisons and marriages of convenience, the Dalling family had survived. There were some still living in South Africa, said Father Rogers, and they occasionally came over to visit the ancestral home. 'Nice people,' he said, 'but not the quality.' She wondered what he meant, until he described the last Lady Dalling to live at the hall. She had been renowned for her good works, her care of the sick and poor in her parish. She read that the nineteenth-century Lady Dalling befriended a celebrated freak, a man with a grotesque head and body, who came to stay with the gamekeeper's family on the estate to escape the painful sideshows where he was exhibited for money.

'We've lost that sense of duty and charity,' Father Rogers said, shaking his head.

'Oh, I don't know,' said Lois, thinking about her mother, who spent long hours in a charity shop in Tresham sorting smelly old clothes and books that other people had chucked out. 'Maybe it turns up in different places,' she suggested, and Father Rogers nodded.

'Quite right, my dear,' he said. 'It is important to be charitable in thought as well as deed.'

Lois had had enough by now, especially if he was going to start sermonizing. 'There was one thing I wanted to ask you,' she said. 'Hazel told me that Dalling church isn't used by many people. I expect you wonder if it's worth going there?' She knew she was risking another homily, but had to get to the subject somehow.

To her surprise, he laughed. 'Absolutely,' he said. 'So much so, that once or twice I have completely forgotten the appointed day!'

'Oh dear,' said Lois, thinking it was just as well. She hated to think of the old boy coming across a gorilla raiding the tombs. 'Was there a queue waiting for you?' she said, leading him on.

'Good gracious me, no,' he said. 'It is an evening service, and Mr Betts with his key is usually the only one in the congregation.'

'Mr Betts?' said Lois. Her voice was sharp with surprise. 'Does Mr Betts open up the church?'

'Oh yes, he's the churchwarden there. He's interested in the history and so on, and offered to take it on. Not easy to find churchwardens these days,' he added wistfully. 'I have my own key, of course, but Mr Betts always brings his too, knowing my dreadful memory!'

This odd piece of information settled uneasily in Lois's mind. She needed to think, to see if this was more than just coincidence. But she couldn't leave abruptly. Father Rogers had been kind, and so she accepted a cup of tea, and chatted amiably for half an hour more. As she left, she thanked him with genuine warmth for an interesting afternoon, and drove back to Long Farnden at speed, anxious to be there before the children returned home.

The telephone was ringing as she unlocked the door, and she rushed to answer it.

'Lois? It's Mum here. Just ringing to see how you are, all of you.'

'Why?' said Lois sharply to her mother. 'Is something wrong?'

'No,' said her mother, puzzled. 'Just a quick ring, that's all. I often do.'

Lois subsided on to a chair. The threat to harm her kids was getting to her, hanging over her. 'Right, Mum,' she said. 'It's just that I'm tired. Not thinking straight. Dick Reading's death has . . . well, you know.'

They chatted for a few minutes, and then her mother said, 'Look, Lois, would it help if I came over and stayed for a week or so? Just while you get back to normal? You've got plenty of room now, and I'd keep out of your hair. I could be there for the kids, and Derek and me get on all right. I'm sure he won't mind. What d'you think of the idea?'

It was such a good idea that Lois felt tears of relief welling up. 'When can you come?' she said.

'Next bus,' said her mother, hearing the wobble in her daughter's voice. 'I'll be with you directly,' she added, and put down the phone.

Twenty-Four

'Fancy goin' out tonight, Lois?' said Derek. He had had mixed feelings about his mother-in-law coming to stay. He got on with her well enough, and over the years she had stood by the family, a pillar of reliability when Lois had asked for help. But Gran was a lonely woman, still full of energy and in good shape, and not at all the sort to sit back with her knitting. Lois being an only child meant all her interest was focussed on the Meade family, and occasionally this became oppressive. Still, he had only to drop a hint, and she backed off at once. No, all in all, Gran was a good old gcl, and he was fond of her. Now she was here, he meant to make the most of it and see that Lois took some time off to enjoy herself. She'd definitely been looking peaky lately.

'Yes, you go, Lois,' said Gran. 'Me and the kids want to watch that quiz on the telly, and we can do it without you and Derek fidgeting about, disapproving.'

'Right, if that's how you feel,' said Lois, taking mock offence, 'you're on, Derek. Where shall we go?'

'Pictures?' said Derek. 'There's that new fantasy movie at the Sol Central.'

Lois shook her head. 'Don't fancy that,' she said. 'How about a good laugh? There's this daft thing on at that little theatre in Tresham . . . all supposed to be amateur actors puttin' on plays. The manager at the hall saw it, and said he'd never laughed so much . . .'

'Blimey!' said Derek. 'Doesn't sound like my idea of a good night out . . . nor yours, for that matter. You got an ulterior motive again, Lois, by any chance? Somethin' connected with your precious inspector?'

Lois was about to cave in, but her mother interrupted.

'Yeah,' she said, 'there was a woman at the Oxfam shop had seen it. Said it's a real scream. Her daughter's in it.'

'Wonderful,' said Derek. 'Amateurs playin' amateurs. Should be a night to remember.' He was silent for a few seconds, and then shrugged. 'Well, if that's what you want, Lois, we'd better do it. Your treat, supposed to be, and I can always have a snooze.'

But the whole thing turned out to be a pleasant surprise for Derek. The entire evening, with all its joke stage effects and really good acting – acting bad acting – was a riot. The audience was mopping its eyes by the end, and Derek held Lois's hand for support. 'Come on, gel,' he said, 'let's get a drink. That was the best laugh I've had for a long time.'

Lois had laughed too, but not so wholeheartedly. All the time the players were on stage, she was looking at them closely. None were familiar, except that client, Mrs Jordan, who'd known the major. She was playing the prompt, and had a real gift for comic ridiculousness. It was not until the last play – there were four short dramas – that she saw Gary. Some of the jokes in the Shakespeare skit went over her head, and she suspected Derek was the same, but he was on a roll and now couldn't stop laughing at whatever was said on stage. And in any case, her attention was on Gary. She watched him closely, first suspecting his loony performance as Testiculo the clown was aided by something not entirely spontaneous; and then decided that he was just good at the part. I'm beginning to see drug addicts round every corner, she thought. Then right at the end, when the cast was taking the applause on stage, she caught sight of another familiar face. A stage hand appeared very briefly to release one of the curtains that had hooked itself round a chair. In those few seconds, Lois knew for sure that it was Mr Betts.

'Could've been him,' said Derek, on the way home. 'He's the sort, isn't he. Schoolmaster, an' that. They like that kind of thing. Anyway, so what? I don't see it's all that important.'

'Seems you liked that kind of thing too,' said Lois, leaning over and giving him a quick peck on the cheek.

'Now, now,' he said, 'no distractions when I'm drivin'. Wait 'til we get home, then I can concentrate. Good thing you put Gran in the back bedroom . . .'

It was not late when they drove into Long Farnden, and there were lights on all over the house. 'Not like Gran,' said Derek, 'to waste all that electricity.'

'What d'you mean?' said Lois sharply, her reaction immediately one of anxiety. Anything out of kilter in her house triggered an alarm.

'Don't mean nothing,' said Derek, 'just it's not like Gran to waste electricity.'

He looked at her curiously, wondering at her white face. 'Lois, is there something you've not told me?' he said suspiciously. 'Because if so, you'd better come clean right now, before we go inside to hear the latest instalment of telly rubbish.'

'No, no, let's go in,' she said. 'I was just worried in case you're not really happy about having Mum with us. You put the car away and I'll go ahead,' she added, and got quickly out of the car and ran towards the house.

'Everything all right?' she called, as she went into an empty kitchen.

Her mother appeared at once. 'Of course it's all right, Lois,' she said, frowning. 'Why shouldn't it be?'

'Oh, no reason,' said Lois, visibly relaxing. 'Kids been good?'

Her mother nodded. 'We watched our quiz. Really good tonight. Pity you missed it. Still, did you have a good evening?'

By now Derek had come in, and took over from Lois, who went off to put on the kettle. She could hear him giving Gran a blow by blow account of each of the four little plays, and wondered how her mother was standing up to the strain. But she was an old hand, and would listen carefully and ask all the right questions, and not look bored or distracted. Why don't I take after her, with all that calm and wisdom? she thought. Then she remembered the time Josie had gone missing when Gran was in charge. She'd gone off with her boyfriend overnight, and Gran had gone completely to pieces. So there it was . . . she needn't feel so guilty about panicking over the kids. It was perfectly natural, with that ugly threat from Joanne bloody Murphy hanging over her.

It was *not* perfectly natural, though, to keep it all to herself and not tell Derek. Lois shook her head, as if to rid herself of unwanted thoughts. Better make the tea and be as normal as possible, she told herself. Derek already had his suspicions, and she did not want to add to them. A call to Cowgill in the morning would reassure her, she hoped. She had reason to speak to him, reckoning that Mr Betts's presence at the theatre was one coincidence too many.

She sat down with her tea in the kitchen, listening to the rest of the family chatting with the television still churning on, and tried to sort out some of the muddled facts which had come her way. Two killings now, apparently unconnected. The major's death probably had some sort of ritual meaning – him being dressed up in a suit of armour and stuck on top of a tomb, like some old sacrifice. Poor old Dick Reading – no, she couldn't think of him like that. Wicked Dick Reading, then. He had been tied to a tree, but more to keep him upright and in a position to frighten someone – her? – than anything to do with . . . what was it? Somebody with an apple on his head? Lois chuckled to herself, and then felt ashamed, thinking of Bridie and Hazel in a state of shock, regardless of how much they hated him.

Then the drugs. Prue Betts had most probably taken the wrong thing, or too much, and ended up in hospital. Joanne Murphy's cigarette smoke smelled of something suspicious, and she lived in the kind of squalor that Lois associated with dozey druggies. Gary was much too interested in drugs at the surgery, knew Joanne Murphy from the theatre, and had been seen by Derek talking to her by the road. Hazel? But no, Lois dismissed Hazel's involvement. The girl was streetwise, certainly, and probably knew the drugs scene better than Josie, but she was such a sensible girl. Then Lois remembered how she had disappeared at the theatre that night, and returned with no explanation. Had she been backstage, talking to Gary and . . . and who else? Mr Betts? But surely . . .

Lois's head began to spin. It was too late to sort it all out, even in a speculative way, and she got up. 'Time for bed,' she said, joining the family.

Jamie groaned. 'Oh, Mum!' he said. 'Gran said—'

His grandmother interrupted him. 'That's enough of that, young man,' she said. 'You do what your mother says, and do it now.'

Derek looked across at Lois, and smiled. 'Cheer up, duck,' he said. 'With Gran in charge we can all relax.'

If only, thought Lois, but she marched Jamie, still protesting, upstairs, and tried to dismiss all thoughts of galloping majors, knights in shining armour and him with an apple on his head.

Twenty-Five

On Monday morning, the telephone was ringing in Lois's office before breakfast, and she rushed downstairs in the slippers that Derek said would break her neck.

'Hello? Who's that?'

'Mrs Betts,' said an anxious voice. 'Is that New Brooms?'

Lois took a deep breath. Now what? 'Yes, this is Lois Meade speaking. Can I help you?'

After a long, rambling story about an old woman who had cleaned for the Betts's for years, not much good lately, but better than nothing, and now whipped into hospital with a stroke, Mrs Betts finally came to the point: she needed cleaning help, and straight away, if possible.

Heaven sent, thought Lois, and arranged to go and see her after lunch. 'I am sure we can be of service,' she said, making Derek laugh as he brought in a mug of tea.

'Let's have a little service here, then,' Derek said. 'The kids're not up yet, Gran's whizzing around feeding the cat, burning the bacon and yelling in all directions. We need the boss, Lois, so get yourself into the kitchen where you belong.'

Lois turned on him. 'It's only Gran being in earshot that saves you, my lad,' she hissed. But she got going fast, and miraculously everything was in good order by the time the school bus was due.

After everyone had left the house, including Gran, who was due at the Oxfam shop this morning, Lois dialled Sheila Stratford's number. She should be back from the surgery by now, and would be just the right one for the Betts's. 'Just a call in advance of the meeting,' Lois said. 'The Betts's at Waltonby school – you must know them – need a cleaner. I'd like you to take it on, Sheila. I'm seeing Mrs Betts this afternoon, and we can arrange day and time etcetera. No objections?' Lois always put it to her staff in this way, reckoning that it would pre-empt later grumbles. Also, and more importantly, she was anxious to know from Sheila any local gossip there might be about the Betts's.

Sure enough, there was a pause before Sheila answered. 'Ye-es,' she said slowly. 'But . . .'

'But what?' said Lois. 'You'd better tell me now.'

'Well, there is talk in the village about the schoolmaster . . . seems he was pretty unkind to old Mrs Whatsit who cleaned for them. There was a big row, and some of the children heard him shouting at her. You know she had the stroke in the schoolhouse, on her cleaning day? Well, I'd not want anything like that, Lois.'

Lois thought for a moment, then decided to treat it lightly. 'Oh, heavens, Sheila,' she said. 'You needn't worry – I'd be checking on everything, and if there was one word out of place I'd be down on him like a ton of bricks. That poor old soul was on her own, wasn't she? Nobody to speak up for her.'

'Oh yes there was!' said Sheila, laughing now. 'Her son-in-law marched into the school playground next morning and sorted out old Betts in front of all the parents! It was quite a sight, apparently. Nearly came to blows, except for one of the dads stepping in and separating them. If old Betts goes on like that much longer, he'll be out on his ear. The governors won't stand for it. Only got away with it so far because the reverend is past it – doesn't know what time of day it is – and all for a quiet life. He's the chairman of the governors, you know . . .'

She was quiet then, and Lois said, 'Well, would you be happy to give it a try? He'll probably be on his best behaviour after all that.' Sheila agreed, and said she would see Lois later at the meeting.

'Old Betts, eh? Still, could be local gossip. Head teachers are never popular,' said Lois to her empty office, and began to tidy up ready for the staff meeting. She and Hazel did shorter hours at the hall on Mondays, and were back in Long Farnden by twelve. That gave them a good hour to meet the others and sort out any changes needed for the coming week.

It was a beautiful spring morning, blue sky and puffs of cloud sailing on the wind, and when Lois drove out of the village and along the Dalling road, it was some while before she noticed the big car with darkened windows cruising along behind her at a discreet distance. She felt a nasty jolt, like touching an electric fence. She was certain it was the Gorilla, but could not see if the Murphy woman was with him. What to do? It was a narrow road, with high hedges on either side, and nowhere to turn off. She put her foot on the accelerator, and the old car responded slowly. As it gathered speed, Lois steered with one hand and fumbled for her mobile phone with the other. Blast! Why was her handbag so full of junk? She tipped the whole thing upside down, narrowly missing a wandering sheep. She dialled Cowgill's number, and when he answered, said tersely, 'Lois here. Being followed by Gorilla and possibly Murphy. Road to Dalling. Can you get here?'

He wasted no time, but said, 'On the way. Don't panic,' and was gone.

Hazel Reading had gone early to Tresham to pick up some cleaning for her mother, and was travelling fast in her little VW to be at the hall on time. Lois was a devil about punctuality, and Hazel was still wary of her sharp tongue. No doubt about Lois being boss, she thought. Funny how people grew into their jobs. Mind you, Lois Meade had always been bossy! Hazel knew her mum had sometimes resented things Lois had said in the past, but she had been the one they'd turned to for support. And Hazel had seen how Lois's authority had worked in meetings when Gary Needham had got uppity. Yep, she'd better get a move on, else there'd be trouble. She increased her speed, swung round a corner, and came upon a big black car with darkened windows filling the road in front of her.

The VW did its best to respond to the brakes, but Hazel realized too late that she couldn't stop in time. By the time she'd whacked into the black car's rear end with a nasty thump, she had braced herself for the impact. She heard ominous sounds of tinkling glass on the road and sighed. God, of all mornings . . .

The door of the big car was flung open, and an enormous man got out. His head was shaved and in his dark glasses he was very menacing. 'What the bloody hell!' His voice was loud and furious, and Hazel cursed to herself. She stayed in her car, waiting for the man to come up. Then she saw the passenger door open, and a woman walked over quickly towards them. At the same time, she glimpsed an old brown car driving off at speed, soon leaving them behind. Was it Lois? Blimey, she might have stayed to help. Still, Hazel had no doubt that she could cope.

'So,' she said, as the unattractive pair leaned down to knock angrily on her car window. She opened it, and stared at them. 'Well,' she began, 'if ain't Ms Murphy and Minder Tony . . . Can't think of anyone I'd rather bash into. You'd better give me a hand clearing up the glass.'

But after delivering an angry kick that dented the VW's already blemished bodywork, the big man allowed himself to be dragged away by Joanne Murphy, who yelled at him, 'We'll lose her, Tony, for God's sake!' They sped off, leaving Hazel to brush away the broken glass as best she could.

Lois drove into the hall car park and turned off the engine. Sod it! She was sure it had been Hazel's car, and knew she should have stopped to make sure she was all right. But self-preservation was a stronger instinct, and now she sat shaking in her seat, trying to pull herself together. Then she saw Cowgill's car cruising in. He parked next to her, and got out, looking round carefully before approaching her.

'I got away,' she said. 'They were run into by a car behind them. I'm pretty sure it was Hazel, but if you go back along that road you're bound to see them. Check Hazel's OK, too.'

To her surprise, Hunter Cowgill shook his head. 'I saw them,' he said. 'Just coming along as I turned in here. I think they were coming in after you, but then they saw me and changed their minds.'

'But Hazel?' said Lois anxiously.

'Ah yes,' he said, 'Hazel Reading. Yes, well, I think it's time I told you about Hazel Reading. Can you meet me in the woods – half past two? We'd better have a chat, but not here.'

Twenty-Six

Lois was puzzled. What on earth could Cowgill mean? There surely was nothing he could tell her about Hazel. Lois had known her since the day she arrived, premature and squealing like a piglet, in the hospital in Tresham. Bridie had doted on her and Lois had feared that the tiny girl would be smothered with protective love. But both she and Bridie had reckoned without Hazel's iron constitution and bloody-mindedness inherited from her father. She had been determined and competitive at school, and had stood up to her father's excesses since the day when, at three years old, she had bitten his leg as he made to slap Bridie round the face. No, there was nothing Cowgill could tell her about Hazel. More likely the other way round! As a young teenager, Hazel had had several unsuitable boyfriends – skivers, too old, or loafers who had money from mysterious sources, etc, etc – and several times Lois had warned her when her father was on the warpath. But then, you never knew with other people's children. And teenagers could be very secretive, very adept at covering up what they did not want known.

Lois got into her car after a hard morning's work and drove home, looking nervously and more frequently than usual in her rear-view mirror. But no big car with darkened windows followed her, and she arrived home to find the others waiting for her outside the house. She had said nothing to Hazel about the crash, and Hazel hadn't mentioned it. She'd decided to find out what Cowgill had to say first.

'Late again, Mrs M,' said Gary, teasing, but nevertheless standing back politely to allow her through the gate.

'Shut up, Gary,' said Lois shortly, and he raised his eyebrows and shrugged. She saw him and Hazel exchange glances, and wondered again how well they knew each other. 'Now then,' she said when they were settled, 'we have a new client – Mrs Betts, schoolhouse at Waltonby—'

She stopped as Hazel suddenly choked and had to be thumped on the back before recovering. 'Sorry, Mrs M,' Hazel said.

'As I was saying, then, Mrs Betts needs someone urgently, and Sheila has agreed to take her on. Shouldn't be too difficult, as it's not a big house. Built by the squire when he thought his tenants needed educating. Smallish rooms, been modernized. Any comments?'

Once again, Hazel and Gary looked at each other knowingly, and this time Lois said, 'If you two have something to say, please say it. That's what we're here for, to give us a chance for a chat. Come on, Hazel, what is it? Something to do with Prue?'

Hazel shook her head. 'Nope,' she said. 'Mrs Betts always seems a nice enough woman, and Prue's OK now. Goin' off to university in the autumn.'

'And Mr Betts?' said Lois, hoping Sheila wouldn't jump in here.

Hazel shook her head. 'Not my cup of tea,' she said, and hesitated. Then, of course, Sheila began her story of the old woman and the stroke, and the discussion became general.

After a few minutes, Lois said, 'Well, we'll give it a try, and I shall keep a close eye on everything.' Not much forthcoming there, she thought, as they carried on with other matters. Gary was quieter than usual, but that could have been because of the snub she'd administered.

They all left cheerfully enough, and then at the gate Gary said, 'Oh blast, left my notebook in your study, Lois!' He walked back with her into the house, and recovered it.

'You all right, Gary?' said Lois tentatively.

He nodded. 'More or less,' he said, and then added, 'it's just that you've been a bit off with me lately, and I'm not sure what I've done wrong. I know I shouldn't have been reading the doctor's papers, but that wasn't exactly a serious crime . . .' He tailed off lamely, looking down at his hands.

And what about you being buddies with Joanne Murphy?

thought Lois. And what's goin' on at the theatre behind the scenes? And, for that matter, what's goin' on between you and Hazel? She said only, 'Don't be silly, Gary, there's nothing wrong. Had a lot on my mind recently. Just as long as your work is satisfactory, and there's no more leaving taps on, I'm quite happy.' He left her then, but the atmosphere between them was far from warm.

Cowgill was already there at the meeting place. Lois was about ten minutes late, and he looked at his watch. 'For God's sake!' she snapped. 'I've got a business to run, and you're damned lucky I've come at all! Miles out of my way, and washing and ironing to do at home!'

He said nothing, but smiled gently. 'Gran not still with you?' he said mildly.

'Is there anything you don't bloody well know?' she retorted. 'Strikes me you could do without my penn'orth perfectly well. And anyway, what's all this about Hazel?'

'Calm down, Lois,' he said in a firmer voice. 'What I have to tell you is serious, and extremely confidential. If I didn't value your help very highly I certainly wouldn't be giving you this information. So just listen carefully, please . . . and don't smoulder!' he added, touching her shoulder lightly.

'OK, OK, I'm sorry,' said Lois. 'I've had a rotten day so far. Go on, then, cheer me up. What about Hazel?'

He began by telling her more or less the same stuff that Josie had described in the middle of the night. The school drugs scene, the young kids drawn into experimenting by those already hooked, the one or two tragedies. Then he surprised her. 'Hazel Reading was a near disaster too,' he said. 'First came to our notice when we picked her up out cold on the pavement outside that club in Tresham. All her so-called friends had vanished, just left her there, and she was in a bad way.'

'But Bridie never said . . .' Lois had gone very pale. If Hazel . . . and then Prue . . . who next? It was her turn to look at her watch. She must be back for the school bus.

'No, well, she wouldn't, would she,' said Cowgill. 'You were already prepared to wade in and rescue Bridie from her husband, and both Bridie and Hazel were anxious to avoid any more ructions from that quarter. No, Hazel recovered and nothing was said. Except that one day Hazel turned up at the police station, asking for me. Said she'd learned her lesson and wanted to get her own back on the pushers and dealers.'

'But did she know . . . ?'

'Not then. She only knew kids who could get more or less anything . . . at a price. But she wanted to find out more and said she could do it, being part of the scene. I was very doubtful. It's a dangerous world, as you've discovered,' he added, watching Lois's colour come back. 'I told her to take no action – and that was an order – but to keep her ear to the ground and let us know if she heard anything of interest.'

'So, ever since then she's been working for you?' said Lois incredulously. 'My God, she's good at keeping it quiet. I never thought for a minute . . .'

'As you know,' Cowgill continued, 'the theatre in Tresham is a hot spot. Joanne Murphy and the Gorilla – I like that! – are heavily into it, but as I said, they're not the level we're after. Hazel's given us some good stuff, wormed her way backstage with offers of help, and is useful there.'

'And Gary Needham?' said Lois sharply.

'What about him?' said Cowgill. Lois knew by now when the shutters came down, and they'd just clattered into place. She was not going to learn anything about Gary, not now.

'And does Hazel know about me?' she said.

'No,' said Cowgill, 'and that's the way we'll keep it at the moment. She's fond of you, you know, and I don't want her rushing to your defence when it's not needed. Might spoil things.'

'Well, thanks,' said Lois bitterly. 'I'll just keep quiet if the Gorilla has another go at me with Hazel in earshot. I wouldn't want to spoil things.'

And then she took a deep breath, decided he'd probably had a bad morning too, and told him about the Betts's. He nodded, and said 'Good' several times. 'He's in with that theatre lot, isn't he?' said Lois.

Cowgill nodded again. 'Not sure how deep, if at all,' he said, 'but it will be very useful having you in touch there. And you know how to get hold of me. I doubt if Mrs Murphy and the Gorilla will try anything on with you. They'll be off on another tack.'

As she got into her car and drove back towards Long Farnden, Cowgill's last words echoed in her head. What other tack would they try? Where was she most vulnerable? The answer to that was so obvious that she shivered. Her kids. Josie, Douglas and Jamie. It never occurred to her to add Derek to the list.

Twenty-Seven

Sheila Stratford rinsed out the sink and took off her apron. She turned to her husband. 'New job this afternoon, Sam,' she said.

'I know,' he said, from behind the pages of the *Sun*, 'you told me . . . several times.'

'Oh, you,' she said, cuffing him lightly round the ear. 'D'you think I need police protection?'

Sam Stratford put down his paper and looked at her with a frown. 'Wha'd'you mean?' he said. Sam was a farm worker, and expert at handling the enormous tractors, trailers and other fearsome pieces of equipment that had replaced men and horses. He was not so good at handling women. His mother had been a bossy woman, and he had married another. Usually he kept his head down, and said very little around the house, reserving conversation for his mates at the pub, where he went regular as clockwork at nine o'clock every night except Sunday. Now he was surprised into attention at what his wife was saying.

'I mean,' she said with emphasis, 'it was all round the village that old Betts had made poor old Mrs Whatsit have a stroke . . . frightened her nearly to death with shouting and threatening her. *That's* what I mean.'

'Gossip,' said Sam. 'Only ever seen him once in the pub, and he was as mild as milk. Blimey, is that the time?' He folded up the paper and vanished.

As Sheila heard the gate slam shut, she sighed. Sometimes she wished she was small and slim and delicate. Perhaps that would bring out the protector in Sam. Then she laughed, as she caught sight of her ample figure in the hall mirror. Her broad red face laughed back at her, and she smoothed down her mop of wiry hair. No, he wouldn't have married her if she'd been a waif. Needed a good, strong woman, and that's what he'd got.

She arrived at the schoolhouse five minutes early, just as the children were crowding into school after the afternoon bell. She knocked, and the door opened at once.

'Morning, Mrs Stratford!' said Mrs Betts warmly. 'I had no idea you worked for New Brooms, until Mrs Meade called. I suppose I could have come to you direct?'

Sheila walked through to the kitchen, and decided to make the situation quite clear. 'No,' she said, 'I don't do jobs on my own account. Just clients of New Brooms. Then I get the protection of the company if anything goes wrong,' she said firmly.

Mrs Betts stiffened. 'I'm sure nothing will go wrong here,' she said. 'Now, I'll just show you round the house, and then leave you to get on. You know your job better than I do!' she added with an attempt at a smile. 'We miss poor old Mrs Whatsit, but she was getting a bit past it,' she continued. 'And then that nasty stroke. My husband tried his best to rally her, but we had to call the ambulance in the end.'

'Yes, I heard,' said Sheila baldly. 'Now, we'd better get on. I have another job to go to later on.'

The house was neat and tidy, with a chintzy sitting room, a study for Mr Betts where the dining room would once have been, and a modern kitchen. Sheila peered out of the window and saw a path leading from the back door to a gate in the school fence. Teacher's Way, the kids called it. Sheila had been a pupil in the school once, and now had grandchildren there. She knew a great deal more about its past and present than Mrs Betts.

Upstairs there were three bedrooms and a bathroom. 'Master bedroom,' said Mrs Betts grandly. And then: 'Here's the guest room and Prue's bedroom. But I've promised her she can clean that herself. You know what these young people are like, and she's very private. Locks it when she goes out, but when she goes to college I plan to give it a good turn out.'

That'll be a mistake, thought Sheila, but said nothing.

The afternoon went quickly, with a tea break at exactly three o'clock. At half past, Sheila washed out her dusters and hung them on the line in the garden. It was a lovely sunny day, and the children were in the playground greeting waiting mothers and fathers. She waved to her granddaughter and went back into the house. 'That's it, then,' she said to Mrs Betts. 'Mrs Meade will be calling before next week to make sure my work's satisfactory and there's no problems.'

'Oh, everywhere looks lovely!' enthused Mrs Betts. 'There are certainly no problems as far as we are concerned. Only too grateful . . . there's really no need for Mrs Meade to come again . . .'

'She always does,' said Sheila, collecting her jacket from the hall. 'A very good employer, she is. Pity there's not more around like her,' she added, smiling innocently. 'I'll say cheerio, then, and see you next week.' She walked swiftly out and round to the school gate, where she hugged the children and went off to have a cup of her daughter's disgustingly weak tea.

'Hello? Sheila? Lois here. Everything go all right?'

'Fine. Himself wasn't there, o' course. And Mrs Betts fluttered round like a daft old moth. Still, once I got goin' she left me alone. Said she was pleased.'

'Was Prue there?' said Lois casually.

Sheila hesitated. 'No, at school. But her mum said somethin' funny. Said she'd promised her I wouldn't go in her room. Keeps it locked. Wouldn't've catched me letting our Jean lock her bedroom door! Funny, I call it.'

'Mmm,' said Lois. 'Well, I'll drop in and see her at the end of the week. Usual routine call. I don't suppose you'll run into Betts until the holidays, then we shall see. Thanks, anyway, Sheila. See you.' She put down the telephone and sat for several minutes staring at nothing, until Gran yelled from the kitchen that tea was ready.

Twenty-Eight

'Last day wiring at the pub,' Derek said next morning as he kissed Lois goodbye. 'Been a long job, but one more day will do it.'

'Tying up a few loose ends?' said Lois wittily.

'Good God, I hope not!' Derek replied. 'Bit more technical than that, or I shall be in trouble,' he added, and then turned back from his van. 'Just you be careful, my gel,' he said. 'Keep your eye on the road and no thinkin' about Dick Reading or the major or any o' that.' He blew her another kiss, and was gone.

Lois went back into the house. She had given him an edited account of the smash on the Dalling road, chiefly to account for the need to check the insurance on Hazel's car. Had he guessed there was more to it? Anyway, his words were timely. Eyes peeled for the Gorilla and his mate, Lois reminded herself. She had to drive to the wholesalers today to stack up on cleaning supplies, and meant to go round by Waltonby to drop in on the vicar. Just a periodic check, she'd told Bridie, but she had found the Reverend Rogers very pleasant and willing to talk, and with a bit of luck she could steer the conversation round to Mr Betts. She was sure the reverend would not divulge school secrets, but she just might pick up something useful. It was worth a try.

The vicar was in his garden, bent double over a flower bed, and Lois cleared her throat loudly as she approached. Deaf as a post, Hazel had said. He was not, but his hearing had definitely diminished and she did not want to startle the old bloke.

He straightened up with a welcoming smile. 'Good morning!' he said. 'I do hope you have not come to tell me Mrs Reading is indisposed? Or has another job? Or won the lottery?' He chuckled to himself, and added, 'Come along in, my dear. Nice to see you again, and I'm so glad you've come to interrupt me. We can have a cup of tea and a chat.'

'No, nothing wrong with Bridie,' said Lois reassuringly. 'She is very happy working here. No, it is just that I call in on all our clients every so often, just to check that there's no problems.'

He confirmed that there were none, and began to talk about his garden. 'It's much too big for me, of course,' he said. 'But you cannot get help these days, even though so many are out of work. I do get one of the bigger boys from the school to sweep up leaves in the autumn, and sometimes they'll cut the grass. Anything to do with machinery! But as for weeding . . . well, that is too much like hard work, I suspect.'

Keep him on the school, Lois! She poured him another cup of tea from the lovely china teapot that had seen better days, and said quickly, 'That's very thoughtful of Mr Betts to send boys round to help.'

Thc vicar nodded. 'I suppose it is,' he said, 'but to tell you the truth, my dear, I think it more likely that Mrs Betts is the one to think of these things. The headmaster has so much on his hands, always dashing hither and thither . . . not an easy man . . .' He stopped speaking and seemed to fall into a reverie.

Lois began again. 'Gets on well with the parents, does he? My kids went to a big Tresham school, and sometimes the teachers and parents came to blows . . . specially on the Churchill, where we lived.'

He looked up at her suddenly. 'Blows?' he said. 'Mr Betts? Have you heard something, Mrs Meade?'

He had clearly not heard her properly, but she pressed ahead. 'You can't always believe what you hear,' she said cheerfully, 'though my mum always says there's no smoke without fire!'

'I do hope not, though . . .' And once more he tailed off without ending the sentence. She was sure he was well aware of the rumours, and far from being the batty old duffer that Hazel had described, had a cunning look in his eye. 'Well,' she said lightly, 'Mrs Stratford is cleaning for Mrs Betts now, so maybe she will be able to lighten the load a bit. I've heard Mrs Whatsit was not quite up to it, being old, an' that.'

'Poor woman!' said the vicar, suddenly getting to his feet and extending a hand to Lois. 'Must go and visit her. And I expect you'll be wanting to get on,' he added, shaking her hand firmly and moving her gently towards the door, just as he did after morning service when a parishioner talked too long at the church door.

Lois loaded up her car at the wholesalers and started back along the dual carriageway that took her out of the wasteland of industrial Tresham, stopping off at a garage selling cheap petrol. As she came out of the garage shop, she glanced behind her and saw a police car, chequered yellow and blue, parked to one side of the forecourt. It was Keith Simpson, the local bobby from her own district, and a sort of friend. He had been helpful on several occasions in the past, chiefly when Josie had got involved with that Melvyn Hallhouse and run away from home, and Lois waved. He smiled, and got out of the car. Oh blast, thought Lois. She didn't particularly want to be seen talking to a uniformed policeman just at this moment.

'Hi, Lois! How are you . . . and the family?'

'Fine,' she said. 'Got to get going now, children home from school . . .'

'Thought you had Gran living in?' said Keith Simpson, still smiling.

'Blimey!' said Lois. 'Word gets around fast. Anyway, must go—'

'Just wanted to ask you something.' Constable Simpson had stopped smiling now, and seemed to grow a few inches taller. 'I believe you have a Gary Needham working for you?'

Lois nodded. 'So what?' she said.

'I need to have a word with him,' he said, 'about a police matter. He's a bit difficult to track down. Doesn't come to the phone . . . ignores our requests to come down to the station . . . that kind of thing. Don't want to come down too heavy . . . not a serious thing. Could you mention it to him, Lois?'

'Certainly not!' Lois's face was an angry red. 'You do your job, and I'll do mine! Gary Needham is a perfectly good worker and I've no fault to find. If you want him, you get him. I must go now,' she added abruptly, and, getting into her car, drove off without looking back.

Keith Simpson frowned. What was eating Lois? She'd overreacted a bit, surely, considering it was only a matter of going through red lights. And he wanted to take a look at young Needham's car, check that it had got a current MOT, etc. Ah well, Lois had been a tricky one in the past. Women. You never knew which way they would jump. He went back to his patrol car and forgot about the encounter as an emergency call came in.

Lois, on the other hand, did not forget. She wondered what Gary had done. He was a difficult one to sort out. Sometimes he seemed so straightforward, and then at others he was secretive and uncommunicative. The one consistent thing about Gary Needham was his politeness and good temper. Nothing ruffled him, and he took reprimand without argument. Perhaps she should not have been short with Keith Simpson, but tried to find out more. Still, it was a real cheek asking her to intervene. Her loyalty was to her staff, and that would remain a priority until she had some definite evidence that Gary was up to something.

She looked at her watch. Gran would be there in Long Farnden by now, so she decided to call in at the supermarket to get supplies. It was crowded with shoppers, and she had to wait a long time at the checkout. The children should be safely back, she thought, as she drove into Long Farnden. She was dying for a cup of tea. As she turned into the High Street, her heart stopped. Halfway down the street, outside her house, she could see a car parked. It was chequered blue and yellow: a police car.

'Oh my God, the kids!' she yelled, and accelerated. Hardly knowing what she did, she rushed into the house, leaving the engine running and the shopping spilling out of the open car door. 'Mum!' she screamed. 'Mum! Where are you!'

Gran appeared in the kitchen and took her arm. 'I'm here, ducky,' she said. 'And so are all the kids, all fine.'

'But the police . . .'

'Sit down, Lois,' Gran said, gently pushing her into a

chair. 'They've come to tell us there's been an accident. It's Derek . . .'

Lois shot to her feet. 'Where? What's happened? Is he . . . ?'

Gran shook her head. 'No, he's not. But he's very badly hurt, and in the hospital. Now, you'd better have a word with the policeman, if you can manage it.'

It was Keith Simpson, of course, and he had no hesitation in putting his arms round Lois and giving her an unofficial hug. 'It's OK,' he said. 'Come on, love, sit down and we'll have a little chat. Then I'll take you to see Derek.'

After a minute or two, Lois was composed enough to ask what happened. 'The Waltonby crossroads,' he said. 'Derek had finished the job at the pub and left early.'

'Whose fault . . . who hit him?'

'We don't know yet,' said Keith Simpson. 'Hit and run, the bastard. But we'll get him, don't you worry. There was a witness . . . woman on a bike . . . said it was a big black car, with them smoky windows, so she couldn't see the driver.'

Lois was deathly white. 'Oh no,' she said, 'oh my God, not my Derek . . .'

Twenty-Nine

Keith Simpson had a hard time persuading Lois that it would be foolish of her to drive to the hospital by herself. She had insisted that she would be perfectly all right, that she could then stay as long as she wanted, and be no further trouble to him. He said she was in no fit state to drive, whatever she might think, and if she didn't want him to wait, then she could ring for a taxi to take her back home.

'Taxi?' said Lois sharply. 'We're not made of money. No, I'll get a bus. Or ring for someone to come and get me. Hazel would comc,' shc addcd, thinking quickly of likely helpers.

Derek was in intensive care. A senior nurse took over from Keith Simpson, and held on to Lois's arm as she ushered her in to see him. 'Don't be alarmed at all the paraphernalia,' she had warned, but Lois felt a jolt of panic when she saw him surrounded by tubes and plastic bottles and dripping blood. But it was his face that was the most shocking. That's not my Derek! was Lois's first thought, but then she saw that it was. The familiar face, normally so full of colour and life, was paper white. His eyes were closed, and there were bandages everywhere. She choked, and felt the nurse's hand take hers. 'Sit down here for a while.' The calm voice was comforting, and Lois did as she was told.

'Is he asleep . . . or unconscious?' she whispered.

The nurse smiled. 'He's stable,' she said. 'We shall know more later, when he is able to speak to us. It will take time, Mrs Meade, and we must be patient.' Now Lois noticed the heart monitor, with its regular bleeps. She couldn't bear to look at it, in case it stopped or quickened. 'You can touch his hand,' said the nurse, and Lois reached out, resting her hand as lightly as she could on top of Derek's. It was warm and rough, and so tangible a part of the Derek she loved so much that she could not stop the tears. The nurse patted her shoulder. 'A couple of minutes more, and then I should leave him to rest,' she said to the weeping Lois. 'It is a shock, my dear,' she added, 'but next time you come, you'll be a great help to him, I'm sure.'

By the time Lois left the hospital and stood in the car park dialling Hazel Reading on her mobile, she had pulled herself together. 'Hazel? It's Lois. I'm at the hospital, and I need a lift home.'

She did not need to say more, as Hazel answered without questions, 'I'm on me way, Mrs M. I'll pick you up outside. See you soon.'

It was twenty or so minutes before Hazel would be in Tresham, and so Lois walked slowly across to where ambulances stood in a row, their drivers chatting quietly. She went up to one at random. 'Do you know which one of you picked up my husband? Road accident – Waltonby crossroads – Derek Meade?'

The driver shook his head. 'Not me,' he said. 'Ask Jim over there.'

'Yeah, it was me,' the driver said. 'Sorry, me duck. He was in a nasty mess. But they reckon he'll be OK. You all right?'

Lois nodded. 'Was there anybody else involved?' she said.

'Nobody there but the police by the time we arrived. Mind you,' the driver added, 'I think there was a witness. Woman on a bike. The police were talking to her. I think my mate knew who she was.'

'That's right,' said one of the others. 'Lives in Waltonby, friend of my sister. She and her bloke run the pub. Not married, but as good as.'

'Oh, right,' said Lois. She knew her, then. And Derek had often spoken of her as being a nice enough woman, good at the job. 'Thanks a lot,' she said to the drivers, and walked across to the bench by the entrance to wait for Hazel. She sat down and closed her eyes, trying to concentrate. She would get those bastards if it was the last thing she did.

'Lois?' It was a familiar voice, a man's voice. 'Are you all right?' It was Hunter Cowgill, looking exceedingly worried.

'If anybody asks me that again, I shall bash them,' Lois replied, reduced to childish threats. She was so tired, she couldn't think, couldn't work out what Cowgill was doing in front of her asking stupid questions. 'I'm waiting for Hazel,' she said.

'I know,' he replied. 'And here she is.'

Hazel's car pulled up beside Cowgill, and she hopped out quickly. 'Mrs M?' she said, 'are you . . . ?'

'Don't ask,' said Cowgill grimly. 'She'll bash you. Just take her home and make sure Gran's there to look after her. I'll talk to you later, Hazel. Make sure you take care of her, won't you?' He leaned over the seated Lois and touched her shoulder. 'Sorry, love,' he said. 'We'll get 'em.' And he walked away to his car, and was gone.

'Did you ring Cowgill?' said Lois, as they drove out of Tresham.

Hazel nodded, her eyes fixed on the road ahead. 'I thought it best,' she said. 'Hope you're not cross.'

'Then you know about . . . ?'

Hazel nodded again. 'Most of it,' she said. 'There's more to tell, but it can wait. Got to get Derek better first.' They drove on in silence then, and Lois looked blankly out of the windows, seeing nothing.

'Here we are, then,' Hazel said, driving into the Meades' entrance. Gran was standing watching out for her, and by the time the car stopped, she was at Lois's door and helping her out.

'Come on, duckie,' she said. 'Tea's ready, and the kids are waiting. They wouldn't start before you came home. Brave face, now, Lois. That's my girl.'

'She was amazing, Mum,' said Hazel to Bridie. 'Walked into that kitchen, smiled at the kids, told Jamie off for having dirty hands at the table, and ate her entire plateful of tea.'

'Doesn't surprise me,' said Bridie. 'Lois was always the strong one. God help them that done that to Derek.'

'They're beyond that,' said Hazel flatly. 'Only the devil can help them now.'

Thirty

Hazel Reading sat in her car, waiting. She had parked up a side street, close by the little theatre, and locked herself in. It was growing dark, and she knew that anyone sitting in a car – especially a girl on her own – was not safe in this part of Tresham. She had arranged a meeting for nine o'clock, coinciding with the end of rehearsals, and kept her eye on the driving mirror.

It was about ten past nine when there was a tap on her window. She had seen him coming, and now unlocked the doors and motioned him to get in beside her. 'Well?' she said.

'They've got rid of it,' he said. 'It'll never be found. They've done it before, and know the ropes. But what they don't know,' he added, with the vestige of a smile, 'is that I could trace it. No problem. I overheard JM talking to that gormless idiot backstage when they thought nobody was around. So it could be found. Trouble is, it wouldn't take them long to guess who talked. I'm scared, Hazel, I don't mind admitting. It's getting very nasty.'

'Very nasty indeed,' said Hazel grimly. 'And I – we – have to end it. I owe Mrs M. And so do you. You could've been out on your ear if she hadn't given you another chance. So now we have to make a plan, get all the help we can, and fix 'em. Right?'

'Right,' said Gary doubtfully. 'Let me know. You're the brains. Usual contact.'

He scrambled out of the car, and she watched him head back towards the theatre, his head down and his thin legs moving fast. You can see he's scared, she thought. Sticks out a mile. Worst possible thing, with Joanne Murphy and her crew on the lookout.

* * *

Next morning, Lois turned up as usual at the hall and met Hazel at the entrance. 'You didn't have to come, Mrs M,' Hazel said. 'I could've managed . . . done a couple of extra hours. Are you sure you're . . .' She stopped, smiled at the expression on Lois's face, and said, 'Come on, then, let's get going.'

They worked in silence for most of the morning, and then finally, when they were putting away the cleaning tools, Lois said, 'Hazel, we need to talk. Not now. I'm going straight into Tresham from here to see Derek. I rang earlier, and they said he was still out of it, but I just want to be there. So can you come round this evening? Eightish? It shouldn't take long. I know some of it, and you know some of it, and we'll get on a lot quicker if we work together. Forget Cowgill for the moment. He has his uses' – Hazel smiled broadly – 'but I've got an idea of what we can do. It'll need your help, and in particular anything you know that I don't.'

Hazel nodded. 'Righto,' she said. 'Eight o'clock. I'll be there. Give my love to Mr M . . . don't matter if he don't hear . . . just give it him.' A shadow crossed her face, and she turned away abruptly. 'See you,' she muttered, and walked away swiftly.

Poor kid, thought Lois, walking into the car park. Not much of a life so far. But maybe it would get better once all this was sorted out. Bridie would make a new start, she was sure of that, and Hazel could shake the dust of Waltonby off her feet. She was a bright girl, full of spirit, and deserved a break.

As she drove into Tresham, she stopped at a flower shop and bought a couple of bunches of freesias. The scent filled the car. Lois hoped it might penetrate through to Derek. He'd always brought them for her into the hospital when the kids had been born. Freesias had meant something special. She remembered when that kid at Ringford Hall had pinched a load of them from the greenhouse and given them to Derek. He'd been really chuffed, and presented them to her as if he'd actually bought them.

Lois turned into the hospital car park. It's not right, she thought, as she put money in the machine. It irked her that the authorities were taking money from people in trouble, visitors or outpatients who had no alternative but to park their cars here, the hospital being right in the middle of town where there was no possible other parking place. It's a con, she said to herself, walking across and into the entrance. Intensive care: she followed the arrows and stopped at the reception desk.

The woman looked up at her unsmilingly. 'Who?' she said.

'Derek Meade,' repeated Lois. Her heart had begun to race. Why didn't she recognize the name? He must still be here. They'd said on the phone this morning that there had been little change. Oh my God, suppose he'd . . . But surely they'd have let her know . . . The woman consulted a list in front of her.

'Oh yes,' she said in a lofty voice, 'you can go in . . . nurse is in there already. Know the way?'

Lois wanted to strike her, thump her as hard as she could, slap her round the face until she yelled for mercy. But she just nodded and walked on, down the corridor to where she knew Derek, her Derek, unrecognizable and absent, was lying. Not waiting for her, not expecting her, not full of things to tell her or questions about the kids. Just there.

'Ah, Mrs Meade,' said the kindly nurse. 'What lovely flowers – you sit down here, and I'll put them in water.

Lois sat down beside Derek. He looked much the same, if a little paler and the shadows under his eyes deeper. She managed to quell the rising panic as she thought the unthinkable. Of course he was going to get better, come back home, go to work again. She reached out and put her hand on his, and thanked God that it was warm . . . alive.

The nurse returned with the freesias, now in an unsuitable orange pottery vase, but wafting their wonderful scent across the room. Lois smiled at her, showing that she was in control, not about to break down and become an embarrassment. The nurse left, and there were no sounds except the humming of machines and the bleep of the heart monitor which Lois tried unsuccessfully to blot out. Perhaps she should talk to him. Maybe he would be able to hear her, even though he seemed completely unconscious.

'It's me,' she said tentatively. 'It's me, Lois. Sorry about all this, Derek,' she added, and forced back tears. 'You'll be OK soon,' she continued, gaining confidence. There was a young nurse over the other side of the room, attending to another patient, and neither were taking any notice of Lois. 'I brought you some freesias,' she went on. 'Can you smell 'em? Not as good as those from Ringford Hall, but not bad.' She reached out and moved the flowers around, rearranging them.

Derek's hand moved.

'Derek?' Her heart stopped and she breathed in sharply. She looked closely at his face, but his eyes were fast shut. Then his nose wrinkled. She daren't move, but held his hand a little tighter. 'Derek? It's Lois . . . I'm here . . .'

The young nurse had come over now, looking intently at Derek. 'Keep talking, Mrs Meade,' she said. 'I'll go and get Sister.'

Lois gabbled now, saying anything that came into her head, all kinds of rubbish about the kids and Gran. The sister appeared and stood silently at the foot of the bed. And then Derek opened his eyes. He looked straight at Lois, and, seeming to focus with difficulty, he said, 'Good gel . . .' Then he sighed deeply, and his eyes closed again.

For one terrible moment Lois thought he'd gone for ever. But then she saw his breathing was regular, the bleeping steady, and the sister was smiling broadly. 'Well done, Mrs Meade,' she said. 'He's going to be fine.'

'It was the flowers,' muttered Lois, as she fumbled for a tissue. 'He could smell 'em. The freesias . . . they're special . . .' The nurse put a hand on her shoulder, assured her she could stay for as long as she liked, and then left her alone.

After a long time, Lois stood up. 'Got to go now, Derek,' she said. She could have sworn his eyelids flickered. 'See you tomorrow, boy . . . take care.' She walked out of the hospital without noticing anything, not even the old man in a wheelchair who used to live on the Churchill Estate, and waved a palsied hand at her. It was going to be all right. Derek was going to be all right.

Thirty-One

At eight o'clock exactly Hazel's car drew up outside Lois's. She tapped lightly at the back door, then walked in. The kitchen was empty, except for Melvyn asleep in the big old chair. She could hear sounds from the television in the front room, and went through to find Lois. Douglas and Jamie were watching a cartoon, and Gran was reading the evening paper Lois had brought back from Tresham. Lois herself, and Josie, were not there.

Hazel cleared her throat and they all looked round in surprise. 'Anybody could walk in here and steal the silver,' she said with a smile, and Gran got to her feet.

'Is something wrong, Hazel?' she said.

'No, didn't Lois tell you? She asked me to come round for a business chat. Is she upstairs?'

'No, I'm here,' said Lois, appearing at the doorway. 'Hazel,' she went on, 'could you go up and have a word with Josie? She's got maths homework, and I can't make head or tail of it. If you could just give her a pointer in the right direction, I'll put the kettle on. Coffee or tea?'

Half an hour later, Hazel came downstairs with a grateful Josie. 'Dad usually helps,' she said, 'but . . .' She tailed off and looked at her mother.

'It's good news . . . well, goodish,' said Lois. 'Derek surfaced for a minute. Spoke a couple of words, and then went back to sleep. But real sleep, the sister said. So it looks as if things are going to be all right.' To her surprise, the usually cool and unemotional Hazel stepped forward and gave her a hug.

'Great!' she said. 'Now, Mrs M, shall we get started?'

Settled in Lois's office, the light slowly dying in the village outside, the two began to talk. Hazel told Lois what she already knew from Cowgill, but added a few things about the teenage drug scene in Tresham. 'Compared with some places, it's pretty small time, I suppose,' she said. 'But I've seen some bad things, Mrs M. Whole families blown apart . . . And kids who've got no idea how to handle it.'

'*Is* there a way to handle it?' said Lois. She remembered Josie saying there was only one way. Leave it alone. 'Easier said than done for lots of kids,' said Hazel. 'They hang around town, no parents at home, and plenty of offers from their mates who're already using. A lot of it is idle curiosity, with nobody to tell them the dangers. That was me. Mum and Dad were always too busy shouting at each other to notice.

'But your dad found out?' said Lois gently.

'Yep. All hell broke loose. Didn't make any difference. I just went to ground. There are ways of keeping it quiet. Mind you, that last time – when Cowgill found me – was an eye-opener all right. Got some bad stuff, I reckon. I nearly died, they said. Mum was great. She said we'd got to stick together because of Dad, and I was no use on drugs. She said she'd help me if I'd help her, and that's how I kicked it. Dad never forgave me, of course. His little girl . . .'

'And Prue Betts?' said Lois.

Hazel shook her head. 'Not drugs,' she said. 'It was something else, but nobody was talking.' Lois looked at her closely, and was sure Hazel knew more than she was telling. But she changed the subject. She had learned long ago that Hazel could keep secrets better than anyone.

'Now then,' she said, taking the lead, 'we need to talk to the woman at the pub in Waltonby. Seems she saw Derek's accident. She might remember more if we prompt her a bit. Your job really, Hazel. You must know her well. Next time you're on bar duty would be best. Don't want her to think we're snooping. You never know who knows who.'

You're right there, Mrs M, said Hazel to herself. She wished she could tell Lois more than she had, but as yet things were so deadly that she knew it would be best to wait. The time would come – with luck – when they could get it all sorted out. She had been surprised when Cowgill told her that Lois was working for him, and thought privately that it was a big mistake. But who was she to judge? If Lois had a little sideline in private enquiries, then it was nothing to do with anyone except herself. And maybe Derek and the kids. It was dangerous ground Lois was treading, Hazel knew only too well. Oh well, it was up to her to keep Lois as clear as possible. 'Yep,' she said, 'I can do that. What do we want to know?'

'The police will have got the car number,' said Lois, 'if she saw it. And them darkened windows don't give much away. But I noticed the day they were after me that there was a sticker on the windscreen, just in the top corner. It was red, with a white band across it. Couldn't see any words, but it showed up. She might have seen that. And there must have been a dent or something after you'd bashed into them? Ask her about the back of it.'

'Good idea, Mrs M, said Hazel, but added, 'there's only one snag. That car will have vanished. They'll have got rid of it, and by now it will be a different set of wheels altogether.'

Lois stared at her. 'How do you know?' she said.

Hazel shrugged. 'That's what they do, them sort,' she said.

Lois had thought Hazel was on the edge of all this, just keeping Cowgill informed of the small-time drugs pushers and dealers. But it was beginning to look as if she was in deeper. As they chatted on about ways of identifying a vanished car, her thoughts were busy going over what she really knew about Hazel. She loved her mother and hated her father. Gary Needham had been at least an acquaintance for years. She knew her way around Tresham's underworld. She had worked at the pub for some time, was a friend and confidant of Prue Betts, and had experienced the major's overtures at first hand. Her hated father had been murdered, and she was an informer for Cowgill. That all added up to quite a lot. Lois changed gear.

'On second thoughts,' she said, 'I think I might go over to the pub myself. After all, it would be only natural. I met the woman once or twice with Derek. No, you stand back for a bit, Hazel,' she added. 'Ask around the village. Someone else might have seen something. All I want is to find the villains who did that to Derek. Nothing else matters to me. Nothing.' Her voice was firm. Everything else could wait. Maybe for ever. Lois was only too well aware that Derek had been nearly killed because of her involvement with Cowgill. She wasn't ready to face up to that yet, but it would have to come. Meanwhile, she would concentrate on the job in hand.

'I mean to get them, Hazel,' she said coldly. 'Cowgill might get there first, but that's not stopping me. If you can help – and I suspect you can – then I'll be grateful.'

That's that, then, thought Hazel, standing up and getting out her car key. 'See you in the morning,' she said.

Lois nodded. 'There's a big do on at the hall, and they want us to put in some extra time,' she said. 'Be there a bit early if you can. Thanks for coming, Hazel, and love to Bridie.'

Lois sat for another hour alone in her study, thinking. She had to get some things straight in her mind before tomorrow. It was no good trying to think of Derek's accident as unconnected to the rest. Go back to the beginning, that would be best.

A man is killed, a solitary man nobody seemed to know very well, but everyone seemed to think was dodgy in some way. The man is connected to two girls, both been in trouble of some sort, by chatting to them in the pub. The girls' fathers are both known to be at the least belligerent, and at the worst violent. One of them, the violent one, gets killed. There is a connection through Hazel with the drugs scene in Tresham, though Prue was apparently not involved. But what about Josie's story of a very different Prue? Was Hazel lying about that?

And then there was Gary. Had she been deceived by him too, by his undoubted charm and blarney?

And all of them, she suddenly realized, were connected with that theatre. Every single one, including Joanne Murphy and the Gorilla. Prue was perhaps the only exception, but her father certainly had a job there, scene-shifting. It was more than likely that Prue knew the place. Hazel had disappeared backstage that time, and Dick . . . no, perhaps not him. Still, he must have been keeping a close eye on his daughter, and it was a point to keep in mind.

She looked at her watch. Half past nine. It was not too late to ring the pub, and she dialled the number. 'It's Lois

Meade here,' she said. 'Would it be convenient if I looked in tomorrow? Around lunchtime? Just to check that everything's all right with Gary now, after that spot of bother. Fine. Oh . . . Derek? . . . Yes, thanks. He's holding his own. Yes, a very nasty accident. Thanks for asking.' She put down the telephone and went to join the others.

Thirty-Two

The pub was quiet, with only one old man sitting quietly in the corner with his pint. Lois nodded a greeting to him, and then looked around. 'Anybody about?' she said.

The old man cleared his throat. 'Betty!' he yelled in a hoarse voice, then smiled at Lois. 'She'll be 'ere in a minit,' he said. 'You that electrician's missus?'

Well, it doesn't take long for news to travel round villages, and Lois reconciled herself to most of the population of Waltonby knowing that Derek had had an accident on the crossroads, that he was an electrician who had been working at the pub, and that his wife was that woman who ran a cleaning business. Oh, yes, and that the Readings and Mrs Stratford were working for her. She was hoping against hope that this network of gossip would also come up with something useful about the sods who'd rammed into Derek and then driven off.

'Morning!' A plump, blonde woman came in and stood behind the bar. 'What can I get you?' Lois liked the look of her. She was tidy and neat-looking, with a very pleasant smile. I must find out her surname, she reminded herself. Her dealings so far had been with the landlord, and now that she knew they were not married, she did not want to offend.

'I'm Mrs Meade,' she said. 'I rang . . .'

'Oh, of course, dear,' the woman replied. 'Now, how is that husband of yours? We were so sorry . . . But anyway, you came to talk about Gary. Do you want to come somewhere private, where we can talk? You'll hold the fort for me, Charlie, won't you? Give a shout if anyone comes in. Geoff's gone into Tresham,' she added to Lois.

The old man nodded vigorously. 'You go and 'ave a gossip,' he chortled. 'I know what you wimmin are . . .'

Settled with a fresh coffee, Lois relaxed. She'd be able to talk to this woman. 'Betty,' she said, 'I hope you'll excuse me calling you that, but I don't know—'

'You carry on, dear, everyone calls me that. Geoff and me, well, we're not married, but we're more married than some who are, if you know what I mean. My name is really Betty Betts, but everyone calls me Betty Boggis – Geoff and Betty Boggis. It's been that for years.'

'Betts?' said Lois, frowning.

'Yep, the same,' said Betty, smiling. 'He's my brother, but he don't like people knowing it, me being the landlady at the pub. He was the clever one, but I'm nicer!' She laughed now, slapping the table in delight. 'He went to college and I went out to work. Married that stuck-up cow, and left his family behind. Mind you,' she chatted on, 'when his precious Prue wanted to work behind the bar, he'd never've allowed it if I hadn't been here to keep an eye on her. Or so he thought . . . but you can't have eyes everywhere when you've got a pubful on a Saturday night!' She stopped then.

Perhaps because she'd said too much? wondered Lois. The revelation that Betty was Mr Betts's sister had come as quite a shock, and for a moment had driven other concerns from her head. Then she remembered.

'Now, about Gary,' she said. 'Have there been any more problems? I did have a sharp word with him, and he assured me it had been a temporary thing.'

'Nope, no more trouble,' said Betty. 'I said to Geoff at the time, I said that lad's got something on his mind, something bothering him. O 'course, Geoff turned round and said never mind about that . . . he's here to do a job, and I'm paying out good money. I expect the job to be done, and not hot taps left on wasting electricity. You know what men are,' she added confidingly. 'No, Mrs Meade, Gary's fine now. A good worker, really, and keeps himself to himself. Never wants to stop for a chat. So you needn't worry about that one.' She reached forward and patted Lois's hand where it rested on the table. 'And what about that husband of yours? Is he on the mend?'

Lois told her the latest, and then felt quite easy about bringing up the subject of the accident itself. 'The ambulance man said you'd seen it happen?' she said.

'Yes, I did.' All the smiles disappeared from Betty's round face. 'The buggers drove off, you know. Terrible screech of tyres and dust blowing up everywhere, and they were gone. I couldn't believe it. It was me that called emergency on my mobile. Thank God I'd got it with me . . . and it worked for once. Then I stayed with Derek until the ambulance came. It was there in minutes – though it seemed like hours, I don't mind telling you. The police asked me some questions, and then I went back home. I'd been going on to see a friend, but I hadn't the heart. Geoff was good, though. Got me going again, in time for working behind the bar later on! Show must go on, he said.'

'We owe you, then, Betty,' said Lois simply. 'If you hadn't been there, God knows what . . .' She couldn't finish, and they both sat without saying anything for a minute.

'Betty?' Lois spoke first. 'Did you see anything special about that car? What did it look like . . . ? The police haven't told me much at all. I really want to know who could do that wicked thing.' She said nothing about her suspicions, of course. If she just played the concerned wifie – which she was – Betty might be moved to remember something.

'It was black, with them smoky windows. I'd stopped at the crossroads, like always. I don't trust cars, and they mostly don't give cyclists a chance. So I had stopped. I couldn't see anything, but I heard it coming, just as Derek started to drive off. He'd stopped, too, but I suppose he couldn't see nothing either and got going. Me being on a bike, I could hear more, I reckon. Anyway, this great thing comes out of nowhere, at speed. It drove straight at Derek's van and then swerved at the last minute, hitting the side of the van so hard that it tipped right on to its side.'

'Didn't the car stop at all?' said Lois.

'For a couple of seconds,' Betty said. 'Oh, yes, and the window on the passenger side went down a little bit, and then up again fast. I just got a glimpse of a woman's face. Yeah, I'm sure it was a woman. I've only just remembered that. Suppose I was in shock, too . . . Geoff said I was.'

'And the woman?' said Lois, her heart beating fast.

'Could hardly see her . . .' Betty frowned, and covered her eyes with her hand. Lois held her breath. Betty looked up and nodded. 'I did just see a bit of blonde hair,' she said slowly, 'sort of shiny . . . but no, that's all I can remember. Sorry, dear . . .'

'No, don't be sorry,' said Lois. She was thinking that it was just like stupid Joanne Murphy to look out of the window. Probably panicked, thinking they might have killed Derek. They wouldn't want to do that, the bloody cowards! Just hurt him enough to scare me off. She smiled at Betty. 'That's a great help,' she said. 'I get around quite a lot in my job, and you never know who I might see.' It was time to let it go now, change the subject. 'I tell you what,' she said. 'When Derek's home again, we'll come over and he can thank you himself.'

Betty nodded. 'You do that, dear,' she said. 'We got fond of him when he was doing the rewiring. As nice a chap as you could want, Geoff said. And he did a good job. Nothing's blown up yet!'

And now back to Mr Betts, thought Lois, finding on the spur of the moment a good reason to bring up the subject again. 'I must go now, Betty,' she said, 'and look in on the Betts's. I expect you know Sheila Stratford's started working for them? Seems they'd got in a bit of a muddle with cleaning. I just want to check all's well there.'

'Oh, it'll be fine . . . for a while,' said Betty wisely. 'Maybe for a good while, since they had that blow up with Mrs Whatsit. You'd think that their Prue would help out a bit, wouldn't you? But not madam, oh no. Too posh by half to sully her lily-white hands. She wasn't much good to me. More good to the young farmers, as it turned out!' This time she put a hand over her mouth, as if to stem the flow.

'Why? What happened with the young farmers?' said Lois innocently.

'Well, our Prue was begging for it, Geoff said. You couldn't blame the chap . . . nice lad, one of a big family of lads.

Working hard all day and coming in here for a couple of pints and a bit o' fun. Took a fancy to Miss Prue, and she was only too willing.' She got up and walked towards the door. 'I shouldn't say any more, Mrs Meade,' she added. 'Family business, really. All I *can* say is that it weren't no bad case of flu that took her into hospital that time. No, she'd taken matters into her own hands in some back street in Tresham, and it went wrong. Landed up nearly losing her life as well as the . . . well, you know . . .'

Lois nodded sympathetically. 'It's often these kids with over-careful mums and dads who get into the worst trouble,' she said. She followed Betty into the bar, waved goodbye to the dozing old man in the corner, and went out into the village street. So that was it. Prue had had a bun in the oven and tried to get rid of it. And what had Daddy to say about that? And what repercussions had there been? She hardly dared to imagine, but reflected that Hazel must know. She'd have known about it without a doubt, and yet had said nothing. Why?

The schoolhouse was quiet, and there was no reply when Lois knocked. Next door the kids were out to play, and the noise was deafening. She saw a woman out on playground duty, mug of coffee in hand. She didn't know her, and decided that she'd leave her visit to Mrs Betts until another day. There was quite enough to think about after Betty's revelations. A woman with bright blonde hair – almost certainly Joanne Murphy – and then the whole Betts thing. Lois needed to mull it over, and decided to drive over to Dalling on the way home. The church would perhaps be open, and she could sit in one of the pews in peace and quiet. It was unlikely she'd run into the Gorilla again. He and Ms Murphy were probably in Spain by now.

She got into her car and drove slowly back down the street, unaware that Mr Betts, standing at the schoolroom window, was watching her intently as she went.

Thirty-Three

Lois sat in her parked car and looked around her, attempting to clear her mind. She had too many thoughts whizzing around, confused and repetitious. Maybe she would concentrate on what she saw, and then she could describe it to Derek and cheer him up. It was certainly a beautiful day, a day when surely nothing bad could happen in the heart of the country, here in the park with sheep munching and ducks cackling from the lake. There was the church sitting on its mound with a dry moat full of daisies. The sky was blue . . .

It was no good. It *was* a beautiful day, but grim reality would not go away. Lois now knew a number of things which she should communicate to Hunter Cowgill. These new facts and suspicions were what she had come to sort out, and she opened the car door and stepped out into a pile of sheep droppings. That was more like it, more like the real world. She should beware of small, peaceful-looking churches.

She walked up and tried the door. It swung open, and she was overwhelmed by the musty, damp stone smell. She had not been prepared for such a forcible reminder of her last visit. Standing at the top of the short flight of steps leading down into the interior, she looked round carefully, her eyes adjusting to the dim light after the bright sunshine of the park. There was no one there. 'Hello!' called Lois, just to be sure, though if the Gorilla was hiding, he'd hardly be likely to pop up and say 'Hi, Lois.'

She walked down the steps and crossed the stone floor to the tomb where she had first seen him lurking. How had they managed to get the heavy stone top off, and what had they hidden inside it? Supplies of drugs? Weapons of violence? Money? Somehow she knew it was the last. Drugs were guarded closely, and, as far as she knew, Joanne Murphy had an army of only one, and he was the Gorilla who kept his knife about his person. She put her hand on the top of the tomb. It was clever, she had to give them that. Nobody would dream of looking in an old tomb. She wondered if Cowgill had investigated it. She could not remember whether she had told him that part of it . . . She realized now that she had not been all that coherent after the attack on her.

The stone was warming up under her hand. In fact, it had not felt cold when she first touched it . . . It was in a particularly gloomy corner, and she peered at it more closely. Then she scratched it with her fingernail. Grey paint came off on her hand, leaving a white scar. For God's sake, the props department again! Whoever had made the knight's armour had done an equally good job with a stone slab.

She put both hands under the rim and heaved. The slab moved at once. It was very light in weight, and she had no trouble sliding it off and on to the floor, leaning it up against one end of the tomb. She looked around, and saw deep in shadow in the corner, where only spiders and mice would venture, the real stone slab propped up against the wall. How had they managed it without anyone seeing? They must have a key to the church . . . or be in cahoots with someone who had . . .

The tomb was empty, of course. Joanne and the Gorilla would have moved the contents as soon as the police had gone, after the major had been found. Lois stared down into the darkness. Something small and whitish caught her eye and she leaned over, reaching down to pick it up. A tiny piece of paper, but it was too dark to see anything written on it. She replaced the tomb cover without difficulty, and walked over to a pew where a ray of sunlight touched the dark oak. It was very quiet, but full of a presence of something. It was very strong, and Lois shivered. She supposed it must be all those generations of prayers, stored somehow in the old stone of the church. The presence of God, some would say. After all, it was supposed to be His house, wasn't it? She peered without much hope at the scrap of paper. It was the corner of something. At first she could see nothing but then, holding it up into the sunlight, realized there was a very faint pattern of dots and lines and, yes, a tiny circle with the letter 'C', and a couple of words: 'THE GOV'.

Lois got out her purse. She had been right in thinking the tomb was a hiding place for money. The scrap of paper was the left-hand bottom corner of a very worn ten-pound note. She put it carefully in the purse and snapped it shut. So, Joanne and the Gorilla stashed their piles of cash away in the tomb, no doubt returning every so often to collect and move on large amounts. But who did they move it on to? Cowgill knew all about the local small dealers, including Joanne Murphy. He had told her that much. He was after bigger fry, which was why Murphy was still out on a long leash. Lois began to think seriously. It could have been the major, though pathetic, vain men like him never seemed to have the bottle to do anything really big. Dick Reading? Lois silently shook her head. Horrible as he had been, and violent, she could not imagine him masterminding anything. He was a creature of impulse, quick to draw attention to himself with an outburst of temper. It hadn't mattered where the family had been, out for the day on an excursion bus or swimming at Tresham pool, if Hazel or Bridie had annoyed him, even slightly, they would have been sure of a noisy explosion.

No, a mastermind working very much on the wrong side of the law would surely keep his head down. He was very likely operating from somewhere else, miles from Tresham. On the other hand, perhaps he wasn't? Perhaps he was the most obvious suspect, maybe responsible for the murders, too, even if he didn't necessarily carry them out himself. A double bluff? Well, it could be anybody . . . except Derek. Soon be time to go and see him. At least she had one thing clear in her mind. She would not tell him who'd very likely nearly done for him in the accident. It wouldn't help to have a vengeful Derek taking on something that might be more dangerous than either of them knew. But she had to carry on. If she gave up, told Cowgill she'd have nothing more to do with it, Joanne Murphy wouldn't know that. So Lois would still be on the hit list, whatever she did now. And it'd be a lot more useful to help clear it all up than to leave the cops to plod on. Suddenly she felt very alone. On an impulse, she shut her eyes and put her hands together, just like she had as a Mixed Infant years ago. Dear God, she said in her head, please help Derek get better soon. Please.

A pigeon cooed rhythmically outside. It was so quiet. Lois's eyes stayed shut. She saw Prue Betts laughing across the bar at a good-looking young farmer, and followed her as she left with him, out across the back yard of the pub and into a barn full of sweet-smelling hay. Oh yes, it was easy to imagine. Poor kid. And then the panic, and the desperate search for a solution. How did she land up in a backstreet abortion? Was that something else Joanne Murphy dealt in?

'Is that Mrs Meade?' Lois opened her eyes with a start, her heart thumping furiously. 'Oh dear, I do hope I didn't startle you.' The voice was familiar, and Lois struggled to her feet. It was the Reverend Christopher Rogers, and he was smiling at her.

'So sorry to disturb you,' he continued. 'It is not often I encounter people at voluntary contemplation in this church. I am delighted to see you, my dear. Don't hurry away, please.'

She smiled back at him. 'It is so peaceful in here,' she said.

He nodded. 'It's certainly hard to think there's a nasty old world out there,' he agreed. 'May I join you?' he added, and slipped into the pew beside her, dropping to his knees in an attitude of prayer.

A minute passed, and Lois began to feel uncomfortable. Then the vicar sat back in the pew and sighed. 'I heard about your husband,' he said, without beating about the bush. 'I prayed for him, of course, and will continue to do so, my dear.'

'So did I,' said Lois, surprising herself, and then spoiled it by saying, 'might as well. You never know.'

Christopher Rogers smiled. He liked this straightforward young woman, and attempted reassurance. 'We none of us know, that's true,' he said, 'but some of us have faith, and that can be pretty powerful.' Then he slid out of the pew and stood looking at her. 'Is there anything I can do to help?' he said. 'I'd be pleased to visit Derek.'

Lois was not sure about that, and said he was still in intensive care and not really very awake, but promised to ring the vicar and let him know how things were progressing. 'Oh, and by the way,' she added, 'the church was open when I came in this morning. Is it always open?' She remembered that he had talked to her about keys, and thought he'd said that Mr Betts was one of the holders.

Christopher Rogers smiled happily. 'I'm lucky,' he said. 'I don't have to come over every morning and evening. Our churchwarden, Mr Betts, is most obliging and does it for me. Of course, he's home from school earlier than most people finish work! I often think schoolteachers have an easy life, with short hours and long holidays, but I'm sure they wouldn't agree with me.'

He looked like burbling on for a while, so Lois stood up and walked towards the door. 'Must go,' she said. 'I'm off to the hospital to visit Derek. Nice to see you, anyway, Vicar. And thanks,' she added, and walked up the stone steps and out into the sunshine.

All thoughts of Mr Betts were forgotten when Lois walked into the hospital. She found Derek sitting up, still swathed in bandages, but smiling crookedly at her and without question being once more her Derek.

She had been warned by the nurse not to expect him to be too bright [illegible] his memory might be a bit unreliable for while. 'Hi, gel,' he said in a gruffish voice. 'Come and sit down and tell me what the hell's been goin' on. Can't remember much about it . . . Sooner they catch those hit-and-run buggers the better. I didn't see nothin' . . . they were prob'ly miles away by the time the cops got there.' Lois silently took his hand. He squeezed, and said, 'Give us a kiss then,' and she was only too happy to oblige.

Then she sat down and gave him an abbreviated version of his accident. 'Don't let's talk about it, anyway,' she said. 'I've got some letters from the kids here for you. Can you read them, or shall I?'

Thirty-Four

Lois had resolved that the weekend would be for the family. She agreed with her mother that it would be a good idea for her to go back to her own house for a couple of days, just to give it an airing and see to a few things. Derek had asked her to bring the children, and the nurse had said they could visit if they did not stay too long.

'Will he have bandages all round his face . . . just have holes for his eyes, like the invisible man?' said Jamie.

'Don't be stupid,' said Douglas. 'Mum said he's much better. I expect he'll be sitting in a chair with his clothes on and watching telly and having nice things to eat and drink.'

'On the National Health?' said Gran. 'That's a laugh. Anyway, he's not going to want you lot arguing the toss, so just you be good and quiet and don't stay too long.'

Josie had said very little about the accident, and Lois knew that she was more shocked than the boys. Derek tried very hard not to have a favourite, but his girl was special, and she'd always been close to him. She was ready on time, and Lois noticed she had no make-up and her hair was brushed smooth and flat. Her attempt to be a simple, unspoiled teenager for her dad was touching, and Lois took her hand and squeezed it. 'He'll be so pleased to see you,' she said. 'Come on, love, help me get the boys into the car without a fight for the front seat.'

Jamie was missing, nowhere to be found. Gran called all round the house, and finally Lois walked down to the bottom of the garden, where she found him picking all Derek's prize flowers, just in bud and lovingly cared for in time for Long Farnden show.

'Got to take him some flowers,' Jamie said.

Lois took a deep breath. She nodded. 'Right you are, Jamie,' she said. 'Very nice thought. Now go and get in the car and we'll be off.' She hoped Derek would see the massacre with the same understanding.

She need not have worried. Derek was so overjoyed to have the kids around him that he took the bunch from Jamie, winked at Lois, and said, 'Great flowers, James, thanks a lot.' He was looking nearly like his old self, except for a few plasters and a florid black eye. But after half an hour, Lois saw that he was tired, and rounded up the family to leave.

'Hello! We meet again,' said a voice, and there was the vicar, the Reverend Rogers, peering in at the door and smiling broadly. 'Just visiting another patient and thought I'd look in. How are we, Mr Meade? Making good progress?'

The look of alarm on Derek's face made Lois smile, and she said that yes, he was doing very well, but thought they'd all tired him out, and were just leaving. 'I'll walk with you, my dear,' said the vicar. 'Just leaving myself. Now, you be a good chap and look after yourself,' he added, 'and God be with you.'

Derek gulped, blew kisses at the kids and Lois, and said, 'Thanks, Vicar. See you tomorrow, Lois? Might have some news about coming home.'

The Meades and the Reverend Rogers walked down the corridors and out into the car park, the kids all talking at once with the release of tension, and Lois trying to keep them in order. Finally they were all in the car, and the vicar turned to Lois. 'I enjoyed our chat in the church. Any time you feel the need to talk, I'm always available at the vicarage,' he said, and then added, 'and by the way, do you remember I said how lucky I was to have Mr Betts? Well, blow me down if he hasn't tendered his resignation! Wants to leave as soon as he can, without the proper notice. That's put us in a pickle, I'm afraid, and I'm not sure we'll be able to manage! Well, now, off you go, and God bless you all.'

So there's a turn up, thought Lois as she drove off. Betts is clearing out. The kids argued all the way home, but she scarcely heard them. Why was he in such a hurry? As soon as they arrived home, she settled Jamie with a snack in front of the television and went into her office. Breaking her own resolution, she lifted the telephone and dialled Cowgill's number.

It was cool and damp as usual in the wood, and Lois felt a shiver of unease as she approached the meeting place. Last time there had been a nasty surprise. Cowgill had made little of her suggestion that maybe they should find somewhere else. 'After all,' she'd said, 'at least one person knows where we meet.'

'Never heard of the criminal returning to the scene of the crime?' he'd replied airily. 'We might nab him when he least expects it.'

Now she looked apprehensively at Dick Reading's tree, but there were no replacements. Thank God for that. I can do without having to cut down Mr Betts from a makeshift gibbet, she thought. Though perhaps he is the hangman . . . But a village schoolmaster, churchwarden and good family man? Probably not . . .

'Morning, Lois,' said Hunter Cowgill. 'Sorry I'm late. Seen anybody?' She glared at him, and he added hastily, 'How's Derek doing?' She gave him a quick report, and he nodded approvingly. 'We've had no luck tracing the car,' he said. 'But we'll get them, never fear. Murphy and – what d'you call him? – the Gorilla have also disappeared, but we expected that. They won't get far. Now, what've you got for me?'

'More than you've got for me, from the sound of it,' said Lois tartly. She told him about her visit to the pub, and the conversation with Betty Betts. 'It seems our Prue got herself in the club, and tried to get rid of it. Ended up in hospital.'

'Is that so?' said Cowgill crossly. 'That Betts told us she'd overdosed. Said they wanted to keep it quiet.'

'Didn't you check with the hospital?' said Lois, surprised at this lapse.

Cowgill shook his head. 'Bad, that,' he said. 'I should know better,' he added, and rubbed his hands across his eyes. For the first time, Lois noticed how tired he looked.

'That's not all,' she said. 'The old vicar at Waltonby is one of my clients. He found me lurking in Dalling church . . . and he was on about how helpful Mr Betts was, him bein' a churchwarden and that. Then I saw him again in the hospital, and he blurted out that Betts had resigned and was off as soon as poss.' She paused, waiting for his reaction.

He said nothing for a few seconds, and then surprised her. 'Why were you lurking in the church, Lois?' he said. She stared at him. His face was without expression, his eyes very cold. For God's sake, surely he didn't think she was mixed up in it?

'Well,' she said furiously, 'I'd just nipped in to see where I could stash a load of drugs, and maybe a corpse or two.' She turned away from him and began to walk back along the track.

'Lois!' She took no notice and continued to walk. 'Lois! Come back here, or I'll arrest you!' She heard him laughing then, and slowed down. He caught up with her, took her arm and said, 'Sorry, sorry . . . mind on something else. Come on, Lois, what did you find?'

'Who said I found anything?' she snapped.

'I can tell,' he said. She told him about the torn-off corner of a ten-pound note, and he nodded. 'All fits,' he said. 'They handle very large amounts of cash before moving it on. You've done well, Lois,' he added. 'You can see it coming together, I reckon. Not too much farther to go. Keep at it, and we'll have a very useful result . . . quite soon.'

After that, there was no more to say, and they left the wood separately as usual. Lois drove home, wondering what kind of a home life was possible for a man like Cowgill.

It had been a morning for rushing about, first working with Hazel at the hall, then meeting Cowgill, and now getting back in time for the weekly meeting. As she ran into the kitchen, her mother – happy to be back from Tresham – said that the rest were in the office, waiting. 'Here,' she said, handing her a mug of coffee, 'I've given the others theirs. You'll have to slow down a bit, Lois,' she added, 'else you'll be the next one in the General.'

'Don't nag, Mum,' said Lois ungratefully, and went to the join the team. As she walked in, conversation ceased. 'Sorry I'm late,' she said. 'Morning all. Shall we make a start?'

There were no major problems, and Lois noticed Gary sat

very quietly for once, not making his usual witty comments as the girls gave their reports. He looked pale, and kept his head down, not looking at Hazel at all. She, on the other hand, looked at him frequently. Worried about him? And if so, why? Lois tried to concentrate.

Bridie was saying something about the vicar. 'He's quite worried, actually,' she said. 'I hope you don't think I'm gossiping, Lois, but he does follow me about and natter on. Seems the schoolmaster has put him in a fix, handing in his notice. Nobody seems to know in the village, so I've kept it to myself, like you said, Lois. I told him, whatever we hear at work don't go no further, I said. He looked pleased. I don't think he should've told me, actually.'

Sheila Stratford looked annoyed. 'Mrs Betts hasn't said anything to me,' she said. 'She must know I wouldn't pass it on.'

'No, well,' said Lois, 'we must all remember that. Had you heard, Hazel? From Prue, perhaps?'

Hazel coloured, and muttered something that Lois could not hear. She asked her to repeat it. 'No . . . that is, Prue did say something about them not being in a boring little village for ever . . . something like that.'

'Right,' said Lois. 'Now, if we're all done, I'm starving. Any questions, anyone?' There were none, and Sheila rushed off, saying her husband would be waiting for his dinner. Gary sloped off finally, leaving Hazel and Lois together. Hazel started for the door, and Lois said, 'Hazel, can you spare another couple of minutes? Just a word or two, if you don't mind.'

Hazel's expression was mutinous. 'Got to get going,' she said.

'Sit down,' said Lois firmly. 'This won't take a minute. Now then,' she began, as Hazel reluctantly sat on the edge of a chair, 'I want a straight answer from you. Did you know that Prue Betts was pregnant?' A brief nod from Hazel. 'And did you organize that abortion?'

'Christ, no!' said Hazel loudly. 'What the hell d'you think I am? I tried to get her to tell her parents, but she went off on her own and did that stupid thing.'

'In that case,' said Lois relentlessly, 'who did fix it for her?' She waited, but Hazel did not answer. 'Was it Gary?' Lois said finally.

Hazel shook her head. 'Well, not directly,' she said slowly. 'But he knew somebody.'

'And that somebody was?' No answer. 'Was it Joanne Murphy?' said Lois.

Hazel had never seen Mrs M like this before, and she wriggled on the chair, as if to get away from that icy glare. But there was no escape, and she muttered that yes, it had been her and her lousy friends.

Lois walked to the door and opened it. 'You can go,' she said, and Hazel left in silence. Lois lifted the telephone and dialled Gary's number. 'Yes,' she said, 'it's Mrs Meade. I know Gary is not home yet, but when he comes in, please tell him to ring me . . . straight away. And yes, it's urgent,' she added, and slammed down the receiver.

Thirty-Five

It was no more than half an hour later that Gary returned the call. 'You wanted me, Mrs M? Mum said it was urgent . . . hope there's nothing wrong.'

'So do I,' said Lois. 'I need to talk to you, Gary. Can you come over as soon as possible?'

'Um, like tomorrow? After surgery?'

'No, like this afternoon. Let's say half past three. And don't be late.'

'Well, I was going . . .'

'Half past three, Gary. Goodbye for now.'

Lois put down the phone and walked through to the kitchen, where her mother was making a chocolate cake, her speciality. Lois sat down at the table and sighed deeply. Her mother slid the cake tin into the oven and turned around to look at Lois.

'What's up? No bad news from the hospital, I hope?' She wiped her hands on her apron and sat down on the opposite side of the table.

'No, no, it's nothing. Just feeling a bit tired, that's all. I've got Gary coming back soon for a talk, and then I must get in to see Derek. There might be good news about him coming home.'

'Sooner the better, if you ask me,' said Gran. 'You need him here at home.'

'He won't be doing anything at all for a while, Mum!' said Lois, bridling.

'No, but he'll be here, for you to talk to and to give you advice. You won't trust me, and I don't blame you. I've no experience of running a business.'

Lois looked at her mother's kindly face and felt terrible. 'Mum, don't be silly,' she said. 'Of course I trust you. And

I wouldn't have been able to manage without you here, helping with the kids and the cooking, and generally bein' indispensable! But, yes, I do miss Derek. He keeps me straight. You never know how much you rely on a person until they're not around, do you?'

'True,' said her mother, and Lois could have kicked herself. Her parents had been inseparable, and she knew how much her dad was missed. 'Anyway,' Gran continued, 'if you've got that lad coming back, you'd better have something to eat right now. I'll make you a sandwich . . . chicken or cheese?'

'Cheese please, with pickle. I'll be in the office. Got to get some papers together. And thanks, Mum. Thanks a lot.'

Gary was on time, and looking apprehensive. He took a mug of coffee from Gran, and Lois noticed that his hand was shaking. The afternoon sun streamed through the window and fell full on to Gary's face. He was pale, as usual, but Lois noticed new dark shadows under his eyes. Was he using something? She hoped the little fool knew better, but he kept the wrong company, she was sure of that. If only she'd listened to Derek, she wouldn't be faced with this problem character sitting in front of her right now. Still, there he was, and she was going to get some information from him . . . or else.

'You're in trouble, aren't you, Gary,' she said baldly. Shock tactics might work. She knew from past experience that polite handling was useless.

He started, and looked straight at her for the first time for weeks. 'What on earth do you mean, Mrs M?' he stuttered.

'Exactly what I said. You are in trouble, and I know some of it. But I need to know more, and you're going to tell me.'

'But I really don't—'

'Shut up, and listen to me. I know you're up to something in that Tresham theatre, and it involves an evil woman named Joanne Murphy . . .' She noted his choking fit with satisfaction. First dart right on target. 'Drink your coffee,' she said coldly. 'Now, where did I get to? Ah yes, an evil woman named Joanne Murphy, and her unsavoury minder whose name I don't know. That's one thing you can tell me. No, don't say anything yet. I know you are friendly – no, perhaps familiar would be better – with Ms Murphy, because you've been seen talking to her. You can tell me where she is now, and what has happened to that car that nearly did for my Derek. No, not yet . . . I haven't finished. The next thing you can tell me is who fixed Prue Betts's abortion and nearly killed her.' She paused then, and when he said nothing, she added, 'There's been far too much killing, hasn't there, Gary? Or nearly killing, in the case of my Derek and silly little Prue.'

The silence lengthened, and became a pressure that Gary could not bear. He opened his mouth, coughed, and then said, 'All right. There's not much I can tell you that you don't know already. Yes, I met Joanne Murphy at the theatre. She was cleaning and her minder, as you rightly call him, got a caretaking job there. When Prue discovered she was pregnant, Joanne Murphy heard about it somehow and offered to help. Help! That was a joke . . . except that it wasn't.'

'How did you know Prue Betts?' said Lois.

'The club scene in Tresham. I've hung around there, and she was one of those young kids whose parents should lock 'em up. Crazy for anything male, and swallowed anything offered. She looked on me as a father figure, I suppose.'

'Don't make me laugh!' said Lois loudly. 'Father figure? A little squirt like you?'

'No need to be offensive, Mrs M,' said Gary feebly. 'Well, anyway, it was a disaster, as you probably know.'

'And the other questions . . . where is Joanne Murphy now, and where is that car?'

Gary shook his head. 'I honestly don't know,' he said. 'I'd tell you if I knew, what with your Derek's accident . . . but I really don't know. Could be they've vamoosed, but I've no idea where.'

'And the car?' said Lois.

Gary shrugged. 'Easy enough to make it vanish. That minder of hers – his name's Tony, by the way – is an expert, I believe.'

Lois sat back in her chair and looked down at her hands. He was lying, of course. He knew far more than he had told her, and she had to find a way of making him tell. What did she really need to know most of all? Who killed the major and Dick Reading, and why. That was the nub of it. She began again.

'Gary, like I said, I know you're in trouble. For some God knows what reason, I'd like to help you. But I can't do that unless you're honest with me. You and Hazel have some kind of relationship, I know that. Hazel is the daughter of my best friend, and I don't want to see her out cold on a tomb in Dalling church. Or you, come to that.'

'Or tied to a tree, with an apple on my head,' said Gary slowly.

Oh my God, thought Lois. He has all the answers. Shall I just turn him over to Cowgill and wash my hands of him? No, she couldn't do that, though she would hate to have to defend her decision to Derek.

'So what do I need to know to stop that happening?' she said.

'You, Mrs M?' said Gary desperately. 'There's nothing you can do. It's all grinding on like some giant steamroller. I reckon I might be next in its path . . .' At that, he began to tremble, and stood up, looking wildly round him. 'Sorry . . .' he said, and then his knees buckled and he fell quite neatly to the floor.

Thirty-Six

Between them, Lois and Gran brought Gary round and got him stretched out on the sofa in the sitting room. Gran fussed around with cups of sweet tea and cushions, and Lois sat on a chair and looked at Gary closely. 'Are you sure you don't want me to get a doctor?' she said. 'Have you done this before?'

Gary nodded. 'Ever since I was a kid,' he said, but Lois suspected he was lying. She would give him another ten minutes, leave him by himself, and then make the decision. 'It's something to do with circulation,' Gary added casually. He made a brave attempt at a smile. 'Sorry, Mrs M,' he said. 'Give me a few minutes and I'll be fine.'

'But not fine enough to drive home,' said Lois firmly. 'I'm going in to see Derek, and I'll give you a lift. You can leave your car here, and we'll arrange something for tomorrow. Sheila can pick you up on the way to the surgery, if you're OK, and then drop you off here to collect your car after work.'

'No, I'll be able to drive back. I always recover quickly . . .' He tailed off when he saw Lois's expression. 'Well, OK then, I'll come with you and do as you say. You're the boss,' he added wryly, and Lois reflected that he was the kind of idiot who spends his whole life being ordered about by women . . . Joanne Murphy included.

It was as Gary had said. Half an hour later he seemed perfectly restored, and happily helped Gran in the kitchen until Lois was ready to go. 'What a nice young man!' Gran whispered as Lois got her things together. 'Just needs a bit of looking after, if you ask me.'

Lois said nothing. She felt far from motherly towards Gary, but for the moment had decided to let things continue as usual.

One question remained unanswered. What exactly was his relationship with Hazel? In a way, it was none of her business, especially if they'd just had a fling and were still friends. But if the connection between them was part of the network of illegal activity at the theatre and beyond, then she needed to know. Hazel was working for Cowgill, certainly, but the girl wouldn't be the first to sit on both sides of the fence. Double agent, thought Lois, and grinned. Blimey, that was going it a bit.

'Cheerio, Mum,' she said. 'Shouldn't be late back. And bringing good news, I hope.' She kissed her mother on the cheek, and was unexpectedly hugged tight.

'Look after yourself,' Gran said. 'And don't forget to say goodbye to the kids. They're in the garden.'

Lois and Gary drove into Tresham in silence. He reminded her of the way to his house, and when she stopped outside his gate he did not get out immediately. Instead, he turned and looked at her. 'Thanks, Mrs M,' he said. 'Sorry about all that. And don't forget, I work for you and I like your set-up. And,' he added, opening the car door, 'I'm not such a shit as you think I am.' He was running up the drive before she could answer.

As Lois walked down the corridors, now only too familiar, she did a rapid sift through Gary's jobs, just in case he was not up to scratch tomorrow. New Brooms now had a full schedule of clients, and she had begun to consider taking on another couple of cleaners. New enquiries came in every day, and she had had to turn one or two down last week.

'Hello, gel,' said Derek, and got up from the chair by the window to greet her.

'Oh, Derek!' she said, and dropped bags and magazines on the floor to give him the best kiss she could manage without touching his bruises and bandages. 'Look at you!' she said. 'On your feet and back to normal!'

'Well, not quite,' said the nurse coming in behind Lois and smiling at the pair. 'But he is doing very well, Mrs Meade,' she added. 'The doctor wants a word with you before you go. He'll be round shortly, and I know you'll be pleased with his report.'

'Does that mean . . . ?' Lois asked tentatively, but the nurse shook her head. 'Wait for Doctor,' she said. 'He won't be long.'

When she'd gone, Lois asked Derek if that meant he could come home.

He nodded. 'If you can stand it,' he said. 'Shan't be able to do much for a while, and I expect I'll get under your feet. But Gran'll still be there, won't she?'

'Derek Meade!' said Lois, so loudly that a nurse put her head round the door enquiringly.

'All well?' she said. Lois said yes, thank you, everything was perfectly fine. She turned back to Derek. 'Now listen to me, young man,' she said. 'The minute they say you can come home, that is my first priority. And that goes for the rest of us, as well. Gran is staying indefinitely, it seems, and the kids will be over the moon. Between us, we'll look after you so well you'll never want to go to work again.'

He took her hands. 'I love you, you know, Lois,' he said. 'I love you all, but you best. You were my first love, gel.'

'And I'd better be your last, too,' Lois answered in a choked voice. 'Come on, you great softie, let's look in this bag and see what goodies Gran has sent.'

When the doctor came, he talked seriously to them both, and confirmed that if Derek took it very easy, and the family could manage, he'd complete his recovery much more quickly at home. 'We'll arrange nurses to change dressings and you'll have to come back to the clinic a couple of times,' he said. 'But if all's well with you, Mrs Meade, Derek can come home tomorrow.'

When Lois returned home, there was a message on her office answerphone that gave a momentary shock. She played it again. It was from Brown's, the estate agents in Tresham. 'Hello, New Brooms,' a bright voice said. 'Can you give me a ring? We've got a house going on the market, needs a really good clean and tidy-up. It's in Waltonby, and been empty for a while. Used to belong to Major Todd-Nelson – p'rhaps you saw the story about him? Anyway, we'd be glad to hear from you as soon as possible . . . Brown's of Tresham . . .' and she added the telephone number too fast for Lois to write it down.

She sat and thought for a few minutes, wondering why they'd asked her, when they must have regular people they used for this job all the time. Could Cowgill have had something to do with it? Or Hazel? She knew a great many young people in Tresham, and the agents' girl had sounded young.

Or it could be, she told herself, that our reputation for doing a good job has spread far and wide, and there's nothing more sinister to it than that.

She played the message again, wrote down the telephone number, and dialled it.

'Yes, we'd be glad to help,' she said to the girl. 'I'll come in tomorrow morning, and we can sort out the paperwork. Yes, we can do it straight away,' she added, and knew that somehow or other she would have to make time to do it herself. Then she remembered Derek coming home, and closed her eyes against the impossibility of fitting it all in.

'You asleep?' said Josie, coming in quietly. Lois opened her eyes. She looked at her daughter, tall and strong, capable and with nothing to do in the school holidays, and saw an answer. 'No,' she said. 'Just resting my eyes. Now, Josie, I want a word, so sit down over there and listen.'

Josie looked apprehensive. What had she done now? But then her mother began to talk, suggesting that if Josie liked the idea, she could help her in New Brooms until she went back to school.

'Hey, Mum, that's a great idea!' Josie's face was flushed with pleasure. She loved Gran, but was sick of cooking and washing-up. There was nothing to do in Long Farnden, and no means of getting into Tresham unless someone gave her lift. At least this would be getting around with Mum, and seeing some new people.

'We'll have to check with Dad,' said Lois.

'Oh, he'll agree,' said Josie confidently. 'He's always telling me to get out and earn a crust or two.'

'Ah, yes, well, it'll just be pocket money, I'm afraid,' said Lois. 'Rules and regs and all that. But I'll make it worth your while. And just one thing,' she added.

Josie lifted her eyebrows. 'Yes, boss?' she said cheekily.

'You'll have to do as you're told. Without arguing. Have to pretend I'm not your mum.'

'Fine,' said Josie, 'that shouldn't be too difficult.'

Thirty-Seven

Lois awoke to the sound of heavy rain beating against the window, and pulled the covers over her head. Early summer, and the usual reverse of flaming June. The day ahead loomed over Lois, with the excitement of Derek's return a beacon in the gloom. She would need all her wits about her for the estate agents, who were said to pay peanuts. And then there'd be the unknown quantity of Josie doing a good cleaning job. She did precious little about the house, and Lois supposed that was her own fault. Gran had tried to teach her some domesticity, but it was a very reluctant Josie to be found standing at the ironing board. Still, the lure of money might make a difference.

The sound of the milk van chugging outside while deliveries were made up and down the street brought Lois out of a half-doze. Why couldn't he park outside somebody else's house? And half the time his milk went sour before they'd finished it. She had a good mind to get milk from the supermarket, but felt a grudging loyalty to a village service that some of the old people relied on. Oh, well, might as well get up. She slid out of bed and went to the window. The van had moved on, and the street was empty and grey, the rain slanting steadily across sodden gardens, and splashing into deep puddles punctuating the narrow High Street. Maybe we should have stayed in Tresham, Lois thought. Then I wouldn't have got mixed up with all this major business, and Derek wouldn't have had his accident. But then, looking at it straight, we'd still be crammed into a small council house, with the kids fighting for their private space and Derek losing his temper every ten minutes. And I wouldn't have started New Brooms, and I'd still be a skivvy at everyone's beck and call.

'Lois?' The door had opened quietly, and Gran stood there. 'You all right, dear? I heard you moving about and it seemed very early . . .'

'Yeah, I'm fine, thanks. Just woke up early. The rain, I think. Might as well go down and make a cup of tea. D'you want one?'

Gran nodded, and said she'd come down too, and make a start on breakfast. 'With Josie joining the work force, she'll need something nourishing inside her,' she said firmly. She had given up trying to stoke up Lois with bacon and eggs. A piece of toast and cup of coffee was the most that she would have. Still, Derek would be back today, and Gran began planning happily all the appetising dishes she would make for him.

At eight o'clock, Gary was on the telephone, assuring Lois that he was perfectly restored and intending to work as usual. 'They've got a new doctor at the surgery,' he said, 'and Sheila and I have to give the old chap's room an extra going over. And no, Mrs M, before you say anything, I am not intending to read any of the papers or lift any bottles or jars of substances when nobody's looking.' He laughed a little, but Lois could tell he was deadly serious. Gary had had a fright, possibly several frights, and he seemed especially anxious to convince Lois of his respectability.

'Well, if you're sure,' said Lois. 'And anyway,' she added lightly, 'you'll be in the right place if you keel over again.'

As a safety measure, she quickly telephoned Sheila, told her what had happened to Gary, and asked her to keep an eye on him. 'Will do,' said Sheila, 'just on my way now. If anything goes wrong, I'll report back.'

Josie had finished breakfast and was ready to go well before time. To Lois, she looked impossibly young to be cleaning at Dalling Hall, making beds, piling up sheets, emptying bins, sorting out disgusting bathrooms that a pig would have left in a better state. But this was just a try out, she comforted herself. Derek still had to agree to the plan, and it would be useful for them to have some idea of how Josie would shape up. She was fifteen, after all, and some girls were mothers at that age. Lois shivered. Prue Betts might have been a young mother if her own parents had been different, but the idea of Mr Betts tolerating a steadily ballooning daughter in the house without husband or support, was unimaginable.

'Come on, Mum, we'll be late!' Josie stood by the car, waiting to be let in.

'It's not locked,' said Lois.

'It won't lock, you mean,' said Josie, settling in the passenger seat. 'Why don't you get yourself a decent car?'

'Because you lot take all my profits and more beside,' answered Lois equably. 'I don't care, anyway,' she added, 'I like to help Dad with paying for Jamie's bike, and Douglas's football coaching.'

'And my ballet classes,' contributed Josie, and they both chuckled. The classes had been held round the corner on the Churchill Estate and Josie had attended as a plump six-year-old. In a rickety wooden hut that had seen better days as a Nonconformist chapel, an enthusiastic spinster, ballerina manqué, held classes for the local children. She claimed to bring out grace and elegance in any child, but even she had to admit that Josie was never going to make it, except perhaps as a baby elephant in the end of term show. One term had been enough, and then any ambitions mother and daughter had entertained were forgotten.

'I liked the swimming, though,' said Josie, anxious to please. 'We take it all for granted, don't we,' she added, looking at Lois's smiling face.

'Course you do. It's natural. All kids do. When you're a mum, you'll do just the same for your kids, and they'll be ungrateful as hell, just the same.'

Hazel had arrived at the hall, and was gathering equipment in the cleaning cupboard. 'Hi, Josie!' she said, surprised. 'You gonna help?' Lois thought it would be better to attach Josie to Hazel, rather than herself. She knew Hazel was tough enough to make sure Josie worked properly.

'It's just a trial,' she said to Hazel, 'so I want you to treat her like any new girl we might sign on.' And to Josie she said, 'Now you do what Hazel tells you. She's an expert, and you're a raw recruit. No slacking, mind, and Hazel can give me a report at the end of the morning.'

Lois deliberately organized the work so that she was at the other end of the hall, and did not see the others until they met in the cleaning cupboard for coffee.

'She's doing OK,' said Hazel.

'Honest?' said Lois.

'Honest,' said Hazel. 'You know I always tell the truth.' Josie nibbled a biscuit and looked at Hazel with admiring eyes. A spot of hero worship developing there, thought Lois, and hoped this was a good thing. She was not at all sure that Hazel *did* always tell the truth.

Brown's of Tresham had been established for fifty years, and was regarded by most as the best estate agents in town. Their offices were in the main square, and, in a manner that suited their prestigious reputation, their windows contained a small selection of pleasant town houses and expensive country mansions. Inside, they were astute enough to have a wide selection of properties, including unattractive – but at bargain prices – small houses such as the major's. The turnover in these was rapid, as newly-weds moved on to greater things, and elderly couples were encouraged by their families into retirement homes on their inexorable way out. The major's exit, of course, had been precipitous and unexpected.

'I'm afraid it is in a bit of a state,' said the girl apologetically to Lois. 'He went out that day, not knowing he wouldn't come back,' she giggled. Lois did not smile. It was true that this stupid girl had no idea of all the ramifications of the major's death. But even so, a sudden death, a murder, was not a laughing matter.

'We're used to that,' she replied. 'Not that we come across such tragedies very often, thank goodness.'

The girl took the hint from Lois's serious face, and sobered up. 'Quite right, Mrs Meade,' she said. 'Poor man. Never got the person who did it, did they? And then there was that other chap – found in the wood. Honestly, it isn't safe to go out alone round here, is it?'

'Can we get down to terms?' said Lois, deciding enough was enough. 'I'm collecting my husband from hospital this afternoon, and I don't want to be late.'

They talked over the details, and the girl handed Lois the key. 'It's Mrs Reading next door,' she said. 'Do you know her? She's very helpful.'

'She's one of my staff,' said Lois. 'Oh goodness, how convenient!' said the girl. 'Couldn't be better. Let us know if there's any problems, won't you. As far as we know, they're still looking for the major's relations. He was a loner, apparently. Nobody's come forward yet, so you'll not be disturbed.'

Lois stood up. 'Thank you very much,' she said, thinking she'd been a bit cool. This could be a good contact, after all. There must be a steady stream of empty houses needing a smarten-up before selling. 'I'm sure you'll find we do a satisfactory job. I'll be in touch.' She shook hands with the girl, and left the office. 'Now for my Derek,' she said aloud with a lightening heart.

One of the agents' partners nearly collided with her and looked at this attractive young woman appreciatively. 'Good afternoon!' he said. 'I trust you've found what you were looking for?' His mind was on houses, but Lois's was elsewhere.

'Not yet,' said Lois, 'but I'm working on it.'

Derek's bags were packed, and he smiled broadly as Lois walked in. 'All present and correct,' he said, kissing her. 'We just need to tell someone we're going. All the rest's been done.'

It seemed odd to have Derek sitting beside her in the car, and Lois was on edge, driving particularly carefully so as not to jolt him too painfully. 'Car goin' all right?' said Derek conversationally as they proceeded at a steady thirty miles an hour on the empty road between Tresham and Long Farnden.

'Yep . . . why? Can you hear something wrong in the engine?' Lois had an instant picture of them stranded without help, and Derek suddenly bleeding profusely and unexpectedly, and she not able to do anything about it.

'Just wondered what had happened to my speedy wife,' he said mildly.

Lois relaxed, and put her foot firmly on the accelerator. 'It's not easy, you know,' she said. 'You've been really poorly, and now you're my responsibility. Bound to be a bit nervous for a bit.'

'Don't you worry, me duck,' said Derek. 'I shan't fall to bits. You just be yourself . . . I don't want no special treatment.' She was silent, and he added, 'I mean to be careful, don't you worry. Now how's the kids and Gran? Can't wait to see them all, and get stuck into some of Gran's home cookin'.'

As they approached the house, Lois could see the double gates had been shut, and something white was flapping in the wind. The weather had cleared, and the bright sun shone on the boys' newly washed hair as they sat on the wall, waiting patiently. Lois drove up to the gates, and Derek started to say something, then choked. Across the gates a banner had been attached. 'WELCOME HOME DAD' stretched across a long piece of white cloth, the red letters uneven and wobbly.

Once inside the garden, Lois helped Derek out. By the back door stood Gran and Josie, both wearing pinnies of the old-fashioned sort Gran loved. Josie ran round to take Derek's other arm, and together, in an awkward huddle, the whole family moved into the kitchen. There, on the embroidered heirloom tablecloth, Gran and Josie had set out the best tea any of them had ever seen. The centrepiece was a huge, iced cake, bearing the same message as the banner. They stood in silence for a few seconds, and then Derek, having a hard job to keep control, said, 'Thanks. Thanks everybody. And now, Gran, if that kettle's boiling, I'm dying for a cup of good strong tea – no more of that hospital gnat's piss for me!'

Thirty-Eight

Lois knew straight away that the major's house job would be for her, and for her alone. There would be no one in the house, nor would anyone be likely to return unexpectedly. Lois could arrange to go in herself, at a time to suit herself, and know that she would not be disturbed. She had briefly considered taking Hazel with her, but she was still not quite sure about sharing all she knew with the girl. No, if there were any discoveries to be made, it would be better to be on her own.

Derek had been enthusiastic about Josie joining New Brooms for the holidays, and this morning Lois had driven her to Dalling Hall to join Hazel. 'Now you be sure to ring me, Hazel, if there any problems, won't you? Forget that I'm Josie's mother, and treat her as you would a new member of the team. All right, then, I'll come and pick you up at the usual time, Josie.'

Hazel said that it would be quite easy for her to drop Josie off in Long Farnden after work, and so Lois left them to it, not quite fully at ease, but confident that as far as professionalism went, Hazel could not be faulted. She would see that the job was completed up to the usual standard, even if it meant doing overtime to make up for Josie's inexperience.

The morning was then free, and Lois went back home to keep Derek company. He was sure to be bored, sitting reading the newspaper and going for a stroll round the village. This was Sunday stuff for Derek. And even on Sundays he spent a large part of the day up at his allotment or in the garden. She walked into the house and was immediately aware of a loud banging coming from upstairs. 'Mum?' she shouted.

Derek's voice came down the stairs: 'Gone to the shop to get some bread.'

Lois frowned. 'Then what are you doing up there?' she shouted.

'Nothing,' said Derek defensively. Lois started up the wide staircase, and he appeared in front of her, hammer in hand.

'What on earth . . . ?' Lois could not believe it. He had on his working clothes, and held a couple of long nails in the side of his mouth, a habit she had long discouraged but without success.

Now he took them out, and said, 'I'm being very careful, Lois. Just fixing that loose board in the bathroom. No effort involved. Just a few taps, and it's done.'

'But . . .' Lois paused. She was sure the doctor would not approve, but what could she do? She couldn't be here every minute of the day, and in any case, it might be good for him to feel useful. She had wondered how he would manage being a convalescent, a man who was normally for ever on the move, fixing and mending. Now she knew.

'Are you sure that's all?' she said. 'Not thinking of putting in a new bath, or maybe rewiring the entire house before dinner?'

He shook his head. 'I'll put the tools away, and then you can make us all a nice cup of coffee, and we'll sit in the front room and read the newspaper and talk.'

'Mmm,' muttered Lois. 'Go on, then. And if you're not going to be sensible, I shall have to give up work and be your minder.'

That word was a nasty reminder of the day when Derek had nearly been taken away from them for good, and she took his hand. 'You won't be daft, will you,' she said. 'Just take it slowly, and then you'll be back at work in no time.'

Half an hour later, coffee drunk and the sports pages thoroughly gone over, Derek stood up. 'I think I'll walk up to the allotment and see if there's anybody about,' he said. Gran, the traitor, said, 'That's a good idea, boy, the fresh air will do you good.'

Lois sighed. 'Oh well, then, I might as well go over to

Waltonby and have a quick look at the major's house. Might even make a start, depending on what state it's in.'

She had told Derek and Gran about this new job, and they'd been interested. Derek had also been a bit concerned. 'They've never found the bloke who did it, have they?' he said. 'Better be a bit careful, Lois. You never know who might be lurking. You'll be taking someone with you?' She had not mentioned that she intended to go on her own, and did not answer.

Lois drove down the main street in Waltonby, and passed the school. The children were out to play, and she could see the suited figure of Mr Betts talking to a woman, both holding mugs. Playground duty. She used to do it herself as a volunteer, when the kids were small. But their school in Tresham had been a chilly place, overshadowed by big industrial buildings and with large numbers of children milling about. Certainly no time to stand in the sun and drink coffee and chat to another adult. She'd needed her wits about her then. And eyes in the back of her head.

She pulled up in front of Bridie's semi, and parked the car in the lay-by that served the two houses. She was so used to walking up Bridie's garden path that she nearly opened the wrong gate. No good calling on Bridie, anyway. She was off on jobs in Ringford and wouldn't be back until that afternoon.

The major's gate stood ajar, and Lois pushed her way up to the front door, through long grass and weeds rapidly taking over the path. She hesitated. Would it be a good idea to look around outside first? She started off again, round the corner of the house and through a narrow passage. It was difficult to open the rickety gate across the passage, the latch being rusty and crooked. A shed opposite the back door was locked, and the dirty window had been blacked out by something dark hanging inside. Behind the house, the garden was a wilderness. It must have been like this in the major's time, Lois thought, and remembered looking over from Bridie's and seeing a neglected patch. Dick had often complained that the nettles and ground elder came through the fence and invaded his own immaculate garden.

She looked at the keys on the ring the estate agents had given her. Three keys. Front and back doors, and what else? The shed? She tried it, but it was no good. Oh well, might as well go into the house. The key to the back door turned easily, and she stepped inside the kitchen.

The smell was the first thing that struck her. It was overwhelming, and disgusting, and seemed to be coming from a cupboard next to the sink. Holding her nose, she opened the door and was nearly sick. A rat lay on its side, swollen, covered in maggots, and very dead indeed. Poisoned, she supposed. Last time she had seen a rat, it had been in Long Farnden vicarage when she was cleaning for that poor Peter White, and it had been a powdery skeleton, ancient and just about tolerable. This one was horrific.

Even so, Lois, she told herself, you have to deal with it. 'We can tackle anything,' she would say cheerfully to potential clients. Now's the test, my girl. She looked around and found a bundle of old newspapers by the bin. Pulling on rubber gloves, she knelt down with brush and dustpan and eased the rotting object forward. She gagged, recovered, and continued the dreadful task. Finally she had it wrapped in several layers of newspaper and took it out into the garden. It would be no good putting it in the wheelie-bin, since that would not be emptied until a new owner moved in. Bury it. That was the only solution, but she needed a spade. She tried the shed door once more, shoving hard with her shoulder. This time it moved. It was not locked, after all, and she looked apprehensively inside. Nothing sinister here, and on the wall hung the usual garden implements, including a spade.

'We tackle anything,' she said aloud, and dug down deep into the hard, unyielding soil in the back garden. As she shovelled earth back over the corpse, it did occur to her that the police might be very interested in newly disturbed ground, should they return to have another look. Well, good luck to them! Let them come across the body in question, and see if they had stronger stomachs!

At last she returned to the house and opened all the downstairs windows wide. An absolute giveaway that she was here, she thought, but never mind. Better to be healthy and visible, than safely hidden and infected with whatever it was that people caught from rats.

She walked upstairs, opened doors and looked around. All the furniture was as he'd left it. The agents had said it was easier to sell a furnished house than one with bare boards and patches on the walls where the pictures had been. Even his toothbrushes were still in the tooth mug on the bathroom windowsill. Have to get rid of those, and the rows of bottles and jars. She picked one up. Hair restorer. Another was skin lotion, another a guaranteed mixture for improving eyesight. She looked along the row. Every possible remedy for the ageing male! How pathetic, thought Lois. She turned away and opened the medicine cabinet. Of course, the police would have been through all this, but she was curious. Nothing there except innocent painkillers and lozenges for coughs and colds. Mouthwash and plasters, nail scissors and ear drops. The average contents of the average householder's medicine cabinet.

But he had not been the average householder, that was certain. Lois left the bathroom and walked down the landing to a door at the back of the house. She tried the handle, but it would not move. Locked? She took the third key on the bunch and fitted it into the lock. It turned smoothly, and she entered another world.

Dozens of Lois Meades greeted her. She stepped back in alarm, until she realized the room was lined with mirrors. Nothing but her own reflection on walls and ceiling. And the room was empty except for various pieces of gym equipment. An exercise bike, a walking-on-the-spot thing. Weights for lifting, stretchers for pulling on, a punchball in one corner. And hundreds of punchballs disappearing into infinity through the mirrors.

Lois shuddered. What kind of man had he been? All she remembered was a smartly-dressed old bloke standing at the bar in the pub chatting up Prue Betts. Chatting up Prue Betts . . . and Hazel Reading . . . and, no doubt, Joanne Murphy in Tresham . . .

She closed the door with relief, locking it carefully. It was strange that the police had locked it up again. Still, maybe they prided themselves on leaving everything as they found it, unless anything had to be taken away. Had they taken anything? Perhaps it was a forlorn hope that she would find any helpful clues of any sort. She opened all the windows upstairs, and went back to get her cleaning things. In her experience, it was easier to work from the top down, and she intended to start on the bathroom. A door into a cupboard under the stairs caught her eye, and she opened it. An ancient Hoover, box of dusters and a broom were neatly stacked away. Any more rats? It was dark in the far corner, where the underside of the stairs met the floor. She took the broom and stretched it along. It seemed to hit something before it reached the end. She jiggled the broom around, and finally got it around the back of what seemed like a heavy box. But the box disintegrated as she pulled it forward, and became a pile of dog-eared, stained magazines.

Oh yes. So this is it, thought Lois, as she leafed through one pornographic picture after another. She felt sick again, and quickly put back the pile. She noticed that several were the same issue. He had customers, then, and who knows how many helpers doing his particularly nasty paper round. One fell from the bottom on to the floor, and she picked it up, glancing at the picture on the cover. Her nausea turned to alarm. A blonde child, simpering, with her thumb in her lipsticked mouth, postured suggestively at the camera. A brief bikini barely covered the immature little body, but the expression in her eyes was frightening. Lois shoved it back into the pile, and put the whole lot where she had found them.

Something new to tell Cowgill, and maybe something important. It was possible there was more stuff hidden that the police had missed. Well, the best thing would be to clean as thoroughly as she knew how, in every nook and cranny, and then she'd come across it, if it was there. She shut the cupboard door, and began to climb the stairs. A sudden slamming door stopped her in her tracks and set her heart thudding. It seemed to come from the kitchen. The back door? There was very little wind, but it could have been the draught made by all those open windows. She froze, and listened. A footstep on the tiled kitchen floor, and then another. Hesitant footsteps, but coming towards the hall.

'Who's that?' shouted Lois loudly, but there was no reply.

Thirty-Nine

Hazel Reading had dropped Josie off in Long Farnden, and called in to make sure Gran was there and that everything was going smoothly with Derek. She was expecting to find Lois. 'Gone over to Waltonby,' said Derek. 'You'll probably meet her. She was going to that house where the galloping major lived. The house agents want it cleaned ready for sale.'

'*I* could have done that,' said Hazel, surprised. 'It's right next door to me. Me and Mum could have gone through like a dose of salts. Mind you, it would've been first time in there. He never invited the neighbours in for a drink!'

'Perhaps Lois thought you'd got enough to do,' said Gran placatingly. Privately, she agreed with Hazel. It was obvious. Still, no doubt Lois had her reasons, and it was Gran's job to back her up. 'She'll explain, I expect,' she said, as Hazel left, still puzzled.

As she pulled up outside her house, she saw Lois's car. She was still there, then. There was another vehicle, too. An old taxi, with lettering badly painted over. She looked at it curiously, not recognizing it as a regular in the village. Before she opened her car door, someone began to get out of it. Hazel recognized the figure at once. A burly, bald-headed man, with shoulders like a bull. She tumbled out of her car as quickly as possible, and began to walk towards him. His eyes were on the major's house, and she almost reached him before he turned and saw her. 'Bloody hell!' he said, 'Not you again!' He wrenched open the taxi door, crashed into the driving seat and started the engine with a dreadful rasp. Then he was away, his foot down hard to achieve only a modest exit, and disappeared.

Hazel thought of following him, but decided her priority was to check on Lois. Had the Gorilla just arrived, or was he making a second check on whatever he had found? She pushed her way up to the major's door, noticed the open windows and knew that Lois was still there, dead or alive. She stepped carefully through the kitchen, avoiding slimy patches, and then stopped. She was more or less sure that that was Lois's voice. But if the Gorilla had been around, maybe J. Murphy was still on the scene. She waited in silence, and then Lois clumped down the stairs and saw her.

'Hazel! For God's sake, why didn't you answer?'

'Not sure it was you, Mrs M.' Hazel hesitated. Should she tell Lois about the Gorilla, or would it alarm her unnecessarily? No, Lois had to know, in order to watch her back from now on. Since the unsavoury pair had apparently disappeared from the area, she sensed Lois had relaxed. Well, they were back, and now was clearly not the time to be off guard.

'Oh Lord . . . are you sure it was him?' Lois sat down heavily on the stairs.

'Certain,' said Hazel. 'Though how he knew you were here, I can't think. *I* didn't know, and I can't see him calling on Gran and Derek.'

'Damn and blast,' said Lois fervently. 'I'd given up watching out for them. Thanks, love, for scaring him off.'

Hazel suggested she should fetch a cup of tea for them both from next door, and then they could decide what to do. She did not ask Lois any questions, thinking that answers would probably emerge in a chat. 'Better lock the door behind me,' she said, 'and shut the ground-floor windows. You never know.'

When she returned, Lois had cleared a space in the scruffy sitting room, and they sat down gingerly on rickety chairs. 'You'd never think he lived like a pig in shit, not from seeing him all dressed up at the pub, would you?' said Hazel, looking round. 'Have you made a start? Need a hand? I don't have to be at Mrs Jordan's until this afternoon.'

Lois thought for a minute and drank her tea slowly. 'Well,' she said, seeing the mug shaking in her hand, 'perhaps it would be a good idea if we do an hour or so together. Break the back of it. Then I can do the rest myself. You're pretty stretched at the moment.' They chatted about the need to employ more staff and Lois sounded out Hazel about the future.

'I'm happy as I am at the moment,' said Hazel. 'I can't leave Mum on her own until they sort out who killed Dad, an' that . . .' Lois nodded. She asked how Josie had shaped up, and Hazel said fine, she took after her mother and knew her own mind. Then she changed the subject quickly. 'Have you looked around?' she asked. Lois told her about the mirror room, the exercise stuff and the potions in the bathroom. She did not mention the porn under the stairs. 'What a pathetic idiot,' Hazel said.

'So long as that's all he was,' said Lois, and Hazel looked at her sharply.

'What d'you mean?' she said.

'Well, you don't get killed for being a pathetic idiot,' Lois replied.

'Oh, he was a nasty piece of work, we all knew that,' said Hazel cheerfully. 'My dad found out quite a lot about him, and was always threatening to sort him out. But it was all bluster, like a lot of the things Dad said. Violence began at home with him. And stayed there,' she added, her face closing up.

'What did he find out?' said Lois.

'Oh, stuff about him changing his name – his real name was Smith – and how he'd never been in the army and all that major thing was a fraud. In fact, everything about him was a fraud, I reckon. He'd come on all flirty and heavy an' that in the pub, but I never heard that he'd actually done anything. Probably run like hell. That sort always do!'

'Was he in on the drugs scene?' said Lois bluntly.

Hazel shook her head. 'Not that I ever heard,' she said. 'Mind you, I kept conversation light. Prue used to chat to him a bit, but she didn't like him and I don't think he ever gave her anything.'

'Nothing to do with Joanne Murphy and the theatre, then?'

Again Hazel shook her head. 'Well, we all know J. Murphy was supplying, and the major certainly acted in the theatre shows, but I don't know of any connection.'

Lois stared at her. 'Is that the truth, Hazel? All of it?' she said. Here was a girl she had known since birth, and she still couldn't tell from the cool look in her eye whether she knew more than she had said. It was only to be expected, probably. Hazel would have had plenty of practice in editing the truth, acting as a buffer between Dick and Bridie. Poor kid. Lois said nothing more, and the two of them began to clean. It took a long time, scrubbing and disinfecting, and they had just about finished the ground floor when it was time for Hazel to go.

'Take care, then, Mrs M,' she said. 'Lock up when I've gone, and just keep your eyes open.'

It was very quiet in the house, and Lois thought of turning on the radio in the sitting room. But then she would not be able to hear any possible visitors. Common sense told her the Gorilla would be unlikely to come back, but she was taking no chances. She had left the mirror room until last. Should she clean each one? Leave a sparkling, freshly-polished interior for whatever nut was likely to want such a room? I'm just the cleaner, she reminded herself, and set to work, removing spiders and dust and fingerprints . . . fingerprints? Oh well, the police would have done all that ages ago.

She tried to move a large wooden box to clean behind it, but it was too heavy. The lid was not locked and she opened it apprehensively. Nothing but innocent weight-lifting apparatus. She tried removing some of it, to make the box lighter, but failed. Then a glint of glass caught her eye. There was something different at the bottom of the box. She heaved weights to one side, and saw that it was a camera, with the lens glinting in the light. With difficulty she managed to extricate it, and looked to see if it was loaded. The frame counter showed 10. Film still in there then. Lois saw in her mind the thumb-sucking child . . .

She walked over to the window, and looked over the back garden wilderness. Now what? If she left the camera where it was, the chances were that the Gorilla would come back for it. He may well have been looking for it, and not for her, when Hazel frightened him away. If she took it, she could be in big trouble, trouble which could jeopardize New Brooms. There was only one thing to do, though she was reluctant to do it. She fetched her mobile phone from her bag, and dialled Cowgill's direct line.

'Look, I don't want to be seen here with you,' she said firmly. 'I'll tell you where it is, then I'm locking up and going home. Give me time to get away, then you can do what you like.'

'Thank you, Lois,' said Cowgill, with a touch of irony.

She told him about the magazines, and he sounded very interested. 'Now we're getting somewhere,' he said happily.

'It's a pity your blokes didn't spot them,' she said acidly.

'None of us are perfect,' he replied. 'Now, off you go, and I'll be in touch later.'

'Don't "off you go" me!' Lois shot at him. 'It's me the Gorilla wants to get his nasty paws on, not you!'

'Gorillas don't have paws,' said Cowgill calmly. 'See you later, Lois.' He had fortunately rung off before hearing her reply.

Derek and Gran were sitting in the front room, the television on, and both were fast asleep. Gran's mouth was open, and her upper set of false teeth had descended. Derek had a beatific smile on his bruised and battered face. Both were snoring, but not quite in unison.

Lois sighed. She need not have worried. All the way home she had scolded herself for going out working when Derek had only just come back from hospital, and now here he was, already with more colour in his cheeks, and looking wonderfully rested in Gran's tender care.

He stirred and opened one eye. ''Lo, duck,' he said, and closed it again. Lois turned off the television, and the sudden lack of noise woke them both.

'All finished?' said Gran. 'Was it a big job? Why didn't you ask Hazel to help? She dropped Josie off, and said she'd look out for you.'

'She found me,' said Lois. 'And yes, it was a lousy job. The house was filthy. I sometimes wonder why I do it. Must be mad,' she added grimly.

'You didn't have to,' said Derek, wide awake now. 'Hazel and Bridie could have done it.'

'If you want a job done well, you do it yourself,' said Gran, illogically. 'I suppose you didn't want to off-load this nasty one on the others. That's why you're good at your job, dear.'

'And why we all love you,' said Derek, reaching out a hand and patting her bottom. She hated this, and he knew it, and her usual reaction was to fetch him one, if only lightly. Now she stopped herself in time.

'That's taking advantage, Derek,' she said, and finally relaxed and laughed.

'Got to make the most of it,' he said, and pulled her down on his lap. Gran tactfully left the room, saying she was gasping, and it was time to put the kettle on.

Forty

Prue Betts had dropped the bombshell whilst her mother was cooking supper. Her father was, as usual, sitting in the most comfortable armchair reading the *Guardian*.

'Go round the world! What on earth are you talking about?' said her mother, and was in such a dither that she sliced into the end of her finger instead of the potato. After this diversion, with a fruitless search for a sticking plaster ending in Prue raiding the school first-aid box, her father joined them in the kitchen and asked what all the fuss was about.

'Oh, nothing,' said Mrs Betts quickly. 'Just wasn't looking what I was doing,' she added, shaking her head meaningly at Prue. But Prue took no notice.

'I've decided to take a gap year, and see the world,' she said boldly.

'All of it?' said her father mildly.

'There's a group of us going,' Prue continued. 'We've got it all planned out. We'll be off in September.'

'Just one thing,' said her father, still in a calm voice. 'What are you intending to use for money?'

'I've saved enough from the pub for my fare out to Australia, and after that we're going to work our way round.' Prue was beginning to feel nervous. This reaction from her father was not at all what she had expected. 'So you can forget me in your plans for moving,' she added. 'I'll be off to university when I get back.'

'Right.' Mr Betts walked forward and put his hands gently on Prue's narrow shoulders. 'Now listen, Prue,' he said. 'You are not going round the world. You are not even going to the Isle of Wight!' His smile was small. 'You are coming with us to Scotland,' he continued, 'where I have almost certainly secured a good post, and – if I can get old Rogers to release me – we shall be there in time for the new school year in September. You have a place already at St Andrews University, and will take it up in October as planned.' He smiled kindly at her, sure that she would see reason.

She did not see reason. 'No, Dad,' she protested. 'We've decided, me and the others, and it is too good an opportunity to miss.'

Mrs Betts tried diplomacy. 'Shall we discuss it later, dear, when your father and I have had time to think about it?'

'Nothing to discuss,' said Mr Betts quietly, and walked out of the kitchen.

Prue looked at her mother, her face mutinous. 'I don't care what he says,' she blurted out. 'I'm going with the others. And I'll be bloody glad to get away!'

'Prue! Please watch your language!'

'Oh for God's sake, Mum, I'm not a kid any more. I know more about things than you ever did, and as for Dad, he just shuts his eyes and hopes I'll stay his precious little bluestocking for ever.'

Her mother did not answer. She had been well aware that lately her husband had not been himself. In some ways, he had been easier, less dogmatic and more willing to listen to her point of view. He hardly spoke to her, though, and when he did, he seemed preoccupied with something other than the subject in hand. But this new plan of his to go to Scotland had been hatched without any consultation with her, and she was worried. Why did they have to move away so suddenly? Waltonby was such an idyllic village, and the school a privileged place for children and teachers, especially the head, who had almost total control over his little empire. There had been that unpleasant business with Mrs Whatsit, but that was all forgotten now. It had been one of his rare outbursts of temper, and this time, as usual, it had been something to do with Prue. The old woman had been making insinuating remarks. No, now she was getting on so well with Sheila Stratford, and if were not for this strange mood that had descended on her husband, life would be very comfortable. She had heard him say many times in the past that he intended to stay in Waltonby until the great School Inspector in the sky told him it was time to go.

'Leave it now, Prue,' she said wearily. 'I'll speak to him, see if I can get him to discuss it with you, at least. But I don't hold out much hope.'

'Then I shall go without his permission,' said Prue. 'I don't need it, anyway. It would have been nice to have his help and blessing, but I'll manage. Anyway, Mum,' she added, 'what's eating him lately? We can't seem to get through to him at all.'

Next morning, Prue got up late. As she came down the stairs to make herself a cup of coffee, she heard voices in her father's study. 'Who's here, Mum?' she said, going into the kitchen.

Her mother shook her head. 'Don't know who it is,' she said. 'Some woman . . . I suppose it's a parent, but he doesn't usually ask them into the house. She's been closeted in there for half an hour. I expect he'll tell us when she's gone,' she added hopefully.

'Or not,' said Prue. 'On present form, he's just as likely to sidle off back to the school. And who's taking his class while he's in here, anyway?'

'The classroom assistant is holding the fort. He said he wouldn't be long.'

On cue, Mr Betts was heard opening the front door and ushering the woman out. Prue went into the hall, and caught sight of the tail end of a blonde with shiny, curly hair, disappearing up the garden path. Her father said to the retreating back, 'As soon as possible, Mrs Murphy,' then shut the door and turned. 'Not eavesdropping, I hope, Prue?' he said, and added, 'I'd like to talk to you for a minute, anyway.' He went back into his study and she followed.

'Well?' she said. Really, this was ridiculous. See me in my study at ten thirty. Six strokes of the cane for daring to grow up?

With what looked like a big effort, Mr Betts managed a smile. 'Sit down, Pruedy,' he said. He hadn't used this pet name for years, and she was at once alarmed. 'Now,' he continued, 'perhaps I was a bit hasty yesterday. Should have given you a chance to explain. Shall we start again?'

She couldn't believe it, but after a short pause while she gathered her wits, they began to talk. Now he was all sweet reasonableness. It could be a good idea, after all. He remembered having had the same plan in his youth. It had not been possible then, of course, with absolutely no spare money in the family. No, he'd been thinking, and had changed his mind. 'Has Auntie Betty been speaking to you?' asked Prue, wondering if her father had, for once, gone for a pint, and been got at by her aunt. When Prue had mentioned it to her, she'd been all for it. 'Go for it, gel,' she'd said.

But Mr Betts shook his head. 'Good gracious me, no,' he said. 'I don't discuss family affairs with my sister. No, I've just been thinking, that's all. I shall give you all the help I can, and with luck some financial assistance, too. We must have a meeting of everybody concerned – the other young people and their parents, perhaps? – and get the ball rolling.'

Mrs Betts was apprehensive when they both came in for lunch after what seemed like hours in the study. She had been very curious about what he was saying to Prue, and had stooped to listening silently outside the door. But the old doors were heavy, and soundproof, and she could only hear the odd word.

'It's on, Mum!' Prue had burst out, grinning from ear to ear. Mr Betts was more dignified, but smiling, and he put his arm around his wife's waist. 'It'll be just us after September,' he said. 'A dear old couple, you and I, slipping into quiet obscurity in the remote Highlands of Scotland.'

Mrs Betts was not sure she liked the sound of that.

Sheila Stratford heard the telephone ringing, and ran in from pegging out her husband's shirts on the line. There was a good blow this morning, and she hoped the rain threatened by the weather forecast would keep off until the washing dried. She was due at the schoolhouse this afternoon, and made a mental note to check before she left.

'Hello? Oh, Lois, hello. Nothing wrong, I hope?'

Lois assured her all was well. 'I've had an emergency call

from Ringford. They need someone at once, before hoards of guests arrive this evening. It would be quite a good contact . . . local new rich at the old rectory . . . so I thought you'd be the person to impress them!'

'But what about the Betts's?'

'I'll come over and do them. They won't mind, I'm sure. Mrs Betts seems so grateful to get help.'

Sheila was flattered, as Lois had meant her to be, and agreed to be over at Ringford at two o'clock sharp. Lois asked if there was anything she should know about the Betts job. She was perfectly confident that the schoolhouse would not present any difficulties. She had plotted this exchange carefully, meaning to keep her eyes and ears open. The more she thought about the deaths, the more certain she was that the theatre was the common denominator, including Mr Betts. All of them were involved, except perhaps Dick. As far as she knew, Dick Reading had had no connection with the theatre. She could just hear him scoffing: 'You won't catch me anywhere near a load of poofs!' But she was absolutely sure that the two deaths were linked, and the theatre was at the core of it all. Time for a spot more culture.

After settling the details with Sheila, she put down the telephone and picked up the local newspaper, turning to the 'Attractions' column. She glanced down the list of fêtes and car boot sales, and found what she wanted. A larger advertisement announced the latest production at the Tresham theatre: 'LIBEL', it said in large bold type. 'An old favourite with an exciting twist!' Lois had never heard of it, but thought she could probably sit through it. She noticed that it was playing for three weeks, and resolved to ask Derek. If he dug in his toes, perhaps she could persuade her mother to come with her. In fact, it might be better to take Gran anyway, leaving Derek to stay with the kids. She could sell it to her as a treat, a reward for all her hard work in helping out.

This reminded her that some decision would soon be necessary about her mother's bungalow in Tresham. Originally council property, her parents had bought it when her father had retired. Now it was wholly her mother's, and not doing any good standing empty most of the time. She would bring up the subject tactfully. How did she feel about it herself? It had just been a short-term thing, a stopgap, but having Gran there, a solid reassuring presence for the kids, gave Lois a great deal more freedom to run the business more efficiently. She was not bound by school times, and in the holidays there was no problem about children being left alone in the house. On the whole, although there was a small difficulty about privacy, times when she and Derek wanted to be left alone to have a good row . . . or something nicer . . . Gran was an unmixed blessing. Derek was extremely fond of her, always had been, and seemed to have accepted her as a permanent fixture.

She tidied her papers and left her office. Gran was busy in the kitchen, and Lois walked in with a big smile. 'Mum,' she said, 'how would you like to go to the theatre with me?'

Her mother looked up from the pastry board. 'Me? Why don't you take Derek? I can sit with the kids.'

'No, I want you to come,' persisted Lois. 'Sort of thank you for all you've done to help us.'

Her mother looked alarmed. 'Here,' she said quickly, 'you're not chucking me out, are you? Because if you are, you'd better say so straight away, before I put the bungalow on the market. I'd just decided.'

So there it was, thought Lois. No need to broach the subject tactfully. Mum had decided, and now she was sure it was the best thing for all of them. 'Phew,' she said, laughing, 'that's a relief! I hadn't liked to mention it, but we'd hoped you'd want to stay.' She walked round the table and gave her mother a smacking kiss on her floury face.

'Right then,' said Gran, 'now go and do something useful while I finish this pastry.'

Forty-One

Lois arrived at the schoolhouse a few minutes early, and knocked gently at the door. Almost immediately it was opened sharply, and Mr Betts stood there, unsmiling.

'Yes?' he said.

Lois was disconcerted for a second or two, then said pleasantly, 'Good afternoon, Mr Betts, I've come instead of Mrs Stratford. We had an emergency, and had to do some reorganizing. I hope that's OK with Mrs Betts?'

She watched him closely, and thought for one moment that he was going to say that no, it was not OK, and shut the door on her. Definitely not pleased to see me, she noted.

'Who is it, darling?' Mrs Betts came up behind him, and he withdrew. Lois explained again, and this time was welcomed in. 'I'm so pleased with Sheila,' Mrs Betts enthused, 'but I expect from the boss we shall get an even better clean up!'

'Mm,' said Lois. 'Could you just tell me where the things are, and I'll make a start. Anything special you need doing?'

Mrs Betts shook her head. She went over Sheila's routine, and added, 'My husband is in his study at the moment, but he'll be getting back to the school shortly. He likes everything to be left as it is on his desk. Just dust around the heaps!'

After half an hour or so, when Lois was upstairs cleaning the bathroom, Mrs Betts called up that she was going out. 'I'm meeting Prue in Tresham,' she said. 'She went in on the bus, and I promised to bring her back.' She had reached the top of the stairs, and smiled broadly at Lois. 'No doubt she'll lure me into dress shops, and my purse will be much lighter when we come back. But then, you have a teenage daughter, too? You'll know exactly what I mean!'

Lois nodded. 'They don't get any cheaper, do they,' she

said. 'Still, your Prue does work at the pub, doesn't she . . . Josie's too young for that yet.'

'Yes, well,' said Mrs Betts. 'If you take my advice, Mrs Meade, you'll keep her away from pubs. I know all the girls do it, but – as my husband says – it can be a very corrupting influence.'

The study door opened, and Mr Betts came to the bottom of the stairs. 'If you're going, Mother, you'd better go!' he said sharply. 'Don't keep the cleaner gossiping. We're paying good money, don't forget,' and he marched back.

'Sorry,' mouthed Mrs Betts. 'Well, I'd better be off. Do make yourself a cup of tea when you're ready. I've left all the things on the kitchen table.' She hesitated, and then added in a whisper, 'Don't take any notice of Mr Betts. He's not been too well lately.'

Lois carried on in the now silent house. She wondered what Mr Betts was doing in his study when he should have been teaching a class in school. Preparing for his move away? Perhaps he was going to stay in there until she went. Perhaps he had something to hide. Perhaps he would wait behind the door and hit her over the head with the headmaster's cane as she went in . . .

One bedroom door was closed. That must be Prue's. Mrs Betts had warned her that nobody was allowed in there. Everything was now done upstairs, except hoovering the landing. She switched on, and did not hear when Mr Betts lifted the telephone. Time for a cup of tea. She supposed she should ask him if he wanted one, and approached his door. It was ajar, and she pushed it open tentatively. Then she saw that he was talking with his back to her, looking out of the window. She heard him say, 'Right then, Needham, be there at six thirty sharp,' and then he turned around and saw her.

'Did nobody teach you to knock at a private door, woman?' he exploded.

'I'm sorry?' said Lois. 'Are you speaking to me?'

'Well, who else? There is nobody else!'

'I see,' said Lois icily. 'I wondered if you thought I was your wife.' She let this sink in, and then added, 'I'm making a cup of tea, as instructed, and thought you might like one.'

Mr Betts sat without speaking, his colour rising. 'Um, well,' he said, 'er, well, thank you, Mrs Meade. But I must be getting back to the school. Excuse me,' he added, and brushed past her. She heard him going out of the back door and along the path to the school.

Right, thought Lois, now's my chance. She began to dust around the study, carefully examining everything she found. 'Needham,' she muttered to herself. She knew only one Needham, and that, of course, was Gary.

The house was very quiet. In the past, when Lois had been cleaning on her own, she would put on the radio if she was alone in a house. She had to be careful, though, as some clients seemed to know immediately if their radios had been touched, even though Lois made sure she put everything back as she found it. But this house was definitely not one to trifle with. Except that here I am, she thought guiltily, trifling away like anything.

She went through the pile of papers on Mr Betts's desk one by one. Nothing much there. All domestic bills, angry correspondence with insurance companies, and lists of educational books. At the bottom of the filing tray, however, there was something interesting. A brightly coloured travel brochure, featuring holidays in the Bahamas, Haiti, and far-flung Rio de Janeiro. Several of these had been marked in pen with a cross. Fancy that, thought Lois. The Betts's were the last people she would have expected to go to such places. The Lake District or Yorkshire moors were more in their line, surely. Perhaps the old fool was planning a romantic surprise holiday. And pigs might fly. She replaced everything with great care, and then turned to the bookshelves. She put out a hand to take a book entitled *Parenting for the Millennium*, and suddenly froze.

There was a sound, a creak outside in the hallway. In the silent house it was deafening, and Lois's heart began to race. If it was Mr Betts returning, why was he creeping about in his own home? It could be an intruder, hoping for a quick looting and then escape. Or . . . oh God, please not, not the Gorilla . . .

The creak again, and then the door of the study moved a fraction. She hadn't latched it properly. She stared now, transfixed and unable to move. It opened another inch, then two or three, and from behind the desk she could see nothing. Whoever was behind the door was keeping well out of sight. Lois picked up a heavy glass paperweight, and moved fast. As she rounded the corner of the desk, her foot hit something soft.

'Yiaow!'

Lois was quick, but not quick enough to catch a ginger cat that wheeled around and was out of the door and gone before she could grab it.

With shaking hands, Lois put the paperweight back, and sat down heavily in Mr Betts's leather-covered chair. After a minute or so, she took a deep breath, and continued to clean. Guilty conscience, she told herself. Snooping is the first sin in New Brooms's rule book. Nevertheless, she was extremely thorough in finishing Mr Betts's study, but nothing suspicious turned up. From the neat row of labelled files in the cupboard, and books arranged alphabetically in the bookshelves, she guessed he was a very methodical man, and would be unlikely to leave on view anything he didn't want seen. 'I don't even know what I'm looking for,' she said under her breath. She finished the room, and shut the door behind her. Only the kitchen left to do now. She looked at her watch. A quarter of an hour to go. Ten minutes should be enough to finish the cleaning, and then she'd have five minutes or so to check everything was neat and tidy.

Dusters and polishes put away, the coast was clear. Lois found herself going upstairs once more. She walked slowly along the landing, and idly tried the handle on Prue's bedroom door, and pushed. It opened. So Prue had not locked it, after all . . . she must have been in a hurry to catch the bus. Lois tiptoed inside, though there was nobody to hear her. The cat had made her nervous. It was the usual teenage centre of chaos. Clothes on every surface, make-up scattered over the dressing table, jars with lids off; and by the wall, Prue's bed, unmade, a mountain of duvet and pillows.

Only a couple of minutes more, and then Lois would have to leave. She had no doubt that old Betts was at the school window, watching out for her. She turned to go, and her eye was caught by a half-open cupboard door. Jeans were carelessly slung over a hanger, and something protruded from a pocket. Lois gingerly extracted a packet of cigarette papers. She sniffed around, and carefully put it back again.

So, Prue was smoking, and judging by the faint but sweet, lingering smell, it was not tobacco you could buy over the counter in the village shop.

As she drove home, Lois reviewed what she had found. Nothing much, really. Prue pursuing her own life, Mr Betts nervous and bad-tempered and dreaming of holidays under exotic skies, and Mrs Betts defensive and determined to keep up appearances.

And the appointment with Gary Needham. Six thirty sharp. Back in her office, Lois looked at the New Brooms schedules. Gary was working this afternoon for a bachelor in Fletching. He would be through by five o'clock, and back home by half past. If he went home, that is. He could be meeting old Betts anywhere. When she rang his house at six thirty, he answered the telephone. So it wasn't today. She made up some excuse for calling him, and then decided to shut down for the day, join Gran and the kids and Derek, and concentrate on the family.

'Here you are, then, me duck,' said Derek, stretching out a hand from his prone position on the sofa. 'Come and give us a kiss.'

'Oh God!' said Josie. 'You two are the only old people I know who still snog in public.'

When Gran roared with laughter, all three kids looked at her in surprise.

Forty-Two

As Lois and Gran – the latter dressed to kill for their night out at the theatre – drove into Tresham, Lois was quiet, sorting out unconnected snippets of fact and suspicion, hoping something would emerge tonight to tie them all together.

'You all right, Lois?' said her mother finally, having failed to get a conversation going.

'Fine,' said Lois. 'Look, there's a space. We'll park here and walk round the corner. It's not far.'

The little foyer was crowded, with loud voices greeting each other across the milling theatre-goers. More like a club, really, thought Lois, guiding her mother across to where they had to pick up their tickets. Local worthies supporting their friends and relations. No doubt it was the thing to do in the Tresham culture set. Well, they were welcome to it, on the whole. Mind you, both she and Derek had loved that last thing. A good laugh, and no mistake. She was not so sure about tonight. *LIBEL*, a courtroom drama, it said in the programme. Judging from a couple of photographs of the cast in costume, it had been written in the year dot. Well, she was not here to be entertained, and with luck, it would appeal to her mother.

'Right, Mum,' she said, 'let's find our seats.'

'Can't we have a drink first?' said her mother, glancing round at gins and tonics being consumed at a great rate. 'Oh, come on, Lois, let me treat you.'

Lois looked at Gran. Her face was carefully made up, and she'd been to the hairdresser that morning. Her shoes were killing her, Lois knew, but she was determined to be smart. This was supposed to be a treat, Lois reminded herself, and felt ashamed.

'No, you're spending nothing, Mum,' she said, and smiled. 'What'll you have?'

By the time they took their seats in the glowing red velvet interior, Lois's mother was already having a great time. She opened the box of chocolates Lois had given her – 'So as not to disturb people once the play gets going' – and settled back into her seat. 'Oh, look, Lois, there's that woman from the library,' she said loudly, the gin and tonic having done its work, 'you know, the snotty one who never smiles.' Heads turned, and Lois was relieved to see most faces were amused.

The play was set in a courtroom, and seemed to be about a problem of identity. There was this bloke, Sir Mark Loddon, who'd come back from the war and there was some problem about whether he was the real thing. Lois's concentration slipped, and she found herself thinking about the Betts's and Gary Needham. So far, she hadn't recognized Gary in any of the characters. Betts was backstage, anyway. Why had they met at six thirty somewhere? What could Betts want with Gary? Surely nothing to do with the play. That would all be taken care of at rehearsals.

The lights went up for the interval, and Gran was smiling broadly. 'It's really good, Lois, isn't it? What do you think? Is he the real Sir Mark Loddon?'

'Um, I'm not sure,' said Lois. 'I expect all will be revealed a few minutes before the end.' She stood up. 'Shall we have another?' she said tentatively.

Gran bounced to her feet. 'Why not!' she said. 'Might as well be hung for sheep as lambs.'

They made their way out to the bar, and Lois settled her mother in a corner whilst she got the drinks. When she came back, Gran was talking animatedly to another woman of her own age. 'Ah, here she is,' she said. 'Now Lois, guess who this is?'

Lois shook her head. 'Go on, tell me,' she said, smiling at the other woman.

'It's Olive Morton, used to live next door to us. You remember, Lois, you used to play with her Jean, then they moved away.'

Lois did not remember clearly, but said that of course,

now she recognized her, and she hadn't changed a bit. This set off another chain of reminiscences, and Lois saw her opportunity.

'Mum, if you and Olive are all right, can you spare me for a while? Just got to check something out. Shan't be more than a few minutes.' The two older women scarcely noticed that she had gone.

It had begun to rain, and Lois slithered down the dimly-lit passage leading to the stage door. She knocked, and as before, the bright lamp overhead was switched on. 'Sorry, love,' a man's voice said, 'can't see anyone during the interval. No problem, is there?'

As Lois cast about desperately for a reason for being there, another head appeared. 'Mrs M? What are you doing here?' It was Gary. He must have heard her voice, and when she said it was urgent, and wouldn't take more than a minute, he pulled her inside, shut the door, and led her through costumed actors staring at her in nervous hostility, and out into a stone-floored passage. He opened another door, and they went in. It was the props room, and so crammed with what looked to Lois like crumbling junk, that there was very little room to move.

'Right,' said Gary, 'can I help? What is it? Is there an emergency?' He looked very agitated, but then this was halfway through a performance. She noticed that he was dressed in an old-style army uniform.

'Are you on stage next?' she said. He nodded, waiting for her to explain.

She hesitated, searching for an opening. Not easy, when she wasn't sure what she was looking for. 'Um, well – my goodness, they could do with New Brooms in here!' she floundered.

Gary did not smile. 'Better hurry, Mrs M,' he said, 'else we shall have old Betts in here. He's in charge of props.'

On cue, the door opened, and there stood Mr Betts, glowering at her. 'What on earth are *you* doing here?' he said, and turned to Gary. 'You're wanted,' he said. 'Now.'

Gary looked uncertainly at Lois. Then he shrugged helplessly. He pushed past Mr Betts, retreated into the passage, and disappeared.

'Now, madam,' said Mr Betts, 'you can make yourself comfortable, and I'll deal with you later.' Before she could move, he had taken the key from the door, and followed Gary out of the room. She heard the key turn in the lock. Lois was alone, and very frightened.

Forty-Three

The bell for the end of the interval sounded twice, and Lois had still not returned to Gran and Olive. 'You go, dear,' said Gran, 'else you'll miss the beginning of the second act.'

'Oh, it's all right, they never start on time. I come here lots, and they always allow a few minutes grace for dawdlers.' Olive looked around. 'Shall I go and see if she's locked in the Ladies?' She laughed, but Gran did not join in.

'Not like our Lois to be late,' she said, looking worried.

A plump, middle-aged man with rimless glasses approached them. He looked important, and Gran stood up. 'Are you Mrs Meade's mother?' he said.

She nodded, and said quickly, 'What's happened? Where is she?'

'Oh, nothing's wrong! She sent a message to say would you two like to go in, and she'll join you. She's just met one of her cleaners, and they have to fix something important for tomorrow.'

Gran sighed with relief. 'Right, come on then, Olive . . .'

'I wonder if you two would like to sit together?' The man smiled helpfully. 'If your friend would like to sit in Mrs Meade's seat, I can direct your daughter to another part of the theatre when she's ready. Then you can meet after the show.'

The usherette was signalling frantically from the auditorium door that the curtain was about to go up, and Gran and Olive, pleased with the arrangement, went swiftly in to take their seats. As they sat down and Gran put the box of chocolates between them, she leaned over and whispered to Olive, 'Wasn't that the schoolmaster from Waltonby?'

'Ssshhh!'

Gran put her spread fingers to her nose at the man in front, and settled down to follow the convoluted plot.

At least I've got light, Lois said to herself. She had tried the door, but it was firmly locked. Right, first push a piece of paper under the door, then ease the key out of the lock so that it drops on the paper. Then pull it back and Bob's your uncle! Lois remembered all this from her misspent youth, and looked around for a piece of paper. Amidst all the junk, there was not a single magazine, newspaper or any other kind of paper. She opened her handbag. Of course! She grabbed her mobile phone, and switched on. No signal. Shit! She threw it violently across the room, and it clattered down behind a pile of junk. Good riddance! What else? Her diary was tiny, and the chances of a key falling on a page from it were remote, even supposing she could push the key out of the lock.

First things first, Lois. She went over to the door, where she squinted into the keyhole. Fine, wonderful. Thanks very much, Mr Betts. He had, naturally, taken the key with him. Well, that was only to be expected. If she shouted loud enough, someone might come and release her. She could hear nothing from outside. The play must have started again, but it was silent as the grave in the props room. Without much hope, she shouted as loud as she could, but nobody came. Oh God . . . Derek . . . 'Help! Help! HELP!'

Then the light went out.

Lois froze. She could hear a far off sound of approaching footsteps, gradually getting louder. Then they stopped, and she knew those marching feet were right outside the door. The key was inserted, and turned in the lock. Then the door opened, and a torch beam flicked around the room.

'Ah, still here,' said Mr Betts. 'That's good. Now, I must find the fuse box, and then I'll attend to you.' He shut and locked the door, and Lois could hear the key being withdrawn again. She sat absolutely still, perching on the edge of a broken old chair. If he approached, she reckoned her chances were reasonable. Derek had taught her the rudiments of a judo course he'd attended one winter, and she flexed her muscles. One thing about cleaning, it kept you in good physical shape.

Then suddenly the light came on, and she was facing him. He had a torch in one hand and a small pistol in the other. It flashed across Lois's mind that it could be a prop, just as the knight's armour and the tomb cover had been props, but there was no way of telling without putting it to the test. No, stay quiet and don't cross him. Bloody hell, had he flipped? But his face was calm, his eyes almost twinkling. She realized with sudden anger that he was enjoying himself.

She had a struggle with herself to keep quiet. It was just possible that she might encourage him to talk. She was sure now that he was pivotal in the whole sorry saga of the slaughtered knight and the knifed peasant tied to a tree. She hoped the story ended in a lucky escape.

'We have about half an hour, Mrs Meade,' he said conversationally, 'in which time you can tell me just how much you know, and how much of that you have conveyed to your friend Chief Inspector Cowgill. Young Gary has more or less refused to help me any further, and so I am relying on you to fill in these necessary details.' He had become the suave interrogator, lounging back against the door.

Off his trolley, thought Lois. But not enough, perhaps.

She shook her head. 'Don't understand you, Mr Betts,' she said. 'I'm Mrs Meade, boss of New Brooms, client of your wife. Surely you remember that?'

His pleasant look vanished. Now he was the stern headmaster facing a recalcitrant pupil. 'Don't be stupid, woman,' he said. 'And don't waste my time. I know perfectly well that you are a police snout – is that the right term? – and I intend that you shall grass to me as well.' As if in answer to a spoken question, he gestured with the pistol. 'And yes, this is real, and it's loaded. I am not afraid to use it, and have no fear of discovery. I have laid my plans well.'

'I have no idea what you're talking about,' said Lois. 'Give me a clue, and then I might help.' Humour him, she told herself. There was not much else to be done.

'A clue? A clue for the amateur sleuth? Do you fancy yourself as a modern Miss Marple?' She waited for him to go on. He might start making some sense, with any luck.

'Very well,' he said, and she could almost see the ruler

tapping on the blackboard. 'A knight in armour is found dead in Dalling church. A man is found knifed and tied to a tree in Alibone Woods. Nobody has been arrested, and as far as the general public knows, there are as yet no suspects. The police are keeping everything very closely under their collective hats. Now,' he continued, puffing out his chest a little, 'it just so happens that I know quite a bit about it. Probably a great deal more than the boys in blue.'

Oh God, thought Lois, a power freak. Is that what schoolmastering does for you?

'But I do not know, unfortunately, how far they've got in their investigations, and my plans depend on that information. Which is why,' and now his smile was more of leer, 'it was so incredibly lucky that you walked into my parlour, little fly.'

Lois looked surreptitiously at her watch. Five minutes gone. She felt calmer now, and concentrated on steering him round to giving away some of his proudly boasted secrets. What would happen at the end of the half hour, she had no idea. Perhaps his well-laid plans would take care of that. She hoped he hadn't got a mocked-up coffin in the props room.

'So you think I know something about the murders?' she said, with as much innocence as she could manage. 'Don't play games,' he snapped. 'You're no actress, Mrs Meade. You'd never pass an audition in this establishment.' He sniggered. 'As indeed, neither did I. Still, they find me useful backstage, and it is a good place for contacts. I understand you have met Mrs Murphy and her friend?' He made it sound like a cocktail party.

Any minute now he'll produce a dry martini from the drinks tray, thought Lois wildly. She took a deep breath. 'I know Joanne Murphy,' she said. 'She applied to me for a job, the lazy cow. I know she has something to do with this place. *And* I know she pushes drugs to kids. She offered some to my Josie, who had the sense to refuse. I think your Prue knows her, too . . .'

The pistol came up sharply, and pointed directly at her head. 'Leave Prue out of this!' he hissed.

She nodded obediently. 'No offence, Mr Betts, just setting out the facts.'

'The facts are gruesome,' he barked at her, 'gruesome and wicked and sordid! Drugs, pornography, paedophilia . . . you name it, as Prue says.'

'Pornography?' said Lois politely. Was he on a roll now? She stayed very still, waiting. He had ceased to look at her, and his eyes were turned upwards, as if to something very nasty in the far distance.

'Little girls are very, er, physical creatures, you know, Mrs Meade,' he said. 'And if a man is that way inclined . . .' He frowned, and gave a sort of shudder, as if to rid himself of unacceptable thoughts. 'I had an eight-year-old in school . . . her family moved away, thank goodness . . . and she had such a knowing look. The minute she came into my class I knew she was trouble. Always dressed like her favourite pop singer . . . and . . .'

'And you . . . ?' said Lois, very quietly.

'Me?' he said, suddenly snapping to attention. 'Good gracious me, no, woman! Always very happily married . . . no, no, not me.' He paused, and she said nothing, just nodded again, encouraging him to go on.

His eyes returned to the distant scene. 'No, it was our very own knight in shining armour. Very partial to young damsels, that one. I found out from that silly child. She was talkative and precocious. I didn't like her much, to tell the truth. But it is not our job to like or dislike. My job is to educate and protect. Protect every single child in my care, just as if it were my own.'

A shadow of pain crossed his face. He's thinking of Prue, said Lois to herself, and made no comment. Mr Betts closed his eyes for a second or two, but not long enough for Lois to make a move. Then he continued, 'I listened to her chatter – in the playground, in the classroom, everywhere – she never stopped. Most of it was nonsense, but one rainy day when they couldn't go out to play, she confided to me that she'd had her picture taken lots of times, by the major.'

Lois glanced at her watch again. A quarter of an hour gone. 'Told you everything, did she?' she prompted.

'That evil man had lured her in,' Mr Betts replied, his face contorted in disgust. 'Told her she was very, very pretty, and took photographs. She was pleased, proud of it! I asked if she'd told her parents, and she said yes, well, there was only Mum, and she'd just laughed. And so nothing was done. Our knight errant was free to go galloping off after another damsel.'

'And you decided to stop him?' said Lois, and held her breath. At this vital moment, the sound of running feet broke the spell. Mr Betts looked round at the door, then walked over to Lois and put his hand across her mouth, and the gun at the side of her head. His round, rimless glasses glinted, and she could smell his unsavoury breath.

'Hello! Is anyone in there? Mr Betts, are you in there? You're wanted urgently! The witness box has collapsed.' The door handle rattled, and then the footsteps retreated. Mr Betts removed his hand, and backed away slowly, still aiming the gun at her. 'I must go now,' he said. 'No doubt someone will find you, sooner or later. But there's plenty of time for me to put my plans into action. Oh, yes,' he added, as he took the key from his pocket, 'and if you set your policeman on to me, my contacts will know. Your husband's accident was just a warning. Next time, retribution will be carried out.'

Lois flew across the room, but he was quicker. The door slammed in her face, and once more she heard the key turn in the lock. 'Sod it!' she shouted as loud as she could, and carried on shouting until her voice was hoarse. No one came.

Forty-Four

'Can you see her, Olive?' said Gran, standing tall and looking over the heads of the milling crowds in the theatre foyer.

'No, dear,' said Olive. 'Perhaps we'd better wait over by the door, and then we won't miss her.'

They had loved the play, with Lady Loddon's dramatic outburst, 'No! He is *not* Mark Loddon!', and then the old school chum coming into court and Sir Mark remembering his nickname, Loppy, proving that yes, he *was* the real Sir Mark, and everything turning out right in the end. Gran had been so involved in the play that she hadn't looked around to see where Lois had found a seat, and now she began to feel a niggle of worry. Where was Lois? Surely she'd have been looking out for them? She couldn't see that schoolmaster anywhere, either, and watched anxiously as the crowd slowly thinned out and disappeared into the dark street outside.

Olive was looking at her watch, and said, 'I really think I'll have to go now. Don't like being out on my own too late at night.'

'No, that's all right,' said Gran. 'You get along home. I've got your phone number, and we'll meet up and have a coffee. Lovely to see you, Olive,' she added, but was already looking back at the open doors of the auditorium. Left alone, she decided to ask for help.

The part-time volunteer manager was in his office, and came out to see her. At first he was dismissive. 'Oh, yes, madam? I'm sure she'll be with you any minute. Probably gone to the Ladies.'

Gran said she had checked the toilets, and Lois was not

there. 'I've not seen her since that man brought me the message,' she said.

'What message?' said the manager, curious now.

'About her meeting one of her cleaners and having to have an urgent chat. Then he said they'd give her another seat and Olive could sit next to me. I never saw her after that, and now I'm worried. What can have happened to her? She'd never leave me stranded like this.'

The manager looked at her, and saw a nicely dressed, elderly woman, clearly in her right mind, and with reason to be worried. He took up a bunch of keys and said, 'Right, Mrs er . . . We'll do the rounds straight away. I always check on everything after a performance, but usually a bit later on. Won't do any harm to do it now. Come along, this way.'

Under any other circumstances, Gran would have been fascinated by being backstage at the theatre. They went through what the manager called the Green Room, where a few actors were still lingering. 'Anyone seen a lady called Lois Meade?' said the manager, but they all shook their heads. Gran saw Gary, and waved to him. He did not wave back, and his face was unsmiling. Funny, thought Gran, but dismissed him straight away.

Then the manager opened a door and looked down a stone-floored, echoing passage. 'Mmm, we needn't go down there,' he said. 'It's only the props room, and that'll be locked until we put on a new production, or need a replacement.' He began to shut the door again, but Gary Needham walked swiftly across the room.

'Excuse me,' he said.

'Yes?' said the manager sharply. Now was not the time for a complaint from a discontented actor.

'Um, I think we should have a look down there,' he said.

Gran was on to him in a minute. 'Why?' she said. 'What d'you know about it, Gary?'

'Nothing,' he mumbled, 'but I thought I heard some noises coming from down there a while ago. Perhaps it'd be worth a check.'

The manager shrugged. 'Oh, very well,' he said, and all three walked rapidly down the passage.

Lois heard them coming, and redoubled her shouting. It was seconds before the door was unlocked and she saw the three of them. 'What the bloody hell's going on?' said Gran, not mincing her words. She rounded on the manager. 'Are you supposed to be in charge of this place?' she said. Then added, 'Come on, Lois, let's get out of here. I'm gettin' claustrophic. We can sort it out upstairs.'

The manager, with Gary and Lois, followed Gran upstairs and into the foyer. Now Lois took charge, and hissed at Gary that she wanted to see him first thing in the morning. Then she calmed down her mother and placated the affronted manager, who wanted to know what she was doing down there in the first place. She convinced him that it had all been an accident and there was nothing more to be said.

She drove home fast, saying little. Gran kept up a monologue, describing the plot of the second half of the play, and then going over her anxiety and the strange behaviour of Gary Needham, until they reached Long Farnden.

'You have a cup of tea, Mum,' Lois said, as they walked into the kitchen. 'I just have to make a call. Something for the cleaners tomorrow. Shan't be long.'

Derek settled down with Gran to listen to an embroidered account of the evening's events, and Lois shut herself in her office. She dialled Cowgill's number, and waited impatiently for him to answer.

'Hello? Yes, it's Lois. Just listen until I've finished and don't interrupt. I think it's urgent.' She gave him the whole story, and followed it up with a guess as to where Betts might be going. 'No, I don't know why,' she said, 'I think he was going to tell me when they yelled for him to repair something on stage . . . and no, I don't know when he was planning to go. That's why I think it's urgent. He knows it all, I reckon, the whole rotten mess.'

Cowgill was calm and decisive. He took everything she said very seriously, and when she had finally finished speaking, he told her to be within call for the next twenty-four hours. He might need her. And then he added, 'Not hurt in any way, are you, Lois?'

There was real concern in his voice, and she was reassured.

'Nope,' she said. 'I'm fine. Cheerio.' She squared her shoulders, took a deep breath, and went to join Gran and Derek in the kitchen.

Gary Needham walked slowly out of the theatre and along the shadowy street towards his car. He was in trouble, deep trouble, and had no idea how to get out of it. If only he'd never met that Joanne Murphy with her hideous henchman. He had gone along to the theatre one idle evening, and met a friend who was a member of the company. Persuaded to join them, he'd discovered he had a natural talent for performing on stage, particularly in comedy parts. Even with a mass of faces watching him, somehow he found a freedom to open up in a way he could never manage in his family life or even with close friends. Acting was wearing a mask. It wasn't Gary Needham who had to account for himself. It was someone else, a character he could bring to life and then dispose of until he chose to resurrect him.

Oh my God. Thoughts of life and resurrection brought him rapidly back to the present. Old Betts and Hazel's dad had recruited him for their rotten little plan at a time when, for once, he'd found a job he liked to do, with a boss – Lois – he respected and who inspired him to do his best. And now, back there in the theatre, he'd been so scared of Betts that he'd nearly left her to rot in the props room! Why had he found it so difficult to tell them where she was? Because he was a weak no-good, and he'd certainly blown it with Lois now. He thought back. He'd never have agreed to help those two vengeful old buggers if he'd been in his right mind. If only he hadn't been half-stoned on one of Joanne's little handouts. And then it had gone so wrong. That had been the beginning; and then Dick Reading's death had plunged him into a worse nightmare.

Just as he'd got into his car, a familiar voice broke his reverie. 'Out of it again?' said Joanne Murphy as she slid into the passenger seat beside him.

'Get out!' he yelled at her, suddenly frantic.

'Now, now,' she said. 'Calm down, sonny boy. I'll go when I'm ready. But first you have some talking to do. I need to know exactly what happened tonight, and where old Betts has gone. If he's done a runner, then we have to stop him, don't we? So fire away. Plenty of time,' she added, and Gary saw her glance at the big shape of her minder leaning nonchalantly against the lamp post a few yards ahead.

'After all,' continued Joanne, 'this car's not going anywhere, is it? Let's have a nice little talk, and then we can see what's to be done.'

Forty-Five

Hazel Reading was now almost certain she knew who had killed her father, but had told no one. She was waiting, knowing that the culprit would be caught very soon. She wanted it to be a well-planned discovery, causing as much terror to the killer as possible. Quite often lately she had thought about her violent, tyrannical father, and instead of remembering the frequent family rows, the terrified Bridie cowering in the corner of the kitchen, with herself standing defiantly between the two of them, she recalled scenes of family accord. She saw again the long-awaited visit to the London Zoo, with her father taking photographs of her and her mum talking to the chimps, and the picnic lunch afterwards on the grass in Regent's Park. She felt a stab of pain as she had a quick picture of him, laughing with his head thrown back, as a passing dog stole their ball and disappeared.

Her childhood had been punctuated far too often with tears and blows, but Bridie had stuck to Dick, and Hazel realized now that her mother had never ceased to love him, always hoping that things would improve. Although Hazel could neither love nor forgive, she hoped that his murderer would suffer as much as her father must have done, faced with a knife that was about to end his life.

It was getting late, and as she and her friend came out of the Tresham Odeon cinema, they went quickly across to where her car was the only one left in the park. 'I'll drop you off home,' Hazel said, brushing aside the offer to take a bus. 'It's not too far out of my way. You shouldn't be out on the streets alone round there, anyway!' She was only half-joking, knowing that the back streets around the theatre boasted the highest incidence of mugging in the town.

The friend safely inside her front door, Hazel turned down the theatre street and headed for home. It was not well-lit, but as she approached a car parked at the side of the road, she looked again. Surely that was Gary Needham's old banger? Then she jammed her foot on the brake. Not only was it Gary's car, but that was Joanne Murphy's bruiser, leaning against a lamp post. So what was Gary doing there? She parked fifty yards up the road and stopped the engine. The bruiser hadn't moved, so it was unlikely that he had recognized her car. Think, Hazel. If Joanne Murphy had had a mutually agreed meeting with Gary, why was the bruiser standing on guard? She had a feeling in her bones that Gary was in trouble, and she had to do something about it.

She looked in her driving mirror. Nothing had moved, but she could now see two heads in the car, silhouetted against the street light. So Joanne was in the car with Gary.

He must need help, Hazel decided. And if he doesn't, they'll soon tell me to shove off. She made a quick call on her mobile, then started her engine, and drove slowly forward. Turning round at the end of the street, she switched off her lights and returned, still at a crawl. At the last minute, she put her headlights on full beam, accelerated and then screeched to a stop exactly parallel with Gary's car. She saw his face as he turned to look, and knew she had been right. Pale and frightened, he recognized her, and at the speed of a terrified rabbit, he flung open his door and was sitting beside her in a heap, screaming at her to get moving. She didn't need telling, and missed the leaping minder by millimetres. She saw in her driving mirror that he crashed to the ground, and had no compunction about leaving him there. J. Murphy could look after him, though she didn't give much for his chances.

'How did you get yourself into that one?' she said acidly to Gary. They were out of the theatre area now, heading down town through night-time empty streets. He was breathing rapidly and didn't answer.

'Where're we going?' he said finally. He had straightened up, and although his hands were clenched into two tight fists, he seemed to have himself in control.

'You'll see,' said Hazel. 'And save your breath now. There's a lot of talking to be done, but not just yet.'

'Well, this is not the way to my house,' he said, but without much interest. He was grateful to Hazel for rescuing him, but had little hope that his situation was much improved.

Hazel slowed down, and came to a halt by the kerb. 'Right,' she said. 'Come on, let's go in.'

'For Christ's sake, Hazel! It's the bloody nick!'

'Yep,' she said equably. 'Shouldn't be too busy. And they're expecting us.'

As they climbed the steps into the brightly lit police station, Hazel caught a glimpse of two people, visibly restrained, being manhandled out of a police car behind them. It was Joanna Murphy and her minder. Cowgill had acted quickly, thank God. A busy night ahead for us all, thought Hazel, and took Gary's arm.

Forty-Six

In the schoolhouse in Waltonby, Mrs Betts looked at the clock on the kitchen mantelshelf. It was late. Where was her husband? He was usually home from the theatre much earlier than this. Prue had gone off for a few days to join the friends who were planning the round-the-world trip, and the house was unnaturally silent.

The sound of a key in the front door brought her to her feet. 'There he is,' she said, and went to meet him.

Half an hour later, they were standing in the hall, suitcases hurriedly packed and carrying their coats.

'I still don't see why . . .'

'You don't need to see why,' Mr Betts said. 'I have decided we are going up to Scotland tonight, and will stay there for a few days to spy out the land and possibly find a house. You like looking at houses, don't you? Well, now is our chance to find something really nice. I have decided not to occupy another schoolhouse. Too close to the job . . . living over the shop . . . known to be a mistake.'

Mrs Betts thought he sounded odd. The whole thing was odd. He had marched into the house and started issuing orders straight away. There had been no explanation, only a stern determination to get her to do what he said without questions. Just as if I was one of his schoolchildren, she thought. But she knew it was pointless to argue. He would only lose his temper and shout, and then shut himself in his study and not get any sleep, and neither would she. So she went along with it until they were ready, standing in the hall as if it wasn't the middle of the night, but a normal off-on-holiday day. She tried to summon up some enthusiasm, and suggested preparing food for the journey. After all, they would be driving through the night, and it would be vital for the driver to keep awake. Then her enthusiasm evaporated. It was *very* odd.

As if he could read her thoughts, he said, 'I'll tell you all about it in the car. Now, are we ready? I've arranged for a substitute in the school, and we can ring Prue in the morning. Right!' he added, and smiled a wild smile at her. 'Off on an adventure!' He locked the door behind them, and struggled to the car carrying both cases. 'Why did we need so much stuff?' she said. 'We'll be back by the end of the week, won't we?'

'Never know what Scottish weather has in store,' he said in a waggish voice.

They had been going for half an hour, and Mrs Betts felt her eyelids drooping. 'Would it be all right if I had a little nap?' she said. 'Then I could take over the driving for a bit later on, and let you sleep.'

'Good idea,' he said, and turned to smile at her. 'We'll be fine,' he said reassuringly, and she wondered at his words. Why shouldn't they be fine? Her eyes closed, and in spite of herself, she drifted off.

When she awoke, they were on a motorway. 'Where are we?' she said. He didn't answer, and she glanced out of the window at the approaching road signs. 'Gatwick!' she said. 'What on earth are we going to Gatwick for?' He still did not answer, and she felt a flicker of alarm. 'I said—' she began.

'I heard what you said,' he interrupted. 'And you will soon know why we're going to Gatwick. A little secret!' But he didn't sound at all happy about it, not like someone about to spring a pleasant surprise on his wife.

'Pull in here,' Mrs Betts said urgently, seeing an exit coming up. 'I need the toilet.'

'Can't you wait until we get there? It's not much further . . .'

'No, I can't. Please, dear, I won't be long.' She felt increasingly apprehensive, and found herself humouring him, jollying him along.

They parked in the services area, and he switched off the lights. 'Now,' she said gently, 'perhaps you'd better tell me what this is all about.' She put her hand over his, and squeezed. 'We don't have secrets from each other, you know,' she added, and waited.

Mr Betts rubbed his eyes. He said nothing for a full minute, and then he began to speak, not looking at her, but staring straight ahead at the shadowy car park.

'We never meant to kill him, you know,' he said. His voice was strained. 'It was supposed to be a kind of punishment.'

Mrs Betts' heart was beating so fast that she felt faint. She took several deep breaths, desperately anxious not to interrupt him. The shock was tremendous, but she still had enough reason left to know that she must appear calm.

'A kind of punishment,' he repeated, 'for what he had done. And a warning that it must all stop. No more photographs, no more contacts with small girls, no more . . .' He hesitated, then continued, 'And no more assignations with our lovely daughter.'

'Prue?' Mrs Betts could not help herself.

'Oh yes,' he said. 'It was him, you know. He made her pregnant. Filthy devil. So we decided to teach him a lesson.'

'Are you talking about the major?' said Mrs Betts quietly. Her husband had become silent again, and she risked the gentle prompt.

'Of course!' he said. 'The so-called major! Name was Smith really. Well, anyway,' he continued, 'I decided to teach him a lesson. Dick Reading hated him as much as I did, and though I didn't care for Reading much – vulgar, and reputed to be a wife beater – I enlisted his help. He was only too willing! Said he'd wanted to have a go at the bugger for a long time . . .'

'No need to swear, dear,' said Mrs Betts automatically. She heard herself uttering this banal comment, and waited for an explosion. But he laughed, and she realized he wasn't really listening to her. It was a spine-chilling, mirthless laugh, and she shivered. 'Go on, then,' she said. 'What happened?'

'Well, I suppose for the first time in my life, I failed to teach a lesson successfully.'

'But the knight's armour . . . ?'

'From the theatre,' he said. 'I got young Gary to help. I know quite a lot about that lad, and it wasn't difficult to persuade him. The three of us, Dick and me and Gary, got the suit of armour from the props cupboard. It was made of some lightweight stuff, so not difficult.'

'But didn't he struggle, or shout or something?'

'Drugged, fast asleep,' said Mr Betts, and his voice was firm. 'Oh yes, my dear,' he added, 'Gary was useful in more ways than one. Knew where to get the necessary. That Mrs Murphy at the theatre, the cleaner, was involved. But I left that side of it to him.'

'How do you know the major was the one who made Prue pregnant?' said Mrs Betts cautiously.

'Obvious,' said her husband dismissively. 'She wouldn't tell me, of course, but I didn't need to be told.'

'Did you mean to . . . well . . .'

'To kill him?' Mr Betts' voice was light. 'No, of course not. We were going to leave him in the church, and then when he came round he'd have the devil of a job getting free. But it was possible. We made sure of that. Tried it ourselves. Trouble was, he didn't come round. The dog did, though,' he added inconsequentially.

'Oh, my God,' said Mrs Betts, and covered her face.

In the Ladies, after she had made sure nobody was around, she took out the mobile that she had vowed so mistakenly was a waste of money, and dialled clumsily, with shaking fingers, the number she found under New Brooms.

'Is that Mrs Meade? Ah, good. I'm so sorry to trouble you, but I need some help. I can't think of anyone else who could . . .'

Her voice broke, and Lois, startled, but immediately alert, said, 'Of course I can help. What is it, where are you?'

Mrs Betts pulled herself together rapidly, aware that time was short. She told Lois in a few brief sentences the bare outline, and then stopped, sadly aware that she had no idea what Lois could do. She had seemed such a nice woman, and so well organized, but . . .

'Carry on,' Lois said urgently. 'Do exactly what he wants. It could be hours before your plane goes – wherever it's going – and we'll be there. Try not to upset him, and don't worry.'

Explaining to Derek was difficult. 'I don't see why you have to go,' he said. 'Just tell your pal at the police station. Let him get on with it.'

'I have to go,' Lois said, 'because I told her I would. She rang *me*, Derek. I've phoned Cowgill already. He's picking me up. Should be safe enough in a police car, shouldn't I?' She tried a smile, but was overwhelmed by the certainty of impending tragedy for people she knew and liked.

'I'll ring you from the airport,' she said. 'When it's all over.'

Forty-Seven

'What time does the plane go?' Mrs Betts felt momentarily reassured, pinning all her hopes on Lois Meade, a woman she scarcely knew. She had not been able to ring the police, though she knew this was the rational thing to do. She tried to order her thoughts, but failed. Who would be rational in my place? She stared out of the window at the passing traffic. I am in a dark car on a dark motorway, heading for Gatwick airport, with a man who has technically committed murder, and that man is my husband. She glanced at his profile beside her, and saw that he was perfectly calm. There was even a half-smile on his face, lit up by passing traffic.

'Oh, not for hours yet,' Mr Betts replied. 'We have to check in two hours before the flight, but we shall be there long before that. I thought we might have a meal . . . Are you hungry, dear?' He sounded so normal, so concerned for her.

Mrs Betts had never felt less hungry, but said that she probably would be by the time they got to Gatwick. 'Why do we have to check in so early?' she said. 'After all, we're going on an inland flight.' She was not at all sure these went from Gatwick, but could not be certain.

'Security,' her husband replied. 'It's all been tightened up since the terrorist attacks. Good idea, in my opinion.'

We needn't have left in such a hurry, then, thought Mrs Betts. They had left like thieves in the night. And what would Prue think, if she telephoned them and got no reply? She asked how long before they got to Gatwick, but Mr Betts was concentrating on his driving. He opened a window, admitting a blast of cold air. 'What's that for?' said Mrs Betts, pulling her coat around her.

'To keep me awake,' he said shortly. His mood had changed again.

She said in a neutral voice, 'Would you like me to take a turn driving? You could pull off on to the hard shoulder?' Again no reply.

Mrs Betts sat in a miserable huddle, doing her best not to cry. She wanted to go home, to find her daughter waiting for them, she wanted to be told it was all a bad dream, and it was time for school. But it was not a dream. She faced this, and began once more to go over what he had told her. Then she realized that there was a big gap.

'There's something I don't understand,' she said as neutrally as she could, 'something you didn't tell me. Can you close that window, dear. I can't hear myself think.'

Mr Betts closed the window, and said, 'What is it? I am trying to concentrate, you know. I don't want to miss the exit, and then have to go on for miles to turn around.'

'This is very important,' Mrs Betts said. 'You haven't told me what happened to Dick Reading. Perhaps you don't know?' she added hopefully.

'Oh, I know all right,' he replied. 'Stupid fool panicked. He said the police were getting close to finding out about the major and our part in it. Said Gary Needham was unreliable, and the others at the theatre couldn't be trusted with anything.'

He was silent for a few seconds, and Mrs Betts prodded him on. 'So what happened?'

'He had to be silenced,' Mr Betts said.

'Who silenced him, then?'

'I did.'

Mrs Betts gasped. Then she began to scream, a terrible, terrified scream. She struck at her husband wildly, causing the car to swerve across the lanes. He managed to control the car, and get them back into the slow lane. He came to a stop on the hard shoulder and turned to face her.

'Settle down, dear,' he said, as if she was a naughty child in class. 'You asked me to explain, so try to listen. It was easy,' he continued, 'especially after he said that our Prue was a little slag, and got what she was asking for. We were backstage at the theatre, just Gary and me. Everybody else had gone, and I had the key to lock up. Then Reading came in and began yelling that he'd decided to go to the police and tell them we didn't mean to kill the major. I knew I had to act quickly, and grabbed a knife left on the table by the woman who does refreshments. It was over in seconds, and Gary never moved a muscle to help.'

'How did you manage to get him out?' asked Mrs Betts, in a flat monotone.

'Gary helped then. He had to, though he was scared to death. It was my idea to take Reading to the woods and tie him to a tree. I'd discovered the spot where Lois Meade – did you know she was a police informer? – had meetings with her inspector. A little surprise for them both. Rather good, that, don't you think? Kept up the theatrical theme. I was rather proud of that. We had the devil's own job cleaning up, of course. Messy business. Still, Gary was perfect for that. New Brooms came into its own!'

Oh, dear God, come and help me, please, please. Mrs Betts mind was floating now, and her body frozen into a solid lump. She knew she could not move, not even to defend herself. She was sure that it might now be necessary. Her husband had clearly lost his reason, and she had no idea what he would do next.

The motorway unrolled before them, and round and round in Mrs Betts's head went the words 'New Brooms'. Now she knew Lois Meade had a connection with the police, she was certain help would be on the way. But would they arrive in time? Please God, she repeated, help me, please.

And then there it was, the turning to Gatwick airport. Her husband drove slowly now, following signs to the long stay car park. In a daze she got out of the car, waited for him to make the necessary arrangements, and then they caught the bus that took them on a rattling ride to the terminal building. He kept up a running conversation, amiable again and chattering about nothing in particular. He seemed not to notice that she was silent.

Lois had never travelled so fast in a car. On a motorbike, yes, when she was about sixteen and then it had been decidedly illegal. She sat in the back, where she could only guess, but reckoned they were doing at least a hundred. Chief Detective Inspector Hunter Cowgill's tall figure in front of her obscured the view. When he turned to talk, she could see his shadowy face, and his expression was surprisingly relaxed. When he spoke, it was about anything other than the business in hand. 'You'll see, Lois,' he said in answer to her questions. 'All will be revealed. We're nearly there.'

'No, sir, we're not,' said the driver, and Cowgill raised his eyebrows.

'Nearly to the conclusion of the case, I meant,' he said sharply. 'Just keep your eye on the road, Sykes, and leave the talking to me.'

'Sir,' said the driver stiffly.

'So it was Betts,' said Lois. She refused to be silenced by Cowgill. It seemed to her that this was the ideal time to get as much information as possible. 'Do you know exactly what happened?'

'More or less,' said Cowgill. 'We have one or two gaps to fill in, but I'm afraid you'll be looking for another cleaner.'

'Poor Gary, is he up to his neck?' said Lois. 'And Hazel?'

'A good girl, Hazel,' said Cowgill. 'Now Lois, tell me about that husband of yours. Is he making a good recovery? And what did he think about this midnight jaunt of yours?'

'Oh, he was over the moon, naturally,' said Lois crossly. Nothing like a bloody cop for caution. Never give too much away, no matter how in debt you are to a perfectly honest woman trying to serve the cause of justice . . . She broke into a sudden laugh, thinking that not even her mother would recognize that description. 'You're not goin' to tell me *anything*, are you?' she said. 'Can't think why I'm here.'

'Because you'll be needed. Just have patience, Lois,' Cowgill said. 'We've warned Gatwick to keep a close eye on them when they arrive, but not to confront them unless they are actually about to take off for Rio.'

'It's Rio, is it?' said Lois. She remembered again the holiday brochures. So he'd planned an escape route well-used by other criminals. 'Not very original,' she said. 'I'd go somewhere nobody would think of looking.'

'Like?'

'Oh, I dunno. Iceland, the South Pole, somewhere like that. Have we got much further to go?'

'Patience, Lois,' said Cowgill.

Mrs Betts sat opposite her husband in the airport cafe, staring at a plate of pasta bake, wondering how she could get rid of it without actually eating it. Every time she got a forkful of the stuff up to her mouth, her stomach turned over and she felt violently sick. But he mustn't know how she felt. If he got her talking – something he was very good at – she knew she would spill out the telephone call to Lois Meade, and then he would do something really stupid. When she tried to follow through on this thought, imagining just what he would do, the shutter came down in her brain, and she felt sick again. Perhaps if she concentrated hard on something else she could get some of the glutinous mass down her throat.

She looked across at him, tucking into his food with what could only be called gusto. How is it possible that I have been married to this man for twenty-two years, and now see a complete stranger – no, a *murderer* – sitting across the table? He had been a good husband, if a little bossy at times, but then, you expect that with schoolteachers. And to Prue he had been an excellent father. He had loved her, educated her, protected her. But that was where it all went wrong. She could see that now. He had loved her too much. Not in any unhealthy way, but wanting to keep her as a small child under his protection, long after she should have spread her wings. Then, of course, Prue had made her own escape and gone too far. Even so, it was not unusual these days, nor the end of the world, for a girl of her age to get pregnant.

Thinking along these lines, she got a portion of pasta into her mouth and swallowed quickly. Her gorge rose, but she detached her mind swiftly and thought of the major and Prue. She doubted very much whether Todd-Nelson had been the culprit. There had been that time when he'd brought her home from the pub, but Mrs Betts reckoned she would have known from Prue's face if he had been . . . well, if he'd been Prue's lover . . . Another forkful went down, and this time it was easier. Back to the major quickly. He'd obviously liked Prue, maybe tried it on a bit. But she could have sworn there was nothing more.

Who then? One of those young farmers in the pub, probably. That's what her sister-in-law Betty had told her, cautioning her not to tell Mr Betts. 'We don't want a big scene in the pub,' she'd said, adding that Prue was keen enough, anyway. This had shocked her at the time, but not now. Prue was a young woman . . . Oh no, what was all this going to do to Prue? She felt the tears come into her eyes, and determinedly pushed another load of pasta into her mouth.

'Delicious, isn't it, dear?' Mr Betts said.

She nodded, and, in a kind of desperation, finished up the plateful and put down her fork. 'Is there anything else to do now, before we catch the plane?' she said.

They had spent ages in the queue, checking in their luggage. 'Shame we can't afford business class,' Mr Betts had said, glancing at the much shorter queue. It was then that she had seen that they were, in fact, en route for Rio de Janeiro, and not a friendly Scottish airport less than an hour away. She had not bothered to mention it. Nothing could surprise her now. All she wanted was for Lois Meade to walk across the cavernous entrance to Gatwick airport, accompanied by police officers, and find them sitting quietly at a table, finishing their meal. She could not bring herself to imagine beyond this point.

'Do you think I could have a doze, dear,' she said, and even managed a small smile. 'I am really tired, and I've never been able to sleep on planes. I could stretch out on one of those long seats over there, and you could wake me when it's time.'

'No wife of mine is stretching out on an airport bench like some no-good student,' Mr Betts said firmly. 'Come on,' he added, and got up from the table. 'We'll sit together, and you can lean on me. It'll be just like the old days,' he continued, and took her hand. 'Just like when we were off on honeymoon, do you remember?'

She had great difficulty in controlling her tears now, and hurried over to a likely looking seat. 'This will do,' she said, patting the place beside her. They arranged themselves comfortably, and he said she should shut her eyes and relax.

'I'll keep an eye on the screen for our flight number,' he said. He put up a hand towards her, and she flinched. But he stroked her hair and said, 'We'll be fine, dear. Just leave it all to me.'

Forty-Eight

To a casual passer-by, they were a respectable couple waiting for a plane, the wife asleep on her husband's shoulder and his arm around her. They were not at all noticeable, but they were the first people Lois saw as she and Cowgill, tall and stern in his dark suit, crossed the waiting area.

She put a hand on his arm, drawing him to a halt. 'There,' she said quietly. 'Over there, on the seat.' And then, unexpectedly, sadness overwhelmed her. She bit her bottom lip, and Cowgill looked at her.

'OK, Lois?' he said. 'It's going to be very hard for Mrs B, and you are the very best person to look after her. She remembered you. Don't forget that.'

After a second or two, they moved forward. When they were a few paces away, Mr Betts turned his head and saw them.

In an instant, his alarm communicated itself to his wife, and she was awake, clutching his arm. He shook her off, and pulled from his inside pocket a small gun, pointed it at Lois and Cowgill, and shouted at them, 'Keep away from me, or I shall shoot.'

Lois froze, but Cowgill slowly moved forward. Through the rapidly emptying waiting area, a number of men were now visible, also approaching as if on wheels, so steady was their motion. Policemen, of course. Cowgill will have organized it all, thought Lois. The little bugger doesn't stand a chance. 'I don't think that gun's real,' she said in a low voice, and Cowgill nodded.

'Can't risk it, though,' he replied.

He cleared his throat, and Lois knew that now Betts would be encouraged to do the sensible thing and hand over the gun. She looked at Mrs Betts. A small woman, she seemed to have shrunk to a shadow, still close beside him, her face as white as paper. And then she heard the voice, loud and screaming.

'Dad! Don't, Dad!'

Mr Betts's head shot round to look, and in that moment Cowgill rushed forward and knocked the gun from his hand. Mrs Betts took his arm and pulled him back down on to the seat, where he sat with his head in his hands. Prue and Hazel, running now, hand in hand, came up, and Prue flung her arms around her father. Tears streamed down her cheeks and Cowgill, for once, looked at a loss. Nobody moved.

Then Lois walked forward and put her arm around Mrs Betts's shoulders. 'Time to go, I think,' she said. 'There's a lot of sorting out to do. Prue, you take your dad and mum and go with Inspector Cowgill, and Hazel will take me home. Got your car, Hazel?'

She waited until the family had been slowly ushered away from the now reassembling crowd, and then she turned to Hazel. 'D'you want a coffee?' she said. She looked at her watch. 'Bloody hell,' she said, 'it's the middle of the night.'

'Better call Derek, Mrs M,' said Hazel. 'He'll be worrying, for sure.'

Lois dialled home, and immediately Derek answered. 'Lois? Are you OK?' To her surprise, she found she couldn't answer. 'Lois? Is that you? For God's sake, gel, say something!'

Lois cleared her throat, and finally said, 'Can you check Gran brought the washing in?' There was a moment's silence, and then Derek said, 'OK, me duck. We'll check. See you soon. Love you,' he added, and rang off.

Forty-Nine

Lois arrived home at dawn, and slept, on and off, for twenty-four hours. Derek gave orders to the family that she was not to be disturbed, and Gran took the kids off to Tresham, first to start clearing and packing up in her bungalow, and then on to the movies for a treat. It was Monday when Lois awoke to see Derek standing by the bed, holding a mug of tea.

'Mornin' gel,' he said gently. 'Time to get going.'

She struggled to sit up, and took the tea. 'Ugh!' she said, making a face. 'You've put sugar in it!'

'Phew!' he said, grinning broadly. 'Glad you're back to normal. Come on then, get up, the kids are skulking about looking worried, and Gran's doin' a fry-up to beat all fry-ups.'

He took the mug from her and pulled her out of bed. 'Get moving, then,' he said, making it impossible for her to do so, holding her tight, and added, 'Gran's trying to do everything, there's wet washing on the line . . . Time to get back where you belong, my gel.' He was smiling, but Lois knew he meant it.

'Right,' she said, pushing him away. 'Ten minutes, and then I'm downstairs. You'd better be ready for me. And why wasn't that washing brought in? There was I, stuck in the middle of bloody nowhere, and you couldn't even . . .'

He put up his hands. 'OK, OK, can we have a truce, just for now?' he said.

'Mum!' said Josie, when Lois appeared. 'Where's my library book?'

Jamie sidled up to her and touched her gently. 'You all right, Mum?' he said.

'Fine,' said Lois. Douglas just looked at her without speaking. Lois said, 'Anything up, Douglas?'

'Nothin',' said Douglas, looking innocently surprised. 'Should there be?'

'Now, now,' said Gran, standing over them all with a large frying pan. 'Who's for eggs and bacon, fried bread and sausage?'

The staff meeting was a subdued affair. Hazel still looked bleary-eyed, and sat hunched up between Bridie and Sheila.

'Where's Gary?' said Sheila. 'He didn't turn up at the surgery this morning, and it was all I could do to finish in time. I thought of ringing you, Lois, but held on, waiting for him, and then it was too late, and I thought I might as well carry on by myself.'

'Sorry about that,' said Lois. 'Gary won't be coming back, I'm afraid. He's resigned.' She hesitated, and Hazel muttered something she didn't catch.

'What's been going on?' said Sheila. 'Has Gary done something wrong?' She looked around at the others. Bridie had clearly been told at least some of what had happened last night, and Hazel looked steadily at the floor.

'Probably,' said Lois. 'Sorry, Sheila, can't say any more at the moment. But as soon as I can, I'll tell you.'

'I liked him,' said Sheila stubbornly. 'He was a good lad. Needed some proper mothering when he was growing up, I reckon. He talked to me quite a lot, y'know, Lois, when we had our coffee break, an' that.'

'Yes, well . . .' Lois was determined to change the subject, and said that she would be looking for new staff, and that if any of them knew likely candidates, they were to let her know.

Bridie looked at Hazel, then said, 'Is it all right if Hazel stays on, Lois? I know it was meant to be sort of temporary, but . . .'

'Fine by me,' said Lois. 'But you're young, Hazel, and what with everything being cleared up, an' that, don't you want to go off round the world, or something?'

Hazel shook her head. 'I'm happy if you are, Mrs M,' she said. 'It's a good job, something new every day. And it gives me time to do other things I'm interested in,' she added, without looking at Lois.

After the others had gone, Hazel lingered. 'D'you want a sandwich?' Lois said, 'I'd like a word, if you've got time.'

The house was empty, except for the two of them. Gran had gone off to continue her packing, and Derek was working the other side of Ringford, too far to come home for lunch.

'How're you feeling?' Hazel opened the conversation when Lois came back with the sandwiches.

'Fine,' said Lois. 'But curious.'

'I'll tell you what I know,' said Hazel defensively.

Lois said, 'I don't expect you to tell me everything. It's not like that, I know. But I would like to know more about Gary's part in all of it. And exactly what was the set-up at the theatre. You probably think I'm stupid – Derek does – but Sheila's not the only one with a soft spot for Gary. I suppose what I'm saying,' she continued, 'is that I'd like to help him, if there's anything to be done.'

Hazel looked at her sandwich. Then she took a knife and cut it in quarters and rearranged them on the plate. Finally she looked up at Lois, and her eyes were sad. 'Gary is hooked,' she said simply. 'He controls it well, and can carry on most of the time so's you wouldn't know, unless you could recognize the signs. But it gets to him now and then, and he passes out, or loses it and does something stupid. Joanne Murphy was a cleaner at the theatre, and operated from there with quite a few contacts. That's where Gary met her, and Betts too. Betts wasn't in on the drugs, but he knew about it. He blackmailed Gary into helping him.'

'Sod it,' said Lois. She sighed, and said, 'And Joanne Murphy? She's not the big time?'

Hazel shook her head. 'Just a little frog in a big pool,' she said. 'And now she's out of the way there'll be a few frantic loonies about. But another like her will pop up in no time.'

'But Cowgill said he'd got her boss in Leicester. That'll dry up the supply for a bit, won't it?'

Again Hazel nodded. 'For a bit,' she echoed, and began to eat her sandwich.

* * *

It was Wednesday morning two weeks later, and Lois had three new possible cleaners to see. She arranged her schedule so that she could visit them all in their homes, and was just collecting up names and addresses from her office when the telephone rang.

'Lois?'

'Oh no, not you!' said Lois. 'What do you want?'

'I knew you'd be pleased to hear from me,' said Cowgill. 'It just that we've got this spot of trouble . . .'

'And it's Wednesday,' said Lois, glad that he could not see her smile. She put down the phone.